MW01126709

DEDICATION

To Lorelai, first of our family's new generation.
May the world be kind to you and yours.

The Boardinghouse

Carol Ervin

Printed by CreateSpace, an Amazon Company

The Boardinghouse

Cover design by Victorine E. Lieske

The Boardinghouse

LIST OF CHARACTERS

Characters who are important in this and other books in the series, listed by first name

Barlow Townsend: husband of May Rose; former superintendent of the Winkler Lumber Company, former partner in the Winkler Mine, now an employee

Blanche Cotton Herff: daughter of Simpson Wainwright, mother of three children who are in the care of her father; now married to Charlie Herff

Charlie Herff: ex-cowboy, brother of Will and Glory; lived with May Rose in Fargo until he was 16, married to Blanche

Ebert Watson: farmer, friend of Will, former suitor of May Rose

Emmy and **Tim** Donnelly: Luzanna's younger children

Evie Wyatt: age 16, daughter of Wanda and her first husband, Homer Wyatt

Freddy and **Hettie** Townsend: children of May Rose and Barlow

Hester Townsend (deceased): Barlow's sister, operator of the former Winkler boardinghouse

Irene Donnelly Herff: mother of the Donnelly boys, briefly married to Will's father, Morris Herff

Jamie Long (deceased): May Rose's first husband; Wanda's father

John Donnelly (deceased): Luzanna's first husband; former tormenter of Wanda, May Rose, and the Herff boys (*The Girl on the Mountain*)

John Johnson: bachelor, part-time handyman at the boardinghouse

Lucie Bosell: Wanda's grandmother; mother of Piney, Ruth (deceased), and Wanda's mother (Evalina, deceased)

Luzanna Donnelly Hale: May Rose's closest friend; wife of John Donnelly (deceased) and former common-law wife of Abner Hale

Magda: midwife and medicine woman

May Rose Long Townsend: wife of Barlow and mother of Freddy and Hettie; stepmother of Wanda

Milton Chapman: boardinghouse guest, husband of Rona

Miss Baldwin: teacher, boardinghouse guest

Mrs. Vincent: teacher, boardinghouse guest

Mr. Cunningham: miner, bachelor, evening watchman/resident at the Boardinghouse

Mr. Jones: boardinghouse guest

Mr. and Mrs. Thornton: boardinghouse guests

Otis Herff: young son of Wanda and Will Herff

Piney Bosell Wainwright: Wanda's aunt; wife of Simpson Wainwright

Price Loughrie: one-time marshal; union representative

Randolph Bell: engineer and partner in the Winkler mine

Rona Chapman: wife of Milton, guest at boardinghouse

Ruby, **Robert**, and **Ralphie** Cotton: young children of Raz and Blanche, now in the care of Simpson and Piney Wainwright.

Russell Long: May Rose's brother-in-law from her first marriage; Wanda's uncle

Silby: a lost girl

Simpson Wainwright: miller and carpenter, father of Blanche Cotton; married to Piney Bosell

Smitty: miner, bachelor, day watchman/resident at the Boardinghouse

Wanda Wyatt Herff: wife of Will Herff; daughter of Evalina Bosell and Jamie Long; May Rose's stepdaughter; mother of Evie Wyatt and Otis Herff

Will Herff: Wanda's second husband; father of Otis; doctor and partner in the Winkler Mine

*

Characters in the series, listed by first name, who do not appear in this story.

Alma Donnelly: Luzanna's daughter, age 18

Glory Townsend: Hester's adopted daughter, biological sister to Will and Charlie Herff

Homer Wyatt (deceased): Wanda's first husband

Raz Cotton (deceased); Blanche's first husband

Ruth Bosell: Wanda's aunt (deceased)

Virgie White: young widow, friend of May Rose and Wanda

1

Someone was trying to find me. The letter came from a lawyer's office in Philadelphia, printed by type machine on paper crisp as parchment, dated August 4, 1919, and signed in elegant script. The paper cut my finger, a deep, painful slash that dripped blood. I pressed the cut to my tongue while I read the letter again. It did not identify the person inquiring, merely asked if I was May Rose Percy, approximately 38, raised in Stillwater, Ohio, by Burt and Sweet Jonson.

I had no reason to assume the letter meant bad news. It might be seeking information about someone I'd known as a child in Ohio. I was tempted to toss it away, but the paper and signature looked too important to disregard, as though ignoring it might put me—and thereby all of us—at risk.

The idea of being found should not have been frightening. I was innocent of wrongdoing, but knew well that innocence did not always ward off evil. I'd had more than one nightmare in which I was arrested, tried, and judged guilty of being married to a murderer, my first husband, Jamie Long.

Blood dripped on the letter and spread into a blot above my name. I dug in my apron pocket for a handkerchief to press against the cut and tucked the blood-stained letter into my account book. Here was one more troubling thing to discuss with Barlow when he returned from his sales trip. I'd had no letter from him for three days. Surely that meant he was on his way home.

The room where I stood was at a front corner of the boardinghouse, near the wide entryway and across from the parlor. It was meant to be a cloakroom, but on admitting our first residents, Barlow and I had realized we did not want to conduct business in our apartment. We'd taken the coat hooks from the walls and added a small desk, chairs, and a lamp. I usually kept the door open, but today I not only closed the door when I left, I considered locking it. I didn't go that far, but I did carry the account book to the apartment and secured it in our parlor desk. Then I peeked into the children's playroom to satisfy myself that all was well.

Back in the hallway, I hurried toward the kitchen without looking to see or stopping to greet the man starting down the center stairs. I knew, of course, who it was—we had only two guests, husband and wife. He had a heavy tread, and she seldom left her room.

My need for privacy had changed in the three months since we'd accepted strangers into our boardinghouse, and I now understood the adage about familiarity breeding contempt. I didn't want to be well known—or found—by anyone except people I trusted.

Next to our own apartment, the kitchen was my favorite room, partly because my friend Luzanna was almost always there with her welcoming smile and help for any urgent need. With Barlow on sales trips, I'd quickly found I couldn't manage the house, the cooking, cleaning, laundry, and our two small children, even with only two guests, so I'd hired Luzanna and her daughter Emmy. Less than two years after selling his share of the Winkler Mine, Barlow had gone back to work for his former partners, not as business manager, but as a salesman. In our present circumstances, we were lucky he had this job, but it had never been part of our plan. We were supposed to operate the boardinghouse together, making decisions and doing most of the work ourselves. I'd expected to have abundant time to spend with Freddy, nearly three, and Hettie, who'd just learned to stand alone. My husband wasn't meant to be gone for weeks at a time.

Luzanna was leaning on our kitchen worktable, turning pages of yesterday's *Fairmont West Virginian*. "The Women's Christian Temperance Union is for giving us the vote," she said, keeping her eyes on the paper. In June, the federal government had approved the 19th Amendment to the Constitution, acknowledging that no citizen could be barred from voting on the basis of sex. Now it had to be ratified by the states. Many had already done so, and West Virginia newspapers were full of comments and notices of rallies.

She turned another page, still not looking up. "I like how the WCTU says women has better morals than men and will elect better leaders. I'd say the morals part is true, judging by men I've knowed. What do you think?"

"Umm. I haven't thought about it." Our countertop egg basket was empty. "The egg and butter man was here today, wasn't he? Where did you put the eggs?"

"Cellarway. Our morals *is* better than men's, wouldn't you say?"

"I'm sure I admire more women than men, but except for the men in our families, we never get to know their minds or natures very well. Not like I know you and you know me and we know Piney and Wanda and the rest of us. Egg salad for lunch, all right with you?"

"Seasoned with a little bacon," she said. "I'll whip up the dressing. I'd like a man who's as good as my friends."

"What?" Luzanna always said she'd had enough worthless husbands and would not waste herself on another. I waited until she glanced up from the paper, then said, "I'm not going to forget that."

"Bacon? Dressing?"

"That you'd like a husband."

"Whoa, Nellie. I mean I wish my husbands had been as good to me as my friends. Lord, can you imagine me with more kids? I'm better off as I am. I like this work."

"Which is my good fortune," I said. If she married, she might leave me and concentrate on her own household. But like every woman who's happy with her husband, I wanted the same good fortune for my friends.

Our work in the boardinghouse was unending, but Luzanna claimed its steadiness and dependability was easier than gathering up and washing laundry from the town bachelors and sewing gloves late at night. Since she and her children had begun taking most of their meals in our kitchen, her cheeks had filled out and at times she looked almost as pretty as her girls.

She re-folded and smoothed the newspaper, making it suitable for the parlor table. "Women against the vote talk like all of us has a good man to lean on. I bet a nickel all of them against it has rich husbands or fathers and maids and such and never worked a minute in their lives. Like our Mrs. Chapman."

We continued to speculate about the vote and about women of leisure as we prepared lunch for Mr. and Mrs. Chapman, my children, Luzanna's two, and ourselves. Work being necessary for our security, we were perplexed and irritated by the idleness of our current guests. I didn't know if Mrs. Chapman had opinions. Indeed, I had no idea what she did in her room all day long.

"She's an odd one," Luzanna whispered.

"In her place, I'd go mad." Rona Chapman was the second woman I'd met who didn't work morning to night, the other being Barlow's first wife, Alice, who'd seemed to crave an important duty but found no dignified opportunity. Childless like Mrs. Chapman, Alice had spent her day reading and worrying about the news and forming her strong opinions. Barlow's sister Hester had not approved of her, but both Alice and Hester would have wanted the right to vote.

Since building the boardinghouse, I'd thought and spoken often of Hester Townsend. We'd modeled it after the one she'd operated nearly on the same ground. Too late, I'd learned that my memory of her boardinghouse was not entirely correct—it had not paid for itself, though it had seemed busy and prosperous. The difference, Barlow explained, was that he and his sister had not borne the cost of building and furnishing it. Much of that had come from his two elderly cousins, who'd become its permanent residents.

Thus far we'd not had enough guests to meet expenses. Instead of being able to work with my husband every day, my ambition to operate an enterprise like Hester's now separated us for weeks at a time. Already I wondered if we should give it up.

~

Often in dreams I seemed to be someone else, wandering on unknown paths and cliffs, searching, following or hiding from unknown groups of people, traveling on, never knowing where. Now with Barlow away so many lonely weeks, I sometimes dreamed of the two of us, heated and desperate to cling together, frustrated because people were in our room, watching.

That night my dream frightened me awake, for I'd been myself, and parts of the dream had been too real. I'd seen the chinked walls of the mountain cabin, the skillets hanging on the wall above the stove, the butchering knives on rawhide ropes. Cold air had rushed through the open door, and I'd risen from the bed in the corner, wondering if Jamie had come home in the night or if he'd gone out and left the door open. I'd called his name but couldn't hear my voice over the shrill of wind. I'd stood in the open door, searching the dome of starry sky and untracked blue-white snow, but Jamie was nowhere to be found, and I knew he'd run away, and maybe that was why a logging train had stopped on the tracks near the cabin. There could be no other reason, for trains never went down the mountain in the middle of the night. The flat cars were piled high with logs and men who laughed and pointed but made no sound, and I closed the door because I was naked and cold.

Then Jamie had appeared, wearing his sheepskin coat, but the day was too hot for a coat and he'd thrown it on the floor and taken off his shirt and stepped out of his trousers and pulled me to the bed. This bed, the one in the boardinghouse, with everyone watching.

Afraid to go back to sleep, I sat up until I had a good sense of what was real and what was not. This dream of Jamie was not as terrifying as the one where I kept trying to fasten the cabin door against a pack of wolves, and not nearly as frightening as the one in which I stood helpless as Freddy fell under the hooves and wheels of a horse-drawn wagon. Barlow's arms had helped me recover from those dreams, but even if he were beside me now, I couldn't tell him about this one.

~

Learning that someone was trying to find me was only the start of disturbing events. The next afternoon while Luzanna and I were shredding cabbage and peeling potatoes for dinner, my stepdaughter rushed into the kitchen, looking like she'd had a fright.

"Wanda, my goodness me," Luzanna said.

Wanda breezed past us to the hallway door, motioning me to follow. "Let's talk a minute." She was out of wind, like she'd run all the way from her house or from the company store where she worked when she wasn't helping her husband in his medical practice.

I wiped my hands and hurried after her into the hall, concerned that she needed to relay something not only urgent, but too private to share even with Luzanna, our closest friend.

Wanda passed the door to my apartment, glanced into the parlor and continued to the front porch, where she stopped and scrutinized the landscape. Apparently satisfied that no one else could hear, she plopped in one of the porch rockers like her legs had given way.

She'd made me too anxious to sit.

"You won't believe this," she said. "It's impossible. Guess who showed up?"

Her eyes shifted back and forth, a nervous habit I thought she'd conquered. The afternoon was hot, but my skin turned cold and damp. I could think of only one person whose impossible appearance would make my voice tremble like hers. I whispered, "Jamie?" From where I stood I could see the spot where I'd seen him for the last time, the back gate of Hester's boardinghouse. Railroad employees had brought out the dead and injured after a trestle collapsed, plunging a train into a gully, but they'd not found one passenger, assumed to be Jamie Long, wanted for murder.

Occasionally when I was feeling blessed to be with Barlow, I'd have a brief fear that Jamie would appear, expecting us to take up as before, even though his brother said he'd found and buried him, even though Russell had brought me the money from Jamie's coat and said he'd kept Jamie's gun. I knew where Jamie had gotten the money and I knew he'd had a gun; he'd shown it to me.

Wanda fanned her face with her hand. "Pa? No. Someone way worse."

For me there could be no one worse. If Jamie Long should turn up alive, Barlow and I might not be legally married. I didn't know the law. Jamie had been presumed dead for nearly 20 years.

Wanda's usual manner in confronting a problem was to attack it head on or dismiss it with a wave of her hand. She now waved it in a confused way, as though her hand could help get her words out. "It's old Mrs. Donnelly," she said.

I had not recovered from the terror of Jamie ruining our lives. "Not...?"

"The very same. Calls herself Mrs. Herff, now, but I recognized her right off. And I guess she could be Mrs. Herff if she married nobody after Will's pa died."

My feelings about the woman were deeper and more bitter than Wanda's. Irene Donnelly had repeated the lies that I'd displayed myself without clothes to loggers from her husband's camp. She'd called me a whore.

Wanda rushed on. "She must know the old man is dead, 'cause she didn't ask for him—she asked for Will. Can you beat that? Lordy, she's still Will's stepma. My step-ma-in-law! I can't bear it."

I dropped into a chair and squeezed the arm rests. The Donnellys had plagued our earliest days in Winkler. I hated that the mother of the clan was making a claim on Will, especially considering her family's damage to his. "Do you suppose we'll have to tell Luzanna? And if we do, what will we say?" Unfortunately, our friend had been married to Irene's older son, John Donnelly.

Wanda got up and paced on the porch. "We never told Luzanna that her husband's ma was married to Will's stinker of a pa, did we? I almost forgot it myself. Will said them two wasn't together much more than a month before her and her boys was kicked out of town."

"I told no one." It was an easy secret to keep, because we didn't like to think about it. We hadn't even told Luzanna we'd known her husband when he was a boy, partly to protect her and her children and partly to protect ourselves.

"I don't think I blabbed," Wanda said. "No, I'm sure I didn't, but sometimes when I think I've forgotten something it pops out, loose-like."

"I wonder if Irene knows Luzanna and her children are here."

"I'd say she don't, 'cause she would of asked for them too, wouldn't she? She come into the store half an hour ago, and age ain't improved her. She walks like she can hardly put one fat foot in front of the other. I don't think she recognized me, though there's no reason she should, 'cause I grew up and she just grew old. Will was out on a call, so I told her to come around later. She said she'd heard somewhere that her stepson had made himself a doctor and owner of a coal mine to boot. She sat down at the store table, said she'd just wait. There's other clerks there today so I left her. What do you think she wants?"

"Nothing good." The last time I'd seen Irene she was threatening to shoot Will's father with a shotgun. In those days, the town belonged to the Winkler Lumber and Logging Company. The town guard had said if she didn't take her boys away he was going to send them to reform school.

"If she sticks around, she'll find out about Luzanna's Emmy and Tim. Poor kids, to have such a granny. At least their pa can't come back, can he? Lu's sure he's dead?"

"Killed in a mine, John and his brother both. She saw the bodies."

Wanda puffed a loud breath of air. "I know it ain't right to say I'm glad somebody's dead, but I can't help it. If that woman lets loose one word of brag about her boys, I might spit out what they done to us."

I'd had too many bad thoughts for one day. "For sure, we have some confessions to make to Luzanna."

"Maybe not yet. Probably the old woman's just come to get money from Will. Maybe she'll leave and we won't have to explain a thing. All right. Gotta go." Like everything was now settled, Wanda bounced up and rushed down the path.

I did not return to the kitchen when Wanda left; I went to my apartment. I needed to hug my children and I needed my husband to come home. This house we wanted so much had separated us, sending him to sleep in hot hotel rooms, ride dusty trains and wait every day in the offices of power plant operators for a chance to ask them to buy coal from the Winkler Mine. I was the lucky one. While he was on the road, he lived without the consolation of family, but I could hold Freddy and Hettie at any time.

The children were sitting in a circle on the playroom floor with Emmy, Luzanna's daughter, who every day looked more like a young lady. I stood in the doorway as she put a block in Hettie's hand and helped her set it on Freddy's stack. At her age, Hettie did not have the coordination to build, but she'd learned how to destroy, and she liked the effect. With a swing of her arm, she tumbled Freddy's blocks across the floor. Freddy yelled, leaned forward and gave his sister a shove. Emmy caught her, but Hettie cried anyway.

Emmy looked at me like she needed to be rescued. "Go keep your ma company," I said. "I'll stay with the children for a while."

At three and one, my children did not play well together, but at 13, Emmy seemed extraordinarily grown-up. She was also patient and good-natured. I did not want her to learn the bad things I knew about her father and his family, just as I did not want her to hear the bad things they'd said about me.

2

Much as I needed the money from their two rooms, I wished Milton Chapman and his wife would leave. He watched me all the time, appraising me up and down when I walked into the parlor or met him in the hall. Estimating his chances, pulling on his silky mutton-chops or shifting his unlit cigar between his teeth, not taking the step back to allow a polite space between us. So certain of himself in his long motoring coat and cap or in the golf knickers he called plus fours, though there was no golf course in Winkler nor in any other town in the region. Trying to convince us he was a somebody in a place he called the backwater of nowhere.

Thus far I'd been able to compose my face and act like I didn't know what was on his mind. I thought often of Hester Townsend, a well-preserved unmarried woman who'd had to deal with difficult boarders and must have learned how to fend off unwanted advances. I tried to imitate her stiff posture and confident tone, but the colder I became, the more he twisted his thin lips in a smile.

He seemed to know how to find me alone, like that afternoon. In the middle of most days, Luzanna went home to see if her boy Tim was into any mischief, and sometimes to lie down for a rest, because her days in the boardinghouse were long.

I was chopping potatoes for salad, standing at the long porcelain worktable in the center of the room when the door from the dining room swung open.

"So this is where you keep yourself." Milton Chapman stepped into the room, letting the door swing shut behind him.

In hot weather we kept only the smallest fire in the cook stove. A fan in the corner moved air in my direction, yet my face was moist, my underarms sticky, and on both my chest and back, beads of sweat rolled down beneath my chemise.

I dabbed my forehead with a dish towel, giving myself a moment to hide my irritation. "May I help you?"

He leaned against the dish cabinet like he intended to stay and chat. I'd never known a man who had no apparent occupation other than a nightly attendance at the roadhouse, and I resented the way he lounged in the parlor and lurked in passageways. Always underfoot, in Luzanna's words.

His only response was a smile that to me looked wicked.

"Please tell Mrs. Chapman I've set iced tea in the parlor," I said. "You might like to take your glasses outside. The summer house is the coolest spot this time of day." I knew this from Emmy's report, for I seldom had time to sit there myself. Barlow and I had imagined the lattice-walled summer house as our daily retreat, a place to rest on chintz-covered chairs, watch the river splash over its rocks, and enjoy the shade while the children played on the cool stone floor.

Milton Chapman shrugged. "Rona is resting in her room. I can't explain it, can you? She does nothing, yet she's always tired." He had the look and stature of a man who might be my age, but his wife looked older.

I had no explanation, and I'd wondered too, but it didn't seem proper for him to speak about her to anyone but the closest family. "Then we'll see you at dinner," I said. "Six o'clock, as usual." He didn't need to be reminded; I was dismissing him from the room.

He didn't move. "You're looking fine this afternoon. A drop of moisture on your cheek, a loose strand of hair, there by your ear. I could write a poem."

I pressed my hands on the table between us, rejecting the kind of sharp response that would put him in his place, wondering what Hester would do. She'd say something that wouldn't sound defensive but would catch him off guard. "Mr. Chapman, are your accommodations satisfactory?"

His look changed to one of pretended surprise and injury. "Most certainly, quite satisfied. I should say *very*. Have I implied that anything is wrong?"

"If you intend to continue as our guest, you must respect the privacy of everyone in the house, including mine. At the present time, I need this kitchen to myself." I did not worry about offending him; it was unlikely he and Rona would leave until their house was finished, which might be as late as next spring. When construction began, they'd stayed with her brother's family, an arrangement she claimed did not suit them, as though it was not good enough. Getting to know Milton Chapman, I suspected her brother had asked them to leave.

"Anything you like," he said. "Will it be all right if I pass through the kitchen to get to the summerhouse?"

"The summerhouse is nearer the front. There's a flagstone path from the porch."

At this moment, Luzanna entered the kitchen from the back door. She stopped and looked from me to the unwelcome guest.

"She wants the kitchen to herself," he said to Luzanna. "We'll meet at dinner, then." He stopped and reversed his course. "I'll carry out a glass of tea from the parlor, as you suggested. Taking the route from the front this time, never fear."

Luzanna and I sighed together when the door closed behind him. "I hope you lock yourself in at night," she said, "and not just with one o'them old skeleton keys."

"There's a deadbolt." I hadn't shared my apprehensions about him with anyone, but Luzanna didn't have to be told.

"I met the telegraph boy out front." She held out the unmistakable brown paper. "It's for you."

I had to sit down. A third piece of disturbing news might do me in.

"It don't have to be something bad," she said.

"Of course not." I opened the seal, unfolded the paper and let my breath go. "It's from Barlow. He's coming home!"

"All's well then," she said.

So it seemed.

~

Only memories of Hester Townsend got me through dinners alone with Milton and Rona Chapman. In the early days of their stay I'd smoothed my hair and changed for dinner, but now if my dress was not stained or sweat-ringed, I merely patted my face dry and removed my apron. One reason for my carelessness was Milton Chapman's excessive compliments about my appearance, and the other was his wife Rona, who seemed to make an effort to look her worst.

Rona Chapman had features that might have been handsome on a man—a high forehead, a long, slightly bent nose and a square jaw. Curls would have softened her face, but she wound her hair in a bun that seemed to tighten the corners of her eyes and the flesh of her thin cheeks. Even in summer, she wore brown or gray dresses with long sleeves and high collars. She had more attractive clothing—when cleaning her room I'd seen stylish hats and bright, filmy dresses, reminders that I knew nothing about her. Our evening dinner was nearly the only time we were together, and I'd given up trying to engage her in conversation.

"Eat up, my dear," her husband said at every meal. "We're paying for it, you know."

When I greeted Mr. and Mrs. Chapman at dinner that evening, my mind was both uneasy about Irene Donnelly's return to Winkler and excited at the prospect of having Barlow home soon. With no other guests, it did not matter if Milton Chapman dominated the table talk. All I needed to do was ask how the house was coming along and nod at intervals.

"I have to keep right on my builders or they slack off," he said. "Mrs. Townsend, you should ride out with me to inspect it. There's enough framed up so you'll see what a grand place it's going to be. Rona will come too, of course."

I glanced at his wife, but she was picking a fork through her potato salad like she was looking for bugs. I intended to be too busy to go anywhere with him, even if she should come along. I'd never seen them leave the house together, but she often went for walks in the evening when he was out.

"My associates question why I'm building in such a remote area, though Rona's brother thinks his family's land comprises God's finest acres. Ours will be the best house in the county, a proper estate for a judge."

His wife glanced up. "You might tell your *associates* you're building there because the land is my *inheritance*."

In three weeks I'd rarely heard Rona Chapman say more than "If you please," and "No, thank you." Her husband seemed equally surprised. "I thought you wanted to be close to your family. I could have bought land anywhere."

"It will be hard to live where we're not wanted." She now addressed me. "My husband only wants my inheritance because my brother hates the idea of him having it. It's part of the land our father farmed, with cropland, pastures, and a fine barn, built by my brother."

"He shouldn't have built the barn on your portion of the estate," he said.

"My father was alive at the time. The property hadn't been divided."

They weren't talking to each other; this was for my enlightenment.

"The house will be our summer place," he said. "As a judge, I'll need a second home closer to the county seat."

"If he's elected," she said. "Someone might seek the office who actually knows a thing or two about the law."

I nearly choked. With a satisfied look, Rona now stirred her potato salad like she was making soup.

Her judgment did not seem to disturb him. "Some people may think I'm wasting my evenings at the roadhouse, but I'm making friends for future advancement—everyone from lowly miners to newspaper publishers."

I did not doubt the roadhouse had a large clientele. It was not only a public source for illegal whiskey, but a gambling site for wealthier men in the region, and as there were few rooms anywhere else for rent, a well-known place of secret encounters.

"My husband won't be elected from this county unless he wins the endorsement of the miners' union," Rona said. "And if enough states ratify the 19th Amendment, he'll also have to get the women's vote."

He forked a piece of meat into his mouth and spoke as he chewed. "They should be easily persuadable, as very few give signs of intelligent thought. But I understand most decent women are against the amendment. We voted it down before, and I'm confident our legislature will do the same again."

"It's been half a century in coming," his wife said, instructing me. "Fifteen states ratified the amendment almost immediately. We need only twenty more. This time we're going to get it."

Milton Chapman winked. "My wife admires those suffragettes who disrupt political meetings and thrust themselves into prominence by carrying signs on public streets. Personally, she's timid as a mouse."

She made no sign of taking offense. I also admired the suffragettes, but not wanting to prolong the argument, I tried to turn the topic with my own best piece of news. "Mr. Townsend will be with us tomorrow evening."

When they showed no interest, I drifted into my own reverie. Most of the time I thought only of the task at hand, but since yesterday I'd worried more than once about the letter in my account book and the reappearance of Irene Donnelly. Before dinner, Wanda had come again with a proposal that gave me goose bumps. She'd found me in our apartment, feeding the children while Emmy took my place in the kitchen.

"It's business," Wanda said. "You run a boardinghouse, and the old crow is set on living in Winkler. We'll pay you to keep her as a boarder."

Little Hettie's mouth was open, waiting for the spoon I'd paused in midair. My mouth hung open too, stuck dry for lack of words.

"At least say you'll think about it," Wanda said. "She says Will must take care of her. You know how he is, he might let her live with us, but we've no place for her to sleep. He's willing to pay her room and board."

"I can't have her here," I said. "She probably still hates me."

"Well then, maybe Luzanna's the one to take her in. Maybe if we tell Irene about her son's widow and grandkids being right here, she'll want to be with them."

"Please, hasn't Luzanna had enough bad luck? It would be better to pay someone else to keep her, someone far away where she won't bother us."

"I guess we could try that," Wanda said.

"For now we've got to tell Luzanna how we knew the Donnellys and explain why we didn't tell her a long time ago." If we revealed everything, Luzanna would understand why we'd held back the story, but I wasn't sure I could go that far. "I'll tell her in the morning. Do you want to be here?"

"Not particularly. Don't tell the bad stuff them boys did to us."

"Not unless I have to. It would hurt her to know, not that she had any respect for John Donnelly. But I think I need to tell about Jamie, because unless Irene has experienced a miraculous conversion, she'll be stirring all that up again."

~

Luzanna and I always chatted whenever we worked together, but this history required a sit-down. I chose the time immediately after breakfast, when Emmy took the children back to our apartment.

Luzanna's older daughter had gone away to college, and only her younger two lived with her now. Unlike the oldest, Emmy and her brother Tim were John Donnelly's offspring, and I hoped nobody would tell their grandmother about them until I had a chance to warn Luzanna.

We sat at the small breakfast table. Luzanna and I were about the same age, but she'd had a harder life. Her best feature was her voice, soft and warm. She'd been so good to me; I thought I'd do anything to keep her from further harm.

"There's something I should have told you long ago," I said.

She sat straighter and clutched the edge of the table. "Oh my Good Lord. Are you all right?"

"I'm fine. I need to tell you something about my past. I don't like to talk about it, and there's been no reason for you to know."

"But now it's important?"

"It's important, yes. Things are going to come out about me and some others. I'm sorry to say there's a connection to your family."

Her eyes were wide. "A sorry connection to my family, and I didn't know?"

"Here it is. Wanda and I knew your husband long ago, when we all lived in Winkler."

I watched her face. "All right," she said. "That's not too bad, though I can guess that knowing him might not of been a blessing. I'm glad Emmy and Tim don't remember much about him. They was little when him and his brother was killed."

It was terrible to be glad that the Donnelly boys were beyond hurting us, but the years had not softened my feelings about them. "When we knew them, your husband and his brother were in their teens, a few years older than Wanda. I also knew their mother, Irene. Did you ever meet her?"

"I never did, and all I know is John and her never got along. Him and me met in a mining camp. He said his ma moved around, and I don't think he knew where she was."

"She's here in Winkler now."

"She isn't! What a wonder. But I guess this was home at one time. Does she know me and the kids are here? Is that why she come? I wasn't sure John told her anything about us."

"It's Will she came to see, heard about him somewhere. I haven't talked with her. Frankly, she and I did not get on."

Luzanna took a deep, audible breath and blew it out from puffed cheeks. "I guess that's the sorry part, but don't worry, it comes as no surprise. John called her terrible names—his own ma—but maybe him and her was alike. Lordy, I suppose I'll have to meet her. Introduce her to the kids and all. Did she come to Will for doctoring?"

Now I got to the sorry part. "We didn't like keeping this from you, but we thought the less you knew, the better. She and Will's father were married for a short time."

Luzanna knew I'd taken care of Will and his brother and sister to pay my way in Hester's boardinghouse, but she didn't know the end of that story. Mrs. Donnelly had also needed a job, and she not only attacked me for it, she got it by marrying Will's father. The worst effect was not that I lost the small income, but that Will and Charlie had to live with her sons.

"Married!" Luzanna leaned back in her chair and laughed. "My John's ma and Will's pa? A short time? Well I would of loved to know that. Why was it a short time?"

"There was a huge fight. Your husband and his brother were involved. There was shooting, and she left town with the boys to keep from being arrested."

"Shooting—that seems right, knowing John. Do you have any idea if she knows her boys are dead?"

"I don't know. In fact, if she learns I'm here, I'm sure she'll be telling everyone that I was married to the man who murdered her husband."

"Good Lord—this gets worse and worse. Are you saying Barlow killed Will's pa?"

The sun had been up only a few hours, and already I was perspiring from the rising heat, the effort of explaining, and mostly from imagining the trouble Mrs. Donnelly would inflict. "Not Barlow, and not Will's pa. This is all so mixed up, and it's always been terrible to think about. You'll see why I didn't want to tell you. Will's father was Mrs. Donnelly's second husband. My first husband, Jamie Long, worked in the same lumber camp as Andrew Donnelly. They got into a fight, which was probably nothing unusual. I never knew if both had knives or just Jamie, but he won that fight, and he was accused of murder."

Luzanna rested an elbow on the table and supported her forehead with her hand. "Well, this is a lot to take in." Now she was watching me. "I'm sure that was a bad time, and I see why you didn't want to tell it." She reached her hand across the table. "It's got nothing to do with you and me."

"Irene said the fight was my fault. If she slanders me, I'll survive, but unless she's reformed herself, you won't want her anywhere near Emmy and Tim." I wasn't ready to reveal the reason she blamed me, not even to my closest friend.

"You got nothing to be ashamed of. But I doubt she's reformed. People don't change. Who else knows all this?"

"As far as I know, Wanda, Will, and Barlow are the only ones who were here at the time. Will's brother Charlie was here too, but you know Charlie's memory comes and goes. Their sister was just a baby."

"Well if you all don't want to tell her about me, there might be an answer," Luzanna said. "I feel no obligation to her. I could say we're a different bunch of Donnellys, no relation a tall."

"We'd go along with that, but I doubt it would work unless we could get her out of town quickly. Maybe you don't see it, but Wanda and I do. Your Tim is the spitting image of John Donnelly."

3

When Wanda rushed into the kitchen the next morning I took one look at her face and shook my head.

"It's too late to get the old witch away..." She stopped, seeing Luzanna's children at the table. Emmy and Tim stopped eating and got big-eyed.

"Breakfast is done." Luzanna lifted Hettie from the high chair and passed her to Emmy. "Tim, you go to the mill and help Simpson. Mind I said help, not hang about and get in his way. If he's got nothing for you to do, come right back here."

Wanda tightened her lips until the children left the room.

"I told Luzanna we knew her husband and how his father was killed," I said.

Luzanna smiled. "It's all right. I got no hard feelings."

Wanda slid into a chair. "Well, I'd hate Emmy and Tim to know my pa killed their grandpap. Irene hasn't made the connection, yet, 'cause she don't seem to remember me. But if she's here very long she's bound to tumble. And now it's too late to talk about moving her to some other town. That husband of mine is just too good. This morning he took her to one of the empty company houses and said he'd find her a few sticks of furniture. That was after she complained to high hell about sleeping last night on a dusty mattress in our old room in the store."

Luzanna glanced at the wall clock and began to stack our breakfast dishes. "I'm sorry she's giving you grief. I suppose I should take her in, but if she's anything like my kids' pa..."

"We don't want her living with any of our children," I said. "Any time I was close to Irene, she pushed me around or knocked me down, and she abused Will and Charlie. She blamed me for her husband's death, and she took my job. I don't know, but I've always believed it was because of her sons that Charlie ran away. I'm sorry, Luzanna. Maybe you see why we never wanted to talk about any of this."

I hadn't told the worst, but Luzanna didn't need to hear more. "What should I tell my kids? And when?"

Wanda went to the door. "I told mine she's not got all her marbles and to pay no heed to anything she says. And I threatened Otis within an inch of his life if he repeated that to her or anyone else."

"Let's think about it," I said. "Luzanna and I can pretend for a day or two that we don't know she's in town."

~

I did not get even half a day to pretend ignorance. Shortly after lunch, I answered the front doorbell, and there she was, holding her carpetbag and giving me the once-over. My first impression was that she looked about to burst the seams of her dress. The second was that except for being heavier and having gray hair, she looked just as she had when she filled the doorway of

Morris Herff's house. I flinched, fully expecting to be pushed aside.

"I'm Mrs. Herff and I want your best room." Bold as brass, Hester would have said, but that's what she'd said about Wanda, insisting such a ragged, undisciplined girl could not lodge under her roof. As calmly as I could, I directed the woman into our small office at the front of the house. My knees trembled as I sat behind the desk. She'd given no sign of recognizing me, but I'd seen her puffy face and her small brown eyes too often in nightmares to forget her. "A room for one night?" Maybe she only needed a place to stay while Will fixed up her house.

She settled herself in the opposite chair and dropped her bag to the floor. "I'll tell you when I'm ready to go."

I slid our register across the desk and watched her sign "Mrs. Morris Herff." She seemed to breathe with effort, but her hands were plump and smooth and her fingernails were neatly rounded, not bitten off and chipped from work like mine and Luzanna's.

"The rate is a dollar seventy-five for a room and three meals a day if you're staying less than a week, a dollar thirty-five if by the week."

"That much? Well, money don't matter if everything else is good." She glanced from side to side. "This place don't look dirty, but maybe I should see the room and get an idea of the cooking before I pay."

"We require payment in advance," I said. "You may see the room first, then pay for one night, and if you decide to stay longer, we'll adjust the rate. We serve plain food, dinner with everyone in the evening, and items set out at breakfast and lunch for our guests to serve themselves."

"If I don't like the meals or the room's not kept clean I'll ask my money back. Maybe I'll eat somewheres else."

"We serve the same food as we eat ourselves, and you pay the rate whether you eat it or not."

"Hoity-toity, ain't you? Is this how you start off with everyone?"

"Only those who talk about getting their money back before they've paid." I stood, feeling moderately in control. "I'll get someone to show you the room. If you decide to stay, you'll have to come back to this office with your payment."

Mrs. Donnelly placed her hands on the desk and pushed herself to her feet. "I'll see the room."

"Wait here just a moment." I escaped to the kitchen, where Luzanna was swatting flies.

"She's here! *Irene. Donnelly.* She calls herself Mrs. Herff and you go by Hale, so you don't have to reveal yourself yet. We'll have a bit of time to decide about telling your kids." I took Luzanna's flyswatter and missed a fly on the side of the pie safe by at least a foot. "How did all these flies get in? Do you understand? Your ma-in-law is here. I need you to show her a room. She doesn't get to stay unless she pays in advance, so make sure she comes back to the office. If she asks your name, just say 'Luzanna.' Or 'Luzanna Hale.'"

She found her voice. "You changed your mind? Does she know you?"

"I don't believe she does, but we'll deal with that later. I doubt Will sent her—he'd have warned me."

"We'll manage her if that's what it comes to," Luzanna said. "We need boarders, don't we?"

"You're right, of course." Pride and fear had made me say "no" to Wanda's proposal, but I was in no position to turn away new income. Likewise, I was going to have to speak plainly to Milton Chapman, whose payment was two weeks overdue.

"I'm going up the street to speak with Wanda and Will. After Irene sees the room, bring her back down to the office and keep her there until I get back. Read her our house rules and don't let her give you any guff."

Luzanna took off her apron and laid it on the worktable. "I'm kinda curious to see what she looks like. Don't worry about me. I survived being married to her son, and I don't see how anyone could be worse."

I pushed our bicycle to the hard-surfaced road. We'd built the boardinghouse at the northern edge of town, a twenty-minute walk to the company store where Will had his doctor office. I hadn't a lot of practice on the bicycle, but if I didn't spill, it would get me there in less than half that time. I started with a wobble, but soon sped along, cheering myself with thoughts of Barlow's return, and how much less our guests would get under my skin when he was in the house.

Will's waiting room was always crowded with miners' wives and children. As soon as she saw me, Wanda motioned me into the treatment room, followed by grumbles of favoritism.

"It's Irene," I whispered, as she shut the door between us and the complainers. "She's at the boardinghouse, bent on staying."

I was instantly sorry to have bothered Will, who worked long hours and by Wanda's report, suffered when his patients' conditions did not improve. He was younger than Wanda by two years, but already his black hair was turning gray, and his brow always seemed wrinkled. "May Rose," he said, "I left her at a company house up near the school."

"I knew that house wouldn't be good enough," Wanda said. "She's come here to be waited on for the rest of her life. Ma, you're awful red in the face."

I fanned my face with my hand. "I rode the bicycle, and it's hot."

Will led me to a chair. "The last thing I want is to upset you. Someone must have told her about the boardinghouse. If she won't leave, I'll carry her out myself."

"I'm not asking that. If I mean to be in business, I can't be choosy about my guests, providing they follow the rules. But I told her she needs to pay each week in advance. Nine dollars and 45 cents. I thought that might turn her away."

Will reached into his pocket. "I doubt she has a cent. Last night she ate like she hadn't so much as smelled food in days."

"I don't like to ask you for money."

He pressed nine ones and a half-dollar piece into my hand. "You're not asking, I'm offering. And if you're keeping her, I'd say Wanda and I got the best end of it."

"This won't be the end, you can bet on that," Wanda said. "But I guess we're obliged. Do you think Lu will be okay about the kids knowing their granny?"

My sigh was a match for their gloomy faces. "We haven't crossed that bridge yet."

~

Luzanna and I could not decide whether to cross that bridge sooner or later. "We might give her a day to settle in," I said.

"Or longer. Maybe the truth won't come out, but if and when it does, you can pretend we didn't know she was a Donnelly or you didn't know I was the stupid woman who married her son. But oh, May Rose, it raises the hair on my neck, how she reminds me of him! I told her she should wait for you to get back before settling in but she told me how her son who was a doctor and mine owner would be taking care of her bills. Her *son*, not stepson, mind you that. She wouldn't wait in the office—she trotted upstairs and used all the hot water for a bath. In this heat, imagine. She must of filled up the whole tub."

I locked Will's payment in our small office safe, uneasy about my resolution to endure this woman. I wouldn't tell Barlow all our troubles right away, because he'd be tired from his trip and I wanted him to have a few hours to enjoy being home. But before he met her at dinner, I needed to warn him about Mrs. Irene Donnelly, now Herff.

Mid-afternoon, I set the dining room table and breaded the chicken so I could devote myself to Barlow and the children before we had to join our guests in the dining room.

At 3:45 I sent our handyman John Johnson with his horse and wagon to bring Barlow home from the Barbara Town railway station. At 4:30, John appeared at the back door.

"There was no passenger car," he said.

"No passenger car?" I pulled Barlow's telegram from my apron pocket. "This is the right day. And no other train scheduled?"

"So they say." He peered into the kitchen. "I smell fresh bread."

John Johnson had come to Winkler before its revival, an out-of-work miner with a crippled foot who'd squatted in one of Will's old houses and found ways to make himself indispensable. We couldn't afford to hire him full time, but he always came when he was needed, and because he never charged much, we usually tipped him with a slice of pie or a loaf of fresh bread. He was another friend who seemed like family.

Luzanna handed him a loaf wrapped in newspaper. "I knew you was coming," she said.

For the next half hour, I tried to think of reasonable explanations for Barlow's delay. Then the doorbell rang and there he stood, dusty and red in the face, with two suitcases at his feet and his suit jacket over his arm. When I threw my arms around him, he nearly collapsed.

I drew him over the threshold. "You walked! I sent John Johnson..."

He turned to pick up his suitcases but he was slow and I reached them first.

"There was no passenger car. The conductor let me ride in the caboose."

"I'm sorry..."

He kissed my cheek. I closed my eyes, relieved and excited to feel him near, the stubble of his chin

brushing my face, the shock of black hair that swiped
my forehead, the familiar scent of his sweat. "It's all
right," he said.

But it wasn't all right; I'd never seen him look so
tired and tottery. As we went through the hall, Milton
Chapman came down the stairs. "Mr. Townsend, is it?
Yes, it better be, the way our hostess is hanging on to
you. But maybe not. Perhaps you are her father?"

I'm sure my face showed my disgust, and I felt
Barlow straighten beside me. But there was more to
endure. Irene Herff pushed herself up from a parlor
chair. "Strike me if it ain't Mr. Townsend. Without a
doubt it is; you're him. And still doing good for
yourself..." She stretched her arms wide. "...by the look
of all this. So her right there is your missus?"

Barlow went into the parlor and shook hands with
Irene, then with Milton Chapman. "I am Barlow
Townsend, and this lady is indeed my wife."

Milton Chapman stood with his shoulders back
and his legs slightly apart, grinning like he'd just struck
gold.

I hurried the introductions. "Mrs. Herff arrived
today; she's Will's stepmother."

"Mrs. Herff, Mr. Chapman, welcome to the house,"
Barlow said. His innocent tone didn't fool me. He knew
exactly who she was.

"We must go to the children," I said. "We'll meet
again at dinner."

Our apartment door shut out the strangers in the
house and opened us to what we loved best. "All of you
smell so good," Barlow said, stooping and hugging
Freddy. "I shouldn't touch anyone—I haven't had a

proper bath for a week." His eyes drooped, and his cheeks were thin and darkened by a day's beard.

"We don't care. Sit, and I'll put Freddy and Hettie on your lap."

Emmy left to fetch the children's dinner, and we stole a moment to stand close with our cheeks together and our arms around each other before he followed my advice and sat down. He reacquainted himself with the children until Emmy returned, and we did not speak of Irene Herff until he had bathed and rested. He lay on our bed in his underwear, while I sat on the edge and told what I knew.

"You're right, Luzanna must be the one to reveal her relationship to Irene, if she chooses," he said. "And if Irene causes problems, I'll deal with her." He rose from the bed and began to dress, moving slowly.

"I can manage her," I said. I needed to do that, not only to test my mettle, but to avoid putting additional burdens on my husband. He'd come home looking ten years older.

4

At dinner that evening, Rona Chapman sat straighter in her chair and gave greater attention to the conversation, especially the few times Barlow spoke. Meanwhile, her husband and Irene Herff competed in their attempts to rule the hour.

"Mr. Townsend and me is old friends," Irene said, with a self-important nod to Milton Chapman and his wife.

Barlow did not deny or add a comment to her claim.

"And my son is the doctor here, did I tell you?"

"Several times," Milton Chapman said.

Unable to resist, I spoke to Rona, who sat on my right. "Dr. Herff is her stepson. Mrs. Herff was married to his father, about a month, wasn't it?"

Irene peered down the table. "What do you know of it?"

"Mrs. Townsend was here at the time," Barlow said. "We remember the circumstances."

She continued to squint down the table at me, apparently ignorant of the warning in those words. I wondered if I'd changed that much, or if I'd not been important enough for her to remember.

Milton Chapman raised his eyebrows, ready to hear more about the Herff family circumstances. After some silence in which no one elaborated, he turned to Barlow. "So, Mr. Townsend, do you enjoy a game of cards?"

Barlow nodded. "Occasionally." He did not seem to have a good appetite; everyone else had finished, but his plate was half full.

"You might like to go with me to the roadhouse some evening. There's always a game in progress, and a few who play for high stakes."

"I don't think it would suit me," Barlow said. "I play only for enjoyment."

Rona Chapman smiled. "My husband plays for enjoyment too—the delight of winning. You must be warned—his skill at cards is his only claim to success. All that land he won, for example. He sold it to a coal company, and now we're rich." She turned to me, but spoke loud enough for all to hear. "The land included a church and a cemetery, all destroyed now. I knew the family that was evicted."

Her husband made a great display of taking a cigar from his jacket pocket and removing the gold band. "They were nothing to you."

"I am capable of sympathy," she said.

Irene Herff had continued to stare at me. "Now I think about it you do look familiar, but I don't recall Mr. Townsend being married. Seems to me all the women talked about back then was how he was a bachelor and did he have any lady friends."

Barlow remained silent, and I wasn't about to help her memory. I could imagine Milton Chapman's enjoyment, should he hear the gossip as well as the truth about Jamie and me.

"O'course none of us would of been good enough for him, even the lookers, him being the boss of Winkler Lumber and all. So you were here then, Mrs. Townsend? What was your name before you was married?"

I smiled at my husband. "Percy." I wasn't sure that even Barlow remembered the name; back then he'd known me only as May Rose Long.

"Why Mr. Townsend, I believe you robbed the cradle," Milton Chapman said.

Irene picked her teeth with a fingernail. "Happens all the time. Rich men can have any woman they want."

Again Barlow said nothing, and Milton Chapman launched into a long description of his personal wealth, his fine house under construction, the delays and the general unreliability of the workmen. "I'd not stay in such a hole of a town if the workers didn't need regular supervision," he said. "I mean, there's no tailor, and not even a shoe-shine boy!"

Through some of this conversation, Luzanna had cleared the table and brought desert, Barlow's favorite, apple dumplings in cream.

"That was a wonderful dinner," Rona Chapman said to Luzanna.

"Thank you. Me and Mrs. Townsend cooked it together."

"The food here may be all right," Irene Herff said, digging into her apple dumpling. "Though I'd say from the looks of Mr. Townsend's plate he don't care for it."

Barlow folded his table napkin and laid it beside his untouched dessert, then stood and slowly pushed in his chair. "If you'll excuse me."

"And me." I followed him from the room, tired of being pleasant to our rude guests. Before we reached the hall I smelled cigar smoke and heard Irene Herff say smoking at the table was against the house rules. Then she laughed.

I turned back to the dining room in time to see Milton Chapman lighting a cigar for Irene. "Please extinguish those," I said.

He smiled through yellow teeth. "Are you rejoining us?"

"I am not."

"Then there's nobody here to care."

His wife snatched the cigar from his mouth and stubbed it on his dessert plate. "I'm somebody."

He rolled his eyes at Irene, who blew smoke, laughed, and choked.

I stared until she put out her cigar. *Old whore*, I thought, smiling.

~

With Barlow beside me, I experienced no bad dreams, but woke that night to the reverberation of an argument in Rona Chapman's room, directly above our bedroom. Though the words were indistinct, the tone was clear. Something heavy hit the floor, then the door slammed. Soon after, I heard the start of a car engine.

Barlow slept on, stretched on his back as quiet and still as death. I lay awake, certain he needed a long rest at home, uncertain about everything else, including what was going on above our heads. Finally, the kind of fear that creeps in with the stillness of the house drew me from bed. I tiptoed upstairs to Rona's door. There was a strip of light at the bottom, but when I gave the door a soft tap the light went out. I stood a moment in the shadows cast by the small lamp on the hall table. Then the door opened.

"I'm sorry for the noise," she said. "I stumbled over my own feet and fell over a table. The table fell too." With the dark room behind her, I could not see her distinctly, but she looked to be wearing her dinner dress. "I don't believe the table was hurt."

"I wanted to be sure you were all right."

"You're very kind. Please don't worry about me," she said.

~

The morning sky was turning pink and the breeze coming into the kitchen smelled of grass newly cut and dried. I'd gotten up and fed the children without Barlow waking, and Emmy had taken them back to their playroom. Luzanna was rolling out biscuit dough and I was washing dishes. Each day we set breakfast on the sideboard precisely at seven-thirty and luncheon at noon so the guests could serve themselves, but we had coffee ready at any time. Neither Rona nor Milton Chapman came down until mid-morning.

"That was quite a time last night," Luzanna said. "I thought things might blow up any minute. But I'm sorry, I know it must of been hard for you and Barlow." She meant the interactions at dinner; I hadn't told her about the noises from Rona Chapman's room or my suspicion that Milton Chapman had struck his wife.

"Barlow has dealt with irritating people all his life, but my food does not go down well when I have to suffer dinner with them."

"You'll teach them some manners. I don't know which part I liked best, you telling John's ma to put out her cigar or Mrs. Chapman talking back to her husband."

I laughed. "That was a surprise."

"Maybe John's ma and him together was more than she could take. Anyway, I told Emmy about her granny last night. I thought it was best, there being a good chance they'll run smack into each other. Emmy has a fear of mean people, so I straight-out told what her father said about his ma. She'll play dumb until I decide to let John's ma know who we are. Which maybe I won't never have to do."

"And Tim?" I liked the boy, but he was strong-willed, and I was always afraid his father's wildness would come out in him.

"I didn't tell him nothing. I got him up at sunrise and sent him to Lucie Bosell's place to help with the horses and other stock till school starts. He's been wanting to go—he loves them horses."

I experienced a small chink of relief. "This is our house, and if Irene causes trouble, I intend to make her leave. But I don't want her to make your family's life miserable, or Will's either."

Luzanna put a finger to her lips. "Someone's coming."

We listened to the heavy, halting steps in the hall, like someone was dragging a foot. Luzanna shot me a questioning look.

Whoever it was had entered the dining room. Then the door between us swung wide, revealing the bulk of Irene Herff. Seeing her in the doorway brought back the memory of the dimly-lit Herff house when she'd blocked my way to the children. I held her gaze while I lifted my hands from the dishwater and squeezed them dry on my apron, proud they were steady.

"I'll be having breakfast now," she said.

"Good morning, Mrs. Herff. It's early. We lay out breakfast at seven-thirty."

"Don't look like you're doing much for the present. I'd like an egg, fried with a soft yolk. And I'll take some of them biscuits with butter and jam."

"As you see, the biscuits are not yet baked. And we do not serve eggs. Biscuits and sausage gravy will be on the sideboard at the time specified in the house rules."

She didn't move. "If you want more money for an egg, you can put it on my bill."

"Mrs. Herff, we do not make meals to special order. You might find another place more to your liking, or a house where you could cook for yourself." I had little hope she would take that suggestion; as Wanda had said, the woman wanted to be waited on.

She labored into the kitchen and pulled a chair from our family table. "Then I'll sit here and have some o'that coffee. You won't grudge me that?"

Luzanna and I exchanged tight glances as I turned my back to the unwelcome guest and poured her cup of coffee.

"With cream," she said.

I took my time skimming cream from the top of the milk jug and pouring it into a cream pitcher. Then

I carried a tray with the pitcher and her cup of coffee to the dining room door. "Mrs. Herff, we're busy here. I'll set your coffee in the dining room."

She rose like every joint in her body hurt. "Not friendly, are ya?"

"This is a business."

"Ah, right. Not much of one, from the looks."

I set the tray on the dining room table and held the door for her to pass through. "Let me know anytime you want to leave and I'll put your stepson's advance payment in your hands."

"No need to be rude," she said. "There's one more thing. I want a room on this floor. I can't manage them stairs up and down all day."

"I'm sorry, there are no rooms on this floor."

"It's a long set of stairs. Mr. Chapman says you've got lots of space down here."

"Not guest rooms. Let me know if you decide to leave and I'll have your money ready." I let the door close between us.

Luzanna and I worked on without talk, communicating with motions and glances. I took the plates from the cupboard and Luzanna carried them to the dining room. When the biscuits came out of the oven, I fixed a tray for Barlow and left Luzanna in charge of the dining room. Then I put on a confident smile for my family.

In the apartment, I set the breakfast tray on a table beside Barlow's chair and opened the door to our room to see if he was awake. Immediately I knew something was wrong. He lay across the bed with his legs hanging over the edge and his feet touching the floor.

"I'm all right," he said. "My legs gave way."

Gave way? "Is it the flu?"

"My stomach seems fine. Give me your hand and let me try again."

I sat beside him and put my arm around his back as he sat up. He put an arm over my shoulder. "So far so good."

"Are you ready to stand? Not light headed?"

"I'm ready."

As we started to rise together, he bore down on my shoulder. I watched his legs and feet to see if they were steady. He flopped his feet on the floor like he was trying to get a grip, then he leaned heavily on me and I knew we were about to fall together. I pushed my hand against his chest and we fell backwards on the bed. He gasped. "I'm sorry. I don't know what's wrong."

"Travel weakness," I said, like his surprising loss of function was not surprising at all and had nothing to do with my surge of panic. "You'll be fine with a spell of bed rest. Let me straighten you out." I was used to lifting heavy baskets of wet sheets and toweling, and his legs were like that—dead weights. One at a time, I lifted them onto the bed, then helped him scoot to a sitting position. "Is this comfortable? Why not rest and I'll bring your breakfast tray."

He grimaced. "I have to—I have to go."

"Oh." The apartment bathroom was at least 20 steps away.

"A bottle or a pail," he said.

I hurried to the basement and found a Mason jar and the porcelain bedpan Wanda had brought when I was sick with the flu. "What..." Luzanna said, when I carried them into the kitchen.

"Barlow is sick."

Going back through the hall, I met Milton Chapman. Today he wore a striped jacket, those white baggy knickers, white stockings and a strong perfume. "Well, well," he said. "What's this?"

I stuck the bedpan under my arm. "Breakfast has been set in the dining room."

"I trust everyone is well?"

"Perfectly," I said. The walls of our apartment were thick and the door was heavy, but when I closed it, I could still smell him.

I gave the jar to Barlow, then sent Emmy with an urgent note to Will.

5

Any time I am tempted to judge a person by his first impression, I remember my first meeting with Will Herff when he was 11, dirty and surly. He and Charlie were supposed to be taking care of their baby sister, Glory, because their mother had recently died. The boys had imitated their father's neglect, and Glory was seldom changed and fed. In that first impression, I saw no sign of what would turn out to be Will's unflinching loyalty or his desire to improve everything within his reach. Maybe those traits emerged only after he was no longer hungry and beaten, or after his brother disappeared and his sister was adopted. During the years when I lived half a continent away, Will had taken responsibility for his father, then for the entire ruined town, and later for the health of people in the hills around Winkler. Such dedication gave him a constant look of fatigue, yet I seldom saw him agitated or hurried.

I appreciated his steadiness now. I longed to ask what he was learning as he pressed the flesh of Barlow's legs, looked in his eyes and down his throat, listened to his chest, and asked him to whistle.

"I never could whistle," Barlow said.

"It takes practice. I used to whistle for my dogs. Just pucker up and give us some sound," Will said.

The whistle was breathy, but Will said "good," his first comment. I hoped he meant good in all respects.

"Can you take off your nightshirt?"

I moved toward the bed to help, but Will said, "I'd rather he do it."

Barlow lifted his arms and pulled the shirt over his head. Will pressed the flesh along Barlow's spine and the back of his neck, asking "Any pain here? Or here?"

At every touch, Barlow said, "No pain." Will pressed Barlow's arms and fingers with the same response.

"Did you eat breakfast?"

"Part of it."

"Did you piss this morning?"

"Yes."

"Good."

The second encouraging word.

"Let's see you try to stand."

Again, I moved toward the bed, but Will said, "I'll help if he needs it."

Barlow used his hands to lift his legs over the edge of the bed, then leaned forward as if to stand. Will caught him as his legs buckled.

"I see," Will said.

I hoped he saw more than we did, including the remedy for whatever this was. Together we helped Barlow lie back on the bed.

Will pricked Barlow's feet and legs with a pin. "Ouch," Barlow said.

"Good." He took one of Barlow's feet in both hands and pushed his leg. "Now, push it back."

He could not. Will pushed the other foot with the same result.

Barlow frowned. "Is it apoplexy?"

Will sat on a chair beside the bed and wrote for a few minutes in a pocket-sized leather notebook. "I don't think so, but it's too early to tell. Your temperature and pupils are normal, your breathing seems regular though your heart rate is slightly elevated. You have no swelling, you're capable of feeling pain in your legs, you're alert and you have no loss of speech. Have you had any recent injuries?"

"Yesterday morning I slipped on wet pavement—my feet went right out from under me. I sat down quite hard. It was embarrassing," Barlow said, "but the worst part was riding home in wet, muddy trousers."

I watched Will to see if Barlow's fall might be significant.

He didn't react. "Recent insect bites?"

Barlow shook his head, and Will stood. "I'll come back tomorrow, but send for me if anything changes. I'll send over a wheeled chair so you don't have to stay in bed."

I asked, "Perhaps if he exercised his legs?"

"It can't hurt. Try a liniment massage several times a day and work his legs back and forth, as I did."

"Should he try to stand?"

"Let's not risk a fall."

"I'm just tired," Barlow said. "My legs will be fine after a bit of rest."

"Rest is good." Will's smile always looked worried.

I accompanied him to the porch, but because Milton Chapman was there we went on to the end of the path where he'd parked his two-passenger Nash. It was almost hidden behind Chapman's long touring car.

"You have other questions," Will said. "You want to know if he will recover. It's too early to say. This muscle weakness could be many things."

"But you have concerns."

"I'm always concerned. Watch him closely for changes. He could recover in a few days, or this might be the start of something worse."

"Like what?" I wanted to hear of something benign and curable, not creeping paralysis.

"There's no need to speculate."

"But you're speculating."

"It's my job to think of everything. I'll be searching for answers. It will be your job to trust in a good outcome."

"I know, but I can't stop thinking. It will help me—get ready—won't it?"

He took my hand. "It will drive you crazy. Think about your work, your children. Think of ways to keep Barlow's spirits up."

I waved as he drove away, then tried to relax my face before turning back to the house.

Milton Chapman got up from his chair when I reached the steps. "So that was Irene's boy, the rich doctor?"

"That was Dr. Herff, and he's not Irene's boy. As it happens, she and Dr. Herff's father did not get along, and they lived together for only a few weeks. No matter what she says, she is not part of Dr. Herff's family. Naturally, you may believe what you like."

He looked amused. "I'm sure you never speak anything but the truth. So how's the old man?"

"Mr. Herff? He died many years ago."

"*Your* old man, that is."

"I gave him my Hester Townsend stare and let the door slam before he could say anything else.

~

While Barlow was weakened—and Lord forbid, if he continued to weaken—I'd need to be twice the woman I was. I spent the morning disguising my fears while I massaged and exercised his legs and played with the children near his bed.

Clearly he was exhausted, and often he nodded off with a book lying face-down on his chest. When he was awake, he made no demands and kept a cheery countenance, but at one point he said, "May Rose, if I can't work..."

"There's no use to worry ourselves about something that hasn't happened." It seemed dangerous to speak of worst possibilities, though my mind was stuck there.

Just before noon, Luzanna delivered lunch to the apartment. "I should hire someone to help you," I said.

"Me and Emmy's doing fine. We might need another woman on laundry day, especially when the teachers come. O'course that's weeks away, and by then he... by that time everything could be back to the way it was. When school starts, Em can come and help of an evening, and she can help with the kids Saturday and Sundays. Rest of the time, you and me can watch them between us. I'm used to working with little ones under my feet."

"I don't like the idea of taking all the girl's free time," I said. I'd not been much older than Emmy when my aunt's death had left me in charge of the house and my three younger cousins, ending most opportunities to walk and talk with girls my own age. Those years had left me capable, but beyond the house I was shy and uncertain.

"Oh, Em likes being here with us. She's timid, you know, and some of the town kids is rough. I'll slip out today and find us a washwoman. Wanda will know somebody."

That afternoon Wanda drove Luzanna back to the boardinghouse in Will's new car. Strong as I vowed to be, I almost broke down when I saw her in the entryway. She quickly made me smile.

"It's my first time driving," Wanda said. "You see how Lu ain't over it yet."

Luzanna's face was sweaty and sickly white. "I'll be getting back to the kitchen," she said, like she'd been holding her breath.

Seeing Milton Chapman on the stairs, I motioned Wanda into the office and closed the door.

"I told Will it was dumb to buy a two-seater when there's four of us," Wanda said lightly, "but it was a good price and it's right handy when we want to go somewhere quick."

Like to the bedside of a dying patient, I thought. But Barlow wasn't dying or in serious decline. He couldn't be.

"I need to sit a minute 'cause I been on the run today." She dropped into one of the wing chairs. Wanda rarely hid her thoughts, but when she tried, I always recognized the sign—the rapid shift of her eyes.

"Is Will worried about Barlow?"

"He hasn't said nothing like that." Her eyes shifted again, making me think she did not have the courage to talk about Barlow, or didn't want to make me cry, or didn't want to cry herself. My throat dried.

She rose from the chair. "So, Barlow had a little spell, did he? Suppose I could say hello?"

I was sure Will had not said "little spell," but because she offered no worried consolation, I managed to smile. "He'd like that."

We moved to the apartment, and she sat beside the bed and jabbered about the mine and store business as though Barlow were still one of the partners. Seeing the interest in his eyes and hearing his questions and answers, I could believe all would be well.

When Wanda said she needed to go home to feed her family, I accompanied her to the porch. "I'm sorry we've saddled you with Will's stepma," she said. "If she's too much, toss her out. You don't need her hogwash."

"We'll manage."

She narrowed her eyes. "I mean it, toss her out and we'll deal with her. One of us will come to see Barlow every day, and oftener if you need anything. Say the word if he don't want visitors, but I think he liked our talk, don't you?"

"He liked it very much. Thank you, I'm grateful."

"You don't have to thank me. It's not often I can just sit and jaw."

I held off panicky thoughts about our future only by filling my head with immediate needs. There were plenty of those. And I hadn't told Barlow about the letter in the account book.

6

A houseful, that's what I'd thought I wanted. In Hester's boardinghouse, everyone had seemed agreeable, and now I wondered if her influence had made them so. At least my guests had regular habits. Over the next three days, Irene Herff continued to come downstairs before breakfast and drink coffee alone in the dining room, then sit most of the day on the porch or in the parlor with her head back, her eyes closed and her mouth open.

Will came to see Barlow every other day, perplexed but hopeful because though he was no better, he was no worse. Barlow claimed he was enjoying a vacation, but I knew he was bearing up for my sake. I did the same for him.

Irene Herff managed to wake up when Will was there. She scolded if he did not come into the parlor to properly greet his "ma" or inquire with enough concern about her health.

The more my guests revealed themselves, the more privacy I craved. Thus far Irene had not recalled our old connection or learned that her daughter-in-law and grandchild were under the same roof much of every day. Milton Chapman usually left after lunch, supposedly to check on his house, and his wife kept to her room even in the afternoon heat. He began each dinner gathering by asking if Mr. Townsend continued to be in poor health, did I think he was failing or would he be joining them soon? It was hard to give a civil reply.

Irene pressed her complaints at every dinner hour. The stairs were too steep; she'd seen mouse dirt in the bottom of a dresser drawer and the sheets on her bed smelled musty—they could not have been dry when they were put on.

I kept telling myself that I needed a thicker skin. And we'd been open for business only a few months— surely our current guests were not typical. Soon we would be joined by the teachers, who'd be too busy to be pesky. But even when changes were positive and exciting, they required new actions and interactions, all exhausting.

I reserved more time for the children and Barlow, and though the unknowns and challenges of his paralysis were always on my mind, those hours in the apartment helped me endure my encounters with Milton Chapman and Irene, who seemed to look for ways to irritate me. Barlow suggested I kill them with kindness, so I made sure a full pitcher of water sat in the parlor through the hot afternoons and gave each room a second electric fan for sticky nights. Luzanna said our guests did not deserve such generosity. Rona Chapman was the only one who thanked me.

"You understand," I said one night at dinner, "the extra fans belong to rooms currently unoccupied. When new residents arrive, I'll have to restore those fans to their rooms."

Milton Chapman made a show of turning his head like he was trying to see evidence of other guests. I knew his provocations might simply be his way of having fun, but I felt like I was losing a battle for control of my house. After dinner, I asked him and his wife to join me in the office.

Inside, we remained standing. "I must be fair," I said, closing the door. "I need payment for two weeks in arrears and one week in advance."

Rona Chapman pursed her lips and glanced sideways at her husband. He tried to stare me down. "Or?"

"Or you can leave in the morning."

He clicked his tongue. "There's no need to be hasty. You've no one lined up for our rooms, and you know you'll be paid in due time."

"I've given you too much time. No more."

He sighed with a show of sadness. "I suppose you need the money."

"For goodness sake, Milton, own up to your responsibilities," Rona said. "I'm sorry, Mrs. Townsend. Money doesn't easily leave his pocket unless it's destined for a card table."

He fumbled in his jacket. "Very well. I'll write a draft on our bank. And I want a receipt."

"You can give her cash." She turned to me. "You treat us very well. This won't happen again."

Clenching an unlit cigar between his teeth, he opened his wallet and counted the bills into my hand, a transaction that looked so painful that I repressed a smile. I wrote a receipt and followed them to the entryway, where Irene Herff waited by the front door.

"Ready and willing," she said. She wore a wine-colored taffeta dress that smelled of old sweat, exposed her turkey neck and revealed the top of her bulging bosom. "Leave the light burning, 'cause me and Milton is gonna be late."

He turned to his wife. "My dear, will you join us at the roadhouse?"

"Not tonight," she said, equally sweet.

For a change, I had something good and something humorous to report to my husband, but first I needed to help Luzanna with the dishes and put the children to bed. When finally I got to our room, Barlow was reading. He folded the newspaper and set it aside. "At least my eyes are good. And I've still got my mind."

He smiled. "So I believe."

I sat on the bed and spread Milton Chapman's bills before him. "Paid up. I won't let him fall behind again."

He examined the bills one by one. "All good. I don't think he'd deliberately pass counterfeit money, not if he aspires to be a judge, as you say. But counterfeit money occasionally appears at the roadhouse."

He rolled to his side and reached the lockbox under the bedside table. He'd been doing as much as possible to use the parts of his body that were not weak, lifting himself from the bed to the wheeled chair and maneuvering the chair through our apartment. This week I'd suggested that while he was home he manage the boardinghouse accounts. It was not much work, but he understood that he was helping in this small way, and he did not protest my assumption that he would soon be on the road again.

"While I'm here, I'm not going to leave you to dine alone with those people."

I didn't think both of us needed to ruin our digestion. "You've been away from the children so much. It's good for them to have dinner with you."

"We'll take turns," he said, "so you can help Luzanna or stay with Freddy and Hettie."

No one was more considerate.

~

Irene Herff went to the roadhouse every night that week and always had a bit of gossip to pass along at the next evening's dinner. I was especially uneasy at those times, expecting her to reveal something she'd heard about me. While she named regulars at the roadhouse, prominent men—*married don't you know*—who openly petted and kissed their lady friends, I imagined words I might use to defuse her if she began to talk about me. I was certain I'd fail. She and Milton Chapman sometimes smiled at each other like they shared a secret.

"You got a new woman working," she said, after the second washday. "She sneaks around on cat feet, don't she? But she looks like a strong one."

"A handsome woman," Milton Chapman said.

The washwoman moved about the house so quietly we barely noticed her, and she was indeed handsome, her face long and thin but with all the features perfectly in place, her olive skin clear; her hair smooth.

"I'm in need of a maid," Irene Herff said. "I'll try her, see if she suits."

Milton Chapman grimaced. "With what you won last night, you could hire a full staff. Or buy a car of your own. Hire a driver."

She made a snoot. "I might do that."

"You might find a house with no stairs," I said.

She wiggled in her chair, pleased with her prosperity. "I do fancy an egg for breakfast."

Two days later, Irene Herff rapped on the apartment door. "Your washwoman said being my maid won't suit her."

I kept one hand on the door.

"I want someone an hour in the morning to help me get in and outa the tub and into my clothes. Half an hour before dinner, and half before bed. It's all right with me if beggars want to be choosers, but somebody here's got to help me. Maybe that girl that watches your kids."

Her granddaughter. "Impossible," I said. "She's a child, not strong enough to help you out of the tub. What's more, I need her. Please don't approach her."

She held her ground. "Colored women are strong. Get me one o'them."

"Hiring help for guests is not a service we provide. If you had your own house in Winkler, I'm sure you'd find it easier to hire someone nearby to work the odd hours you require."

"If this business was mine, I'd give people what they want." She smirked. "Maybe I'll buy it when it falls through."

"Good luck," I said.

"Don't you worry about me! I'm climbing up in the world."

She never let me have the last word.

Later that day John Johnson and a clerk from the store carried a carton up the stairs to her room. Wanda cornered me when she came to see Barlow. "The old witch bought a safe," she said. "If she's got so much money she's got to lock it up, I see no reason why Will should pay her keep."

"You tell her. I'm trying to convince her she needs to move to a grand place of her own." It might be biting off my nose to spite my face, but I wanted her out. Even if she didn't recognize me now, I was sure she'd meet someone from the hills who remembered the scandal of Jamie Long, his wife, and his whore, and all the gossip about which woman was which.

7

Wanda said doctors might be good at observing what was wrong with a person, but aside from cleaning and stitching wounds, setting bones and giving laudanum for pain, they didn't know how to cure a lot of illness.

Will would say only that Barlow's condition was some kind of paralysis, a disorder of the nervous system, possibly temporary, especially if it was related to his fall. "You might try the mineral baths at Berkeley Springs or White Sulphur Springs," he said. "People take the waters there for weeks or months at a time. There's massage therapy too, and doctors with experience in treating conditions like this."

Like what? Creeping paralysis? Poliomyelitis? Will wouldn't say, and Barlow and I didn't speculate, not aloud.

"Let's wait a few weeks and see if I improve," Barlow said. I knew he was thinking of the expense. I hid my fear, and he hid his.

Every-other evening he wheeled himself into the dining room to preside while I had dinner with the children or took Luzanna's place and served the meal. At those times Milton Chapman appeared not to notice the wheeled chair and made none of his usual insinuations that my husband was failing, poor fellow.

Even confined to his chair, Barlow had a manner that generated respect and tempered Irene Herff's loose tongue. At his instruction, John Johnson had built a short ramp at one side of the porch steps, and Barlow now spent part of each day outside, acquiring a glow of health. Facing an undefined, unspoken threat, we treated each other with great care, almost like we were newly married. Without having to speak of it, we were also careful not to start another baby. Our future no longer seemed limitless.

What keeps a person awake one night may seem unimportant as days go by. I'd dismissed the inquiry from the Pennsylvania lawyer, replacing that curiosity with immediate concerns: the children, Barlow, our finances, and our difficult guests. I'd even forgotten that I'd placed the lawyer's letter in one of our account books until Barlow lifted it from his bedside table and asked if I'd done anything about it. I was massaging and exercising his legs, a task I enjoyed because I liked the feel of his skin under my hands.

"I forgot. The letter came while you were away. I meant to ask if I should reply. What do you think it means?"

"Maybe an old family connection? Do you want me to send it to Cousin Clarence? He could reply, lawyer to lawyer."

"I was afraid it might have something to do with Jamie. Who else would be trying to find me?"

"Oh, May Rose, it couldn't be him. Russell wouldn't lie—Jamie's dead."

"I think Russell might lie to protect somebody. Jamie stole from him, and he was angry about that. But he might have lied so the authorities would stop searching for him. If Jamie is alive..." The thought was like drowning in icy water. I sat on the bed and clutched both of Barlow's warm hands. "I suppose I should find out."

"Shall I forward the letter to Clarence?"

"Yes, please." Whether it was Jamie or someone else, I liked the idea of a stuffy lawyer like Barlow's cousin standing between us.

~

Every time the doorbell rang, I hoped to meet a nice new guest or the teachers, expected soon. Early in September I answered the bell and saw an old friend, Ebert Watson.

In the years since I'd refused Ebert's offer of marriage, I'd seen him only from a distance. In their younger days, he and Will had worked side by side in the lumber mill, and later Ebert had helped Will in the store. I'd known him first as the father of Jonah, one of the boys in my small home school. Ebert hadn't known Jamie, but he'd heard of him, and something in his manner said he'd also heard the stories about me. Ebert had helped make up my mind by indicating he'd marry me despite everything.

"I've come to see my sister," he said, after our awkward exchange of greetings.

"Your sister?"

"Rona Chapman. You didn't know she's my sister?"

Now I saw the family likeness. "I knew she had a brother. I guess I didn't know you had a sister, or... I'm sorry. Please..." I invited him inside.

"I didn't see Milton's fancy machine." He glanced into the parlor, fortunately empty, since Irene Herff had again imposed on Milton Chapman to drive her somewhere. "This is a nice house. I told Rona she'd like you."

I was pleased to think he could still recommend me. When Rona came downstairs, I left them and went to the apartment, half-certain she'd known about her brother and me all this time. If Ebert had also told her about Jamie, she must not have told her husband, for he would by now have used that knowledge for amusement or advantage.

The children were napping and Emmy was helping Luzanna. Barlow had rolled his wheeled chair to our small table in the apartment, where he'd spread our account books. I told him about Ebert and Rona. "I'm tired of pretending I don't know Irene. It will be all right if everything comes out."

"Are you sure? Irene has a loose tongue and a love of scandal. We can count on her to spread our history all over town."

"I suppose her stories would hurt business."

"Which would not be as important as hurting you."

"Or you. Or the children. I know how it was for Wanda, to have her mother known all over town for what she was." I lowered my voice to a whisper. "What if some day Freddy and Hettie hear their mother stood naked to the view of loggers on the trains? It's hard for me to think about those lies, and harder to talk about them. Think what it would be for them."

"When they're old enough to understand, we'll tell them the truth about the Donnellys and their lies." He took my hand and pulled me onto his lap. I closed my eyes and rested my head on his shoulder. Until he'd begun spending weeks away on sales trips, I hadn't known how much I relied on the shelter and support of loving arms. Having him, I should not complain of anything.

"Maybe I'm borrowing trouble. Irene hasn't connected me to Jamie, and even if she does, our word should be better than hers. What do you want to do?"

"We shouldn't let her drive us away."

I agreed. But what would happen, I wondered, if Jamie came to claim me?

I jumped at a knock, though it was only a timid tap. Rona smiled when I opened the door. "I'm sorry to intrude. My brother is traveling north tomorrow. He'd like a room for the night, if that's possible."

For a change, she looked happy. I knew Ebert well enough to know he'd disapprove of both his brother-in-law and Irene Herff. He wouldn't speak publicly of anything that would shame me.

I was a bit flustered as I took Ebert's payment in the office, maybe because he also seemed ill at ease. I showed him to a room and told Luzanna about the additional guest for dinner. Affected by Rona's happiness, I also had Emmy take a note to Wanda, saying their friend Ebert was staying the night and asking if she and Will could come after dinner and give us some music.

Though I was happy for Rona, I begged Barlow to take my place at the table that evening while I had dinner with the children. If I presided, Irene Herff would tune up her bragging for the new man and Milton Chapman would insert insults in his usual manner. With Barlow at the table, he and Ebert could disappoint our tiresome guests by leading the conversation to topics like the price of corn and coal. For that, I'd like a peep-hole.

I did not leave the apartment until the engine of Milton Chapman's car signaled his departure for the roadhouse. Then I met Rona and her brother in the parlor and invited them to join us for the music. I'd already invited Luzanna and Emmy.

"Everyone behaved better than usual," Barlow said, when I asked if anything special had happened at dinner.

"Believe me when I say everything is better when you're at the table."

"Or it may be as you've said, the presence of someone new changes the atmosphere. But I suspect if Ebert stayed, he and his brother-in-law would soon be unable to restrain themselves, no matter who else might be at the table."

Soon after dinner, Wanda arrived with Will, her children, and a surprise—our friend Price Loughrie and his fiddle. I put Hettie to bed and let Freddy sit on the floor with Otis until both were drowsy and fell asleep on the rug. Wanda and Price sang together, and at times we all joined in. Through every song, Rona smiled and tapped her foot. It was the first pleasant time we'd had with guests, and I was glad Rona was not spending another evening alone.

8

I kept extra keys to the front door on a hook in the office, and Milton Chapman always took one of these when he left for the roadhouse. Unless I was having a sleepless night, I seldom heard him return. But that night both Barlow and I woke to a repeated rattle of the doorbell. Barlow sat up and scooted to the edge of the bed so he could lift himself into the wheeled chair.

I put on my housecoat. "No need. I'll go."

"I'm with you." He swiveled into his chair and followed me to the hall.

No one was ringing to get in. Milton Chapman stood in the open doorway, his hand twisting the bell and his legs straddling a mound of loose gray hair and wine-colored taffeta on the threshold. *Irene,* lying face down. Even with the door open, the entryway smelled of alcohol, as though she—and maybe he also—had been drenched in it.

When he saw us, he stepped over the mound on the floor and wobbled toward the stairs, mumbling, "I'm not dragging her another inch."

Barlow wheeled his chair to one side of the threshold where Irene lay, and I stooped on the other side. "Maybe it's not just the drink," I said. "Maybe we should fetch Will."

"We'll see. Can you roll her over?"

I pushed, but she rolled back. The hall clock chimed the half hour, half past two. I pushed again. She grunted.

"Chapman, give us a hand here," Barlow said.

Laughing in a high, crazy way, Milton Chapman grabbed the bannister to keep from falling backward. "You give your wife a hand, cripple. I 'spect that's all you can give her."

Furious now and heedless of what I touched, I shoved one arm under Irene Herff's great belly and another under her bosom and rolled her to her back. Barlow reached from his chair and grasped her wrist, I took the other, and together we pulled her over the threshold.

Barlow wheeled away to get a blanket from the laundry room. I shut the door and went to the bottom of the stairs, where Milton Chapman was traipsing upward, grasping the railing hand over hand.

"Mr. Chapman. Can you hear me clearly?"

He struggled to lift the next foot. "I'm not deaf. You don't have to shout."

"Good. Pack your bags and be gone before breakfast."

He whirled around and fell against the railing. "What's that?"

Rona appeared at the top of the stairs and started down.

"Mrs. Chapman, I'm sorry," I said.

She shook her head. "Don't be, because I'm not. Let me help."

Together Rona and I pulled Irene Herff onto the parlor rug. Barlow returned with a pillow as well as a blanket. When I slid the pillow under her head, her lips twitched into a smile, but she did not open her eyes.

"She looks peaceful," Barlow said.

"Much nicer than when she's awake," Rona said.

I choked back a laugh. Barlow grinned.

A loud bumping and clattering on the stairs drew us back to the hall. Milton Chapman had slipped and now lay sprawled, face down.

"Serves him right," his wife said. "Leave him there."

Barlow nodded toward the top of the stairs where Ebert stood, fully dressed. "I'd rather not. Perhaps your brother can help."

Ebert came down several steps and pulled his brother-in-law to his feet.

"Put him in my room," Rona said. "Mr. and Mrs. Townsend, I'd like to stay on after my husband leaves. Just for a few days."

We assured her she would always be welcome.

When we retreated to our apartment, I said, "They sleep in separate rooms. Why did she want him in hers?"

"Maybe she intends to smother him."

"Ah, that's it," I said.

If Barlow's pride was hurt from being called a cripple, he would never show it. He fell asleep almost as soon as he lay down, but I could not rest. I now hated Milton Chapman fully as much as I detested Irene Herff.

When the hall clock struck five, I got up, dressed, and started toward our office. Irene was no longer on the parlor floor, but had left a pool of vomit drying on the rug. I didn't care whether she'd made it to bed or was lying in the yard.

Luzanna arrived, and I explained the night's drama and why I was rinsing buckets and washing rags in the laundry room at that hour. "If she's soiled her room too, she'll have to clean it herself."

"The teachers won't be happy with that kind of goings-on," Luzanna said.

I hoped they wouldn't arrive today, because I didn't expect Milton Chapman to go quietly. Irene did not appear for her usual morning coffee, and only Ebert and Rona came down for breakfast.

I said goodbye to Ebert when I carried fresh coffee to the dining room, and I was in the office when he and Rona parted at the front door. The office door was open and we were clearly visible to each other, but they made no attempt to keep their talk private. I kept my head down and my hands busy dusting and straightening.

Ebert sounded reluctant to leave. "Are you sure you'll be all right?"

"I packed his luggage and hid it in the car before breakfast. When he wakes, I'll tell him you said there's something at the house we should see right away. He won't remember last night, and I won't tell him he's been evicted until we get there."

"Then what? I don't want him to hurt you."

"He won't try anything in front of the workmen. I'll walk to your house and lock myself in until you or Jonah can bring me back here."

"You don't have to live in a boardinghouse. I'll be home tomorrow. Think about staying with Jonah and me. As long as you like."

"I've never been on my own," she said. "I'd like to try that. And I'm paid up here for another week. Maybe I'll find some kind of work."

"What about your house?"

"It's his house. I don't intend to live in it, but I want my share of the land. I suppose I'll need a lawyer."

I heard the front screen open and close, then muffled talk on the porch, then a squeak of hinges and soft steps. Rona tapped lightly at the office door.

"Ebert has left to catch the train." She nodded toward the parlor. "And I see she moved."

"Unfortunately, only as far as her room." I motioned to the corner chair. "Would you like to sit down?"

"If you're not too busy. Did you hear?"

"I didn't mean to eavesdrop. We could have helped with your husband's suitcases."

"I enjoyed every step, like I was clearing out my life. But I couldn't move two of his trunks. Could you ask your handyman to deliver them to the roadhouse? Milton can get a room there. I understand it's rough lodging, but it's where he belongs."

I promised to send for John Johnson.

"When we get to the house, I'll tell Milton his luggage is in the car and his trunks are at the roadhouse." She sat with her ankles crossed and her hands clasped in her lap. "He might try to worm his way back in here. I'll let him think I'm going to live with my brother, but I'd like to come back while I decide my future."

I placed a door key in her hand. "I've often thought I should keep the front door locked during the day. I'll try to make it a habit."

Her fingers closed over the key. "We've been married eight years, going wherever he could find a card game, living in hotels and boardinghouses. For a country girl, all of that was exciting. Then it wasn't."

I heard Freddy's chatter in the hall. Emmy was taking the children to breakfast.

"You have a fine family and a good man," Rona said. "I'm thankful Milton and I didn't have children. I've always been timid and unattractive. No man wanted me, that was clear, until I met him. It didn't matter what he looked like or what he was. It's been hell." She smiled. "I should not have settled, but I'm wiser now. Being here, watching you, and reading about the women's movement—well, I've broadened my outlook. I want to make it on my own, like you."

She had no idea. "Mrs. Chapman—Rona—I've done nothing on my own. My husband's money built this house."

"But you operate it. You remind me of myself, except that you aren't afraid to have ideas or speak up for yourself. I think you may have been timid as a girl, like me. Ebert said you've been through a lot."

Whatever she knew, it did not make her think worse of me, but I took this chance to shift the topic. "Your brother is a good man."

"He tends to be rigid. I'm afraid if he doesn't marry soon he'll become even more fixed in his views. Unfortunately, I wasn't particular enough."

"You'll always be welcome here."

"I've no money of my own. We women seldom think of making a place for ourselves in the world, do we? I intend to change that. I've kept in touch with one of my former teachers who moved to Charleston to operate a secretarial school. I'd love to be her pupil again." She smiled. "Now I must go and fool my husband. I'm looking forward to it."

We separated in the hall, Rona taking the stairs to begin deceiving her husband, while I went to the apartment to share this information with mine.

I found him sitting at the window, dressed in summer whites as though prepared for a day of recreation and leisure in the sun. He had devised new methods to dress himself, efforts that left him satisfied but tired, because he stretched and positioned himself in uncommon ways. I'd learned to withhold help until he asked.

I bent and kissed his smoothly-shaved cheek, then sat in his lap for a hug and a better kiss. "I could sit here forever," I said.

"When we're too old to do anything else, we'll sit like this all day."

"Until then," I said, "there's the matter of our disgraceful guests. They aren't awake yet, but Irene somehow got herself out of the parlor, and Rona has a strategy to get her husband from the house without a struggle."

"Aha. There's more to that woman than meets the eye."

"She intends to find work. I know how hard that can be. A woman can't earn enough to keep herself."

"Her brother may help."

"I think she wants to be independent."

He tightened his hug.

I was close to tears. "Some women aren't lucky enough to get away from their bad choices and remake their lives. I'm grateful to Rona for ridding us of that man. Every day I know how blessed I am to have you."

"Hmm," he said. "I should probably keep Milton Chapman around to make me look good. But look, what he thinks of me is no worse than what I think of myself. Last night I realized we need a strong man or two in the house, at least while I'm gone."

Gone? I leaned back to see his face.

"I need to walk again, for all of us. I'm going to try the mineral baths."

There was nothing to do but agree, though I was afraid he'd be disappointed. I didn't think I could get through my day if he lost his good spirit. Maybe he was afraid he'd lose it too.

It did no good to look back, but I couldn't stop thinking. Had we continued to live in the small company house instead of building the boardinghouse, we'd now have a comfortable savings, and instead of talking about more weeks of separation, I would be packing up the children and going along for my own rest cure.

9

Luzanna prepared a basket lunch for Rona and her husband, who as she had predicted, was in a hurry to take care of whatever emergency had called him to his house.

"I hope everything goes well," I said. "At the house, I mean."

Rona took the basket with a grim smile. "I'll let you know."

"She doesn't need to know our business," her husband said.

Rain began as he hurried her through the door. I was glad to see it, because the summer had been too dry, but I was afraid they'd turn around and come back. If the rain continued it would slow their trip, and a cloudburst would rut the hilly roads and make the low places a muddy mess.

When they reached his car, wind-driven rain was pummeling them, harsh and heavy. I watched from the porch as Milton Chapman seized the basket from his wife's hands, tossed it in the back seat and hustled into the driver's seat while she ran around to the passenger side, holding her hat on her head. They had to be drenched. Before their car reached the main road, the rain stopped, and just like that, the sky cleared.

I closed the door. One disagreeable guest gone; one more to go. It would be convenient if Irene's needs and vanities lured her to a place she thought was better, but I doubted her departure would happen smoothly.

An hour from now Milton and Rona would reach their house and she'd reveal the changes in his circumstances—their imminent separation and his immediate lack of a place to live. He might react with violence. She probably knew that.

There was never time to dwell on a single problem. Lunch with the children was next. It was an important event, the only time Barlow and I ate together with the children, a time we tried to make happy.

Before Freddy and Hettie, I thought I knew what work was. Now I had a business that claimed me as much as a third child, its needs never out of mind. Managing required thought as well as action, and it was thought that left me tired and frazzled, open as it was to worrisome possibilities. I felt better with Barlow here, not only for his good sense but for his calming influence. Most of all, he was the only other person in the world who put our children first. Now he was talking of going away again.

Luzanna had our lunch trays ready. She wanted to know if Milton Chapman had gone quietly. "For him, like a lamb," I said. "I'm afraid there'll be fireworks when he learns Rona deceived him."

She picked up one of the trays. "I'll carry this one. No sign of our other bad apple?"

"Neither sight nor sound."

"Suppose I should leave everything set out in the dining room?" She winked. "The custard might turn."

"Convenient as that sounds, you best clear it away. We don't need a reputation for food poisoning."

"She'll howl for her food."

"There's none to hear but us." I backed with the other tray through the swinging door to the hall.

Luzanna followed. "Wait till she finds out her ride to the roadhouse won't be here no more."

"Ah yes," I said. "We need to turn her out before the teachers arrive."

~

Irene not only howled; midafternoon she banged on the floor of her room, shaking the dining room chandelier. Luzanna and I were in the kitchen, cold-packing tomatoes. "I suppose I should go up there," Luzanna said. "I think she's calling for help."

"You're not her servant, and she's not your responsibility."

We ducked as something crashed and shattered on the floor above. "We better both go," Luzanna said.

We hurried up the back stairs. When I knocked on her door, Irene howled, "Open the damn door!"

Inside we found the washstand overturned, its water pitcher smashed, the bedding pulled to the floor, and Irene Herff on her hands and knees, peering under the bed, still wearing the taffeta dress and shoes from the previous night.

"I been robbed! My purse is gone! Who's been in here?"

"Since yesterday, only you," I said. "You slept on the parlor floor last night, do you remember? You were passed out when Mr. Chapman brought you home. He was drunk too."

"What do you mean, drunk too? I don't drink, nothing but a little tonic once the while." She pointed at Luzanna. "Where was you last night?"

Luzanna stiffened. "Asleep in my own bed. In my own house!"

Irene shook the gold chain pinned to the waist of her dress. "My purse was right here. Somebody took it off me. Tell Milton I want to see him right now."

"Mr. and Mrs. Chapman left several hours ago."

"Then send him soon as he gets back."

Luzanna turned toward the door. "I'll get on with the tomatoes if that's all right."

"Right. There's nothing for us to do here."

Irene grasped a bedpost, and with great labor, pulled herself upright. "That washwoman. Send her up."

"She's busy. You woke the entire house last night, and this morning I cleaned your vomit from the parlor rug. Now this." Pieces of the pitcher lay scattered in a puddle of water. "You're no longer welcome here. Pack your things and I'll refund the balance on your account."

Her eyes narrowed and her puffy face turned red. "You hypocrite! I know who you are."

Thunder rattled the window panes, the room darkened, and wind rushed through the hall, catching the door and slamming it shut. "I'll send the handyman to carry your luggage downstairs. He'll drive you to the train station or to any of the other towns nearby."

"Didn't you hear me? I said I know who you are—you're Jamie Long's *whore*."

I picked up the largest chunk of the pitcher, a thick sharp shard of pottery, because she looked angry enough to jump on me. "Everyone knows what a liar you are. Every time you lie about me, I'll tell the truth about you and your boys."

"My husband told me what you did. It got him killed."

Rain blew in the window, but I did not move to shut it. "He knew nothing about me. *You* know nothing about me."

She stomped her foot. "I want my money! Someone in this house has took it."

The pottery chip bit into my palm. "If you don't pack your clothes, I'll throw them out the window."

She screamed. "I haven't ate since yesterday, and I ain't going till I see Milton."

"He won't be coming back."

"You're the liar."

"Go to his room and see for yourself."

"You're gonna be sorry. Milton must of stole my purse. Help me get it back and I won't say a word."

"I've told you for the last time. Your behavior has made you unwelcome here. Leave quietly, or I'll call the town guards."

"Do that and I'll tell the world about you. Them men at the roadhouse will love all that. Then where'll you be?"

Her insane grin inspired me. "I'll be here, Irene, but you'll be in a very bad place. Your stepson—you know who I mean, the doctor and coal mine owner—he has the authority to commit you to the Weston Insane Asylum. It won't be hard for people to believe you're deranged, especially if Dr. Herff says so. Being related as you are and all."

"He wouldn't."

"He's partial to me. All I have to do is ask."

Her mouth was open but for once she had no come-back. I left the room and walked with rigid steps through the upstairs hall toward a window where rain was wetting the curtains and puddling on the floor. I shut the window, took off my apron and used it to mop up the floor. Then I went down the front stairs, leisurely sliding my hand along the bannister, enjoying the smell of warm tomatoes and the ticking of the grandfather clock. Before returning to the kitchen, I closed myself in the office and sat at my desk until my heart slowed down.

~

Again, the rain storm was hard but brief.

Luzanna stood with me in the hall as John Johnson carried Irene Herff's small safe down the steps and out to his wagon. She came down as elegantly as she could manage, keeping her nose in the air while she took baby steps and clutched the bannister rail. When I handed her an envelope with the two dollars remaining on her account, she crumpled it and threw it to the floor.

"That better be the last of her," Luzanna said.

I breathed easier when I saw the wagon turn north toward the roadhouse. "Now I need to talk with Will. Keep the door locked in case Milton Chapman tries to come back. Rona wants to stay with us, but she'll be at her brother's house for the next several days."

"Nobody but us for dinner, then?"

"How nice. Nobody but us."

Mist rose from the wet pavement as I pedaled the bicycle to the store. Will was such a straight ticket—he'd not like how I'd used his name. Even so, I couldn't help feeling triumphant: I'd rid the house of a poisonous guest. With good luck, she'd be out of my life forever.

I found Wanda in the store, arranging women's shoes on a rack. Most were brown lace-up or button-up shoes that reached above the ankle, suitable for sloppy weather. She held up one that was low-cut, reddish brown with a white saddle-like inset. "Will you look at this? I don't know who's gonna buy it." Then she frowned. "What's wrong?"

"Trouble with the stepma," I said.

She led me through a connecting door to Will's private office, then left me and continued through another door to his treatment room. I stared at a skeleton in the corner. Long ago I'd heard someone say skeletons belonged to the devil because their souls were no longer in them. Maybe that notion was why Will kept it in his office and not in the treatment room where his patients would see it. People who acted afraid of skeletons never seemed genuine to me, but it wasn't my place to judge. It was always possible that a person's repugnance was based on an experience with grisly remains.

When Wanda returned with Will, I blurted the details of Irene's drunken night, the vomit, and her accusation of theft. "She said she remembers who I am and all that old talk about Jamie and me. She said if I didn't do what she wanted she'd spread that all over town."

"I'll move her out of there tonight," Will said.

He didn't understand, but Wanda did. "Moving's not gonna stop her mouth. Let's drive her into the hills and drop her where she can't find her way back."

Will briefly closed his eyes. "That feels good, but you know we're not going to do it."

"I'm not asking you to move her; she's gone," I said. "I told a fib to keep her from telling tales. I said if she spread that old gossip I'd tell everyone she was deranged. I said it would be easy for you to commit her to the asylum at Weston. I said you'd do it for me."

Wanda whooped. "Good for you!"

Will looked grim. "May Rose, I know people are committed for weaker reasons than threats and gossip, but I can't sign papers unless she's a danger to others. Or to herself."

"It was a bluff. I'm sorry I used your name, but it worked. I don't want my children growing up with those stories about their mother. I'm not asking you to do anything; I've come to apologize."

"The old witch is a danger to our family, whether you see it or not," Wanda said. "I don't want Otis and Evie hearing her tales neither."

"I know." Will swiped his forehead. "Was she really robbed?"

"I think she came back from the roadhouse without her purse. I don't remember seeing it when we dragged her into the house. She couldn't walk, so we left her sleeping on the parlor floor. Milton Chapman was inebriated too, and he didn't seem to remember anything this morning. I'm happy to say we're rid of him—his wife packed his things today and tricked him out of the house. She intends to come back and stay with us until she decides what to do."

"All right," Will said. "You've had a lot to contend with. Thanks for the warning. I'll be around later to see Barlow."

I sighed. "He wants to talk to you about the mineral springs. Please, come to dinner tonight. For once, it's just us."

~

After the day's turmoil, I was relieved to get back to the boardinghouse and find it still standing. But I carried in my pocket something that might mean new distress—mail from Barlow's cousin, Clarence Townsend.

I opened the door to a warm, sweet smell. In the kitchen, Luzanna motioned proudly to 30 shining glass quarts of tomatoes. "That makes 120 quarts and there'll be more. I saved a pot for supper, since it's just us. I dug a few potatoes too."

"Maybe dig a few more. Wanda and her family are coming. We'll put all the young ones in the kitchen, and you eat with us. String beans and light bread, stewed tomatoes and new potatoes—it will be a feast. I'll say a word to Barlow then be back to help."

"Good by me. I miss the old days."

I often missed them too. When I had no children, no boardinghouse, no husband or income, I had time to help and appreciate my friends. Now I had to tell Barlow how I'd threatened Irene. I decided to get Cousin Clarence's letter out of the way first. If it contained good news, Barlow might not care about my lie.

My husband, who'd been manager of the Winkler Lumber and Logging Company and a partner in the Winkler Mine, never thought he was too important or busy for ordinary chores. I found him in the playroom, snapping beans with Emmy and our children. Freddy sat cross-legged on the floor with a pan of beans at his side. Hettie stood by the wheeled chair, stooping to pick up a green pod and rising to release it into the pan on her father's lap. When she saw me, she dropped the bean and toddled across the floor.

Hugging her small soft body was a comfort. It also made me feel protective and somehow, stronger. "There's a letter from Cousin Clarence."

Barlow backed his chair and turned it toward the door. "Let's take it to the other room."

I started to take Hettie with me, but she squirmed to be down. Whatever Freddy was doing, she wanted to do it too. I set her beside Emmy and shut the door behind us.

In our parlor, I put Clarence's envelope in Barlow's hand.

"You didn't open it," he said.

"It's addressed to you."

"We have no secrets."

"I was afraid. Of what it might say."

"Whatever it is, we'll be all right."

"Yes." Even if it took years to overcome.

He slit the envelope with his finger, pulled out the letter and unfolded it to read. "Well. It doesn't say much." He handed it to me. "Only that Clarence wrote to the Philadelphia lawyer asking the nature of the inquiry and the identity of the inquirer."

"So perhaps we'll know soon."

"Very likely. This is a bad time for me to go away. I should be here—if anyone comes."

"It couldn't possibly be Jamie," I said.

"I'm sure it's not. Clarence will let us know if there's anything we should worry about. I'll ask him to telegraph when he hears something."

"That's good."

"Now." He took the letter and returned it to the envelope. "There's something else worrying you."

"I'm already missing you. And I told a big lie today to get Irene out of the house."

"It doesn't matter."

"I don't know. I lied about Will. He wasn't happy when I told him."

"May Rose. He's a big boy now."

"Do you want to hear what I said?"

He kissed my hand. "Not unless you need to tell me."

I didn't.

~

Wanda came at dinner time with her two, but Will was late. "As usual," Wanda said. "He has a hard time getting away from some people."

We fed the children in the kitchen, then sent them to the playroom with Emmy and Evie.

Will arrived an hour later, looking faded and worn as old clothes and deciding he needed to wash up. I hurried to fetch a clean towel for the washroom, then helped Luzanna carry serving bowls to the table.

I'd set out two candelabra to make everything more relaxed and special. As we ate, the day darkened and the candles seemed to glow brighter. Will leaned back in his chair and gave me the smile I'd been eager to see. Luzanna surprised us with canned blackberries and fresh cream, and we finished with coffee. We'd had almost no dinner conversation, with everyone clearly tired and so familiar that silences were never awkward. Rona Chapman might believe I was strong, but I knew I'd be a weakling without these people.

"I've decided to try mineral baths," Barlow said, ending the silence.

In candlelight, all our faces were shadowed, but I saw Will nod. "White Sulphur Springs is closer. I know a doctor there. Six weeks of therapy should be enough for a result."

Six weeks? I'd thought perhaps no more than two.

"If there's going to be a result," Barlow said.

"Correct."

We'd never talked about what we might do if he did not recover, or God forbid, if he got worse. He would be terribly hurt if some day he could not even string beans.

He looked around the table. "I thought while I'm gone we might offer a room to a couple of bachelors, preferably a miner who works the day shift and one who works nights, so one of them would always be here. The small servants' room is empty. We could put two narrow beds there and if the men paid for their meals and laundry, we wouldn't really be out anything."

We hadn't discussed this. In my experience, bachelors were young, unsettled and unpredictable. I didn't want the wrong kind in the house.

Perhaps my face showed my feeling, because Barlow said, "May Rose, you should have someone to help with unruly guests."

I didn't like it, but recent experience supported his decision.

He turned to Will. "I thought you or Wanda might recommend some young men we could trust. I've lost touch with the mine employees."

"No one too young," I said.

Wanda offered to ask John Johnson, who managed the house she rented to bachelors. "Someone there might like a more private place with good food and all."

"I don't want to steal your renters," I said.

"It don't matter none to me—those beds fill up fast, four to a room. John says he always has men asking, even some who work the other mines."

"Getting back to White Sulphur Springs," Will said. "If you decide to go there, I'll ride along. I'd like to see the place, and I could do with a day or two off."

We all said that was a fine idea, without mentioning that Will looked and sounded desperate for a rest.

"Give me a couple of days to make arrangements," Will said. "Then we'll go."

I smiled to hide my disappointment. *Six weeks.*

10

All in one day, my husband left, our live-in watchmen and the teachers arrived, and Rona returned. It was laundry day, so the house smelled like soap and wet cotton. The washwoman was everywhere, carrying bedding, going in and out of the back door and hanging sheets on the lines outside while Luzanna and I prepared meals and dealt with the arrivals. I had no time to cry.

The first of the bachelors came early in the morning, straight from his night shift in the mine.

I greeted him at the front door but did not invite him to step inside, because though he'd washed his hands and the front portion of his face, the rest of him was black with coal dust.

"John sent me. I'm Smitty," he said.

I picked up the guest register and walked him outside and around the house to the back door. Like she was praying for strength, Luzanna closed her eyes as he tracked into the kitchen.

"George Franklin Smith," he said, looking up and down the kitchen walls and peering into the laundry room. "You write it down and I'll make my X." The folds of his knuckles and the edges of his fingernails were black. He dropped his duffle and lunch pail on the floor.

He didn't object when I said he should use the back door, the back stairs, and eat in the kitchen. "This smells a good sight better than where I was," he said.

Mr. Smith couldn't write his name but he counted money in greasy bills and coins for meals and laundry onto the work table where Luzanna was kneading bread.

"This is Mrs. Hale. She runs this house with me and does most of the cooking."

Luzanna looked him over. "Before you come in, brush yourself off on the porch with that there broom. And if you don't mind, leave your dirty clothes outside. You're dropping black grit with every step."

Her voice was none too kind, and he snapped back. "You got a room on that porch for me to change? I may be dirty but I'm no heathen."

"You don't use that bathhouse at the mine?"

"I don't care for it."

I knew men tended to be coarse when women weren't present, so I guessed either Mr. Smith didn't like bathhouse language or he liked his privacy. "Very well. Brush off as best you can outside, and when you come in, wash up and change in the laundry room."

"And you can mop up the floor after yourself," Luzanna said.

"I guess I can oblige, if that's the way things is to be. Now for what you call breakfast. After a shift, I like meat and potatoes."

"Meat's for the evening meal," Luzanna said. "You'll be getting breakfast. It's usually biscuits, grits or oatmeal and sometimes fried mush."

"That ain't much after a night's work. What'll be in my pail?"

I stepped back and let Luzanna deal with him. "It'll have whatever we eat in the evening," she said. "That'll usually be meat and potatoes. If there's soup, I'll put it in a mason jar. Some kind of sweet."

"Bread and butter," he said. "Two slices."

"O'course."

"I guess it'll have to do. Don't forget the water."

"I know how to pack a lunch pail."

"Yes, Ma," he said. I judged him to be near our age. He was a head shorter than both of us, with a broad chest and muscled arms.

"Mind your manners," Luzanna said.

I showed him the laundry room and introduced him to the washwoman, who was running sheets through the wringer. "He'll be washing and changing in here every morning." She nodded, and we waited until she carried the basket of sheets outside.

"Mr. Smith, please leave your dirty clothes in one of these buckets."

"I'm gonna wear them tomorrow. No use to go into the mine clean every day."

"That's your choice, but you'll have to do your changing here. You can hang your clothes on that peg. And..." I pointed to the trail of coal dust. "This will mean extra work for us. We can't have it all over the house. Wipe out the laundry tub after you wash."

"Yes, Ma'am."

"You understand, we're giving you the room free of charge so you'll be here to help, should we have an unruly guest. That might mean we'd wake you in the middle of the day."

"I'm a heavy sleeper," he said. "But I'll come to life right off if that laundry maid gives me a shake."

To his credit, he hadn't said this in her hearing, but I couldn't let it go. "Mr. Smith, I'm not sure this is going to work out."

"It's Smitty. Sure it's gonna work. First, you'll find nobody better, and second, I'll be on my good behavior 'cause I can't wait to get some o'that bread your cook is making, and third, John said I shouldn't make you mad or you'd kick me out and he wouldn't take me back. And usually I don't talk much."

"Well then, seeing as though you've just come from work, I'll ask Mrs. Hale if she might heat up some of last night's supper for your breakfast, just this one time. Your room is directly above the laundry room. If we need you while you're sleeping, we'll strike a broom against the ceiling or pound on your door."

Later we heard boots overhead as he settled into his room. "You got no idea what washing miners' clothes is like," Luzanna said. "I hope these men is worth it."

I hoped we'd never need them, but Smitty proved himself soon after he arrived when we needed to take Barlow to the train station. Waving away Will's help, he lifted him from his chair into Will's car. Then he hopped on the running board to go with them to meet the train.

Barlow waved from his window. "The next time you see me, I'll be walking."

I nodded and waved, my eyelashes clogged with tears. *Six weeks.*

~

The teachers arrived while the children and I were having lunch. "Two women, big and little," Emmy said. "I put them in the parlor."

One of the teachers was plump with gray hair and a pronounced double chin, and the other was tiny, younger, and severe in her appearance. They stood when I entered the parlor.

I invited them to sit so we could chat. "I'm Mrs. Townsend. And you are...?"

The tiny teacher peered at the timepiece she wore on a chain. "Miss Jeanetta Baldwin."

I followed Miss Baldwin's worried gaze from her timepiece to the two suitcases at her feet. "I'd like to unpack as soon as possible," she said.

"It's all right with me if you see to her first," the larger woman said. "I'm Cora Vincent, Mrs., and I'm glad to rest. We walked from the train."

"You came together?"

"We came on the train," Miss Baldwin said. "We are not acquainted." Her tone suggested I was rude to think otherwise.

I motioned Miss Baldwin toward the office, but did not offer to carry one of her suitcases, since she seemed possessive of them.

"I must press and hang my clothes. I assume there's a flat iron?"

"We have an electric iron in the laundry room. I'll show you after I register Mrs. Vincent."

"School begins next week," she said, like she had not a moment to spare. "I hope there are no rowdy boarders here. I'll need quiet to study. Also a bolt on my door. And a fan."

I closed the office door and sat at the desk. "Those are provided."

She remained standing. "And I'd like to be close to the bathroom. There is a bathroom, surely? This appears to be a modern establishment."

"It's in the center of the upstairs hall. There's also a small one here in the hall."

"That's a relief. I've been told there are plans to install washrooms and toilets in the school very soon."

"I hope you're right." I'd heard of no such plans. The four mines in the region cooperated in paying the teachers, but the building was old and the other mine operators did not believe inside plumbing was essential to education.

I turned the register for her signature, then read our house rules.

"You have no nighttime requirement for lights off?"

"It's never been needed."

"I hope you'll consider it. Lights off means people settle down. I like a quiet house."

Oh, Barlow, I thought. How I wanted to tell him about this one. I collected payment for Miss Baldwin's first week, then because the other teacher appeared to be dozing in the parlor, I showed her to her room.

When she'd judged the bed, window, clothespress, fan and door bolt to be satisfactory, I took her down the back stairs and through the kitchen to show our conveniences for washing and ironing.

"Miss Baldwin," I said, introducing her to Luzanna.

"I'll be teaching the upper grades."

"My daughter may be one of your pupils," Luzanna said. "Emmy is thirteen."

"A difficult age. But I know how to handle them. I don't suppose you have an iron I might use in my room this afternoon?"

"No, and the iron is busy at present. Tuesdays and Thursdays are our laundry days. You may use the laundry room any other day, or any evening after we've cleaned the kitchen."

"I suppose that must do. I forgot to ask, do you have male guests?"

"Presently two, but they're partly employed here. As watchmen," I said, a description I hoped would inspire confidence. "You'll seldom see them."

She sighed. "I'm accustomed to a boardinghouse for ladies."

I held the hall door for her to pass through. "Doesn't that sound nice? Though on occasion I've known women to be equally as difficult as men."

"I'm sure that's possible." She lowered her voice to a whisper. "I hope Mrs. Vincent won't be too much trouble. Will we have lunch soon?"

I directed Miss Baldwin to the dining room where Luzanna had set the buffet lunch, then turned my attention to Mrs. Vincent. She seemed an amiable person, though I wondered if she smelled because the trip had given her no opportunity to wash, or if her odor would be something we'd have to get used to.

~

I missed Barlow from the moment he left, but blessed the fact that the boardinghouse and the children kept me too busy to give a thought to the guests I'd evicted, or what Cousin Clarence might discover from the person trying to find me.

Our other watchman arrived just before dinner, clean, quiet and with no demands. "I can't catch onto these new names all at once," Luzanna said, "so I guess you'll know who I mean if I say the day man, night man, little teacher, big teacher."

"The one who will be here at night is Mr. Cunningham. Mr. Smith is the day man."

She scratched her head. "So I'll pack the day man's bucket in the afternoon and the night man will eat dinner in the kitchen. You better stay on top o'me. With them men using the back stairs and the little teacher coming down to do her wash and ironing, there's gonna be a lot of traipsing through."

"The watchmen were Barlow's decision," I said, "or I would have asked your opinion." Luzanna sounded like she was ready to quit. Above all, she was the one I needed to keep happy.

~

Rona returned that afternoon and asked to speak privately. No one else was in the parlor, but I motioned her into the office and closed the door. She sat without invitation, as though exhausted. "Has Milton been here?"

"I've been keeping the front door locked. If he came, he did not ring the bell."

She pulled a handkerchief from her sleeve and blotted her neck. "He laughed when I told him I want a divorce. He said I have no grounds, and I suppose he's right. I pray women will win the right to vote. Divorce laws, wages—everything at present works against us. I have Milton to thank for waking me to that fact."

"I admire your decision," I said. "It can't be easy."

She gave me a look that said she wasn't used to being admired. "Well. I'm coming to know myself. Milton said if you'd truly evicted him—and he doubted me—you'd be wise to reinstate him. He's confident he can be elected judge, you see, and he wants the good opinion of the people of this town. Your endorsement, and your husband's."

"Pardon me for being frank, but surely he doesn't think we'll recommend him for anything."

"I only want to give you a warning; I'm not asking you to endorse him. He told me to say it's in your best interest to introduce him to the voters. You and Mr. Townsend must appear to be his friends. He said you won't want to be his enemies. I'm sorry. My brother is sorry, too. We don't know what to do about him."

I told her about our watchmen. "One will always be here, in case of trouble," I said. "You'll be safe."

"I'm not thinking about me; I'm thinking of those stories about you. Milton wants a meeting to explain how you must help his political ambitions. He says if you cooperate, he'll keep Irene Herff from talking. He's heard none of those stories from me, but I'm curious. Mind, I'm not going to think worse of you. I might even congratulate you. Did you really work in a house of prostitution?"

I nearly fell off my chair. "I did *not*. The Winkler boardinghouse was close to an establishment like that. We knew the operator and her cook." We'd known more, but I did not want to share the fact that I'd visited Suzie's place on sad and regrettable occasions, like when Jamie was hiding from the law and when Wanda's mother was near death. I'd never imagined that over the years, gossip might confuse me with Wanda's mother, who'd serviced men there until Suzie turned her out.

"Once I got to know them, I realized the women in that house were just poor creatures who were trying to stay alive."

"You can't know how well I understand," Rona said.

The more I knew about Rona Chapman the more I liked her, but I had a new surge of hatred for her husband and Irene Herff, and most of all, for Jamie Long. Everything bad in my life had happened because of him. I also hated myself for being the fool who had loved him.

11

On Sunday, Will returned from White Sulphur Springs with a letter from Barlow. The familiar slanted lettering on the envelope made me eager to tear it open.

"It's a peaceful place," Will said. "I wanted to stay, myself. Barlow is determined to make this treatment work, and I believe that kind of attitude goes a long way toward healing."

Because Rona and the teachers were reading in the parlor, I nodded toward the porch. "I'd like to ask a favor. Can you sit a minute?"

"Gladly." He followed me to the two rocking chairs not yet reached by the afternoon sun. "It was good to get away. Most days I wish I was raising goats and building things. Doctoring takes too much of my life, but it's what I wanted. And I still do. It's only..."

"You never have time off." Neither Luzanna nor I rested until bedtime, but in his daily toil Will contended with gruesome illnesses and too many sad conditions he couldn't change.

"I've no right to complain," he said. "Now, what can I do for you? Is my stepma still bothering you?"

"Not at present. I regret that I used your name to threaten her." I didn't look at him as I spoke, because I wasn't sure I wouldn't do the same thing—or something worse—if she threatened me again.

"When she was with Pa, I was an ignorant kid. I knew we had troubles with the Donnellys but I never caught on to the fact that they gave you trouble too. But Charlie knew."

"Your brother knew because he snuck around after them, a dangerous thing for a little boy to do."

"Charlie saved you from those boys. Least I can do is save you from their ma. Is there something legal I can do? Give her a house in another town?"

"Ask Price Loughrie to come and see me."

"This is the favor? Just that?"

"If I need something more, I'll be sure to ask."

"Price comes here most Mondays to meet with the miners' union rep. Will Monday be soon enough?"

"Monday will be fine." I saw his curiosity, but I didn't want to add to his concerns.

"Wanda tells me Irene took a room at the roadhouse," he said. "I hear she's a card player."

"I think she wins a lot. She bought a safe."

He rocked his chair and watched the river. "She must be good. If she's too good, she should watch out for sore losers." He tried to smile.

Will's only apparent similarity to his younger self was an intensity of thought that gave him a look of squinting. The rest of him had become too pale. I was afraid he'd soon wear himself out. "I'm glad you had a rest. I wish you did not work so many hours each day."

"And I wish we had another doctor. I'd like to direct some of my patients to Magda, but I don't know if they could pay her. The miners get free care. They're supposed to pay for their wives and kids, but not many do."

"Magda? Who's Magda?"

"She's that medicine woman in the Gypsy wagon. She came for the last Trading Days, selling remedies, dried herbs and sachets. And she stayed. I spent a bit of time finding out about her to make sure she wasn't selling intoxicants. Turns out I could learn a thing or two from her."

"Does she have doctor training?"

"Just a lifetime of treating people. She's probably as good at it as I am. Hell, most of the time people get well on their own or they die. Either way, the family never credits or blames me. They claim it's God's will."

"Does Magda attend church? She looks quite strange, the way she wears her headscarf and all those necklaces and bracelets and hoops in her ears. If she doesn't go to church, she might be accused of practicing the dark arts."

He chuckled. "In that case, she'll attract even more patients. She might go to the Catholic services. I doubt it matters—every soul here is half religious and half superstitious. They trust every word of scripture and at the same time tell me about ghosts, spiritualists, and the power of curses."

"Also Ouija boards and séances," I said. "If the company hired another doctor, you could move to a farm and go back to raising goats. Keep just a few patients. Like my family."

Will rose and kissed my cheek. "You're my rock, you know?"

"A sponge, I think." And a wet one, too often teary-eyed.

"A rock. You have no idea."

Barlow's letter was tender and encouraging. Before bedtime that night, I sat down and wrote a description of the new antics of our children, adding that the watchmen were settling in and the new teachers were sticklers for rules. If I'd told him my real worry, he'd not only be disturbed, he'd stop his treatment and hurry home to deal with Milton Chapman.

White Sulphur Springs sounded like a nice town. I wondered if it needed a boardinghouse. I wondered if anyone would want to buy this one.

~

Monday I had lunch with Rona and Price Loughrie, who'd come to see me at Will's request. I'd asked Rona to have lunch with us because she'd confided in me.

Had Barlow been here, he'd also have consulted Price, who had a wide acquaintance with bad characters and low places. Price and Barlow had become friends when they worked at the Jennie Town Mine. Before that he'd been a marshal as well as a bootlegger, then he'd lived for a few years with Wanda's Aunt Ruth. Now he worked as a union representative and traveled from place to place either by railroad or on his beautiful black horse. Price was taller than most men, and even in dusty coal country managed to appear well groomed. And though he had a long face and seldom smiled, he won hearts with his patience and gentle manner, his fiddle playing and occasional preaching. He had a quiet way of making people feel happy, though Barlow believed Price was unhappy himself. Politely stated, he had a recurring drinking habit.

Rona and Price remembered each other from our musical evening not long ago. Though I felt I was among friends, I hesitated to explain why I'd asked Price to join us. I waited until we'd satisfied our appetites before I said, "Rona's husband has threatened me."

Price set down his fork and sat straighter in his chair.

"I'm not on his side," Rona said. "He sent the threat through me. It's extortion."

Price had been in this part of the country for a long time, but I didn't know if he'd heard the stories about Jamie and me. I gave him a vague outline, omitting the most embarrassing parts. "I'm convinced that Andrew Donnelly started those rumors, or at least perpetuated them. He was Irene Herff's first husband. Jamie killed him in a fight, and Irene said it was my fault. I think she told all this to Rona's husband."

The thoughtful look on Price's face did not change.

"Mr. Chapman is threatening to revive those stories to damage our business and my reputation unless Barlow and I support his election for judge in this county. We can't do that."

"Such a man must have many enemies," Price said.

Rona shrugged. "He claims to be making friends. He plays cards every night at the roadhouse."

"I thought you might suggest a way to stop him. Barlow's cousin is a lawyer. Do you think a lawyer might help?"

"I've no idea," Price said, "but I enjoy a game of cards. I'll see what I can find out. Meanwhile, I have a request. I need a permanent place to hang my hat. Do you have room for me here?"

This news was a good item for my next letter to Barlow.

~

It took Price only one night at the roadhouse to form a judgment about Milton Chapman. He gave that to us at breakfast the next morning after the teachers left for school.

"I'm sure he cheats, and Will's stepma too," Price said. "I figure they signal each other, but I'd have to watch a while to catch on. Most of the time they win and lose like everyone else, never big money. But twice last night they raised and re-raised each other, with a few of us staying in and adding to the pot until our pockets were empty. When only the two of them were left, she folded. The next time he was the one who gave up. Both times, a lot of money was on the table. I figure they split the pot."

Rona's face reddened. "Tell a lawman. I'd like to see him locked up."

"I doubt the sheriff will come this far to check on a card game. I'm back to work this morning, but I passed my opinion to an acquaintance at the table so he wouldn't sit down with the pair of them again. Let's give it a few days. Next time I'm here, I'll try to get evidence you can use."

"When will that be? Milton plans to address Winkler voters a week from Saturday," Rona said. "Before that time, he says Mrs. Townsend must welcome him back into the house. He also expects her—and me—to sit on the speaker's platform at the meeting. He says she must influence Dr. Herff and his wife to support him as well."

Price pulled a folded paper from a pocket and ran his finger down the page. "I'll ask about him in some of the other mining towns. There's probably stories he wouldn't want told and men who'd like to know where he can be found. Meanwhile, if he wants to talk, tell him you're waiting for approval from Barlow."

That day's other special event was the arrival of a letter from Cousin Clarence. I slid it under my pillow because we had work to do and if the news was bad I wouldn't be of use to anyone.

My less busy time did not arrive until the children were asleep, Luzanna had departed, and the house was dark. Then I studied the envelope and wondered if I should be holding someone's hand when I opened it. If the news was the last thing I wanted to hear, I'd either have terrible dreams or not sleep at all.

I undressed and washed my face, put on my nightgown and peeked in on the children. Then I sat on the bed and slit the envelope.

The letter was full of Clarence's own news—he was getting married—and it had only one line relating to our concern. He'd sent a second request for information, but the Philadelphia lawyer had not responded.

Barlow would enjoy the part about his cousin's marriage. He'd always thought Clarence too stingy and finicky to share his life with anyone.

12

Now that five people needed to eat breakfast and leave the house with lunch in hand, our morning routine gathered speed. The kitchen was often crowded with both the night and day watchmen at the table, Luzanna's children, and my two in their high chairs.

Tuesday morning my children and I arrived late for breakfast. Emmy and Tim were alone at the table, bent over their bowls of grits, eating slowly and quietly. Luzanna was not sitting but bustling around the kitchen, her face as red as if she'd been standing close to a fire. Something had happened, but it didn't feel like my business. I asked anyway. "Is there something I can do?"

Luzanna slopped grits into my children's bowls and let the pot and spoon rattle into the sink. "I suppose there's nothing to be done. I'd still be in the dark if Tim hadn't told."

The boy glanced up. "Miss Baldwin whupped Emmy."

Emmy's head drooped. I was struck dumb.

"Three cracks of the paddle," Tim said. "Took her to the woodshed and made her lift up her dress so it'd hurt more."

Luzanna backed against the sink. "It was on the first day of school, and I'm just now hearing about it." She waved the children to their feet. "Get your lunches and get along. Wait. Carry your bowls over here."

I stood back while they obeyed. Tim pushed past his sister, then both were gone.

"I wouldn't think a thing if it was Tim," Luzanna said. "I want to whup him myself about twice a day. But Em, well you know. She tries so hard to please."

"Did they tell you why?"

"Some boys was pulling on a girl's arms at recess. Em said it was like they were trying to pull her in two. She tried to get the girl away and pushed one of them to the ground. He wasn't no little boy—I had no idea she was that strong. Miss Baldwin must of saw just that part, because Em was the only one that got the paddle. I'd like to throttle her. Miss Baldwin, I mean. Em didn't say but I'm sure the paddle didn't hurt nearly long and hard as her feelings. Now she's scared to death of that teacher, and she's in a room with her half the day."

I hated the injustice, especially since the victim was our Emmy. "I'll have to set Miss Baldwin straight."

"Please don't," Luzanna said. "If anybody, I should be the one, but Emmy don't want no more said about it. And I was brought up not to go against the teachers."

"If that's what Emmy wants." I poured milk over the grits, gave Freddy his bowl, and began to spoon-feed Hettie. "*However.* Miss Baldwin depends on us for a comfortable stay, doesn't she?"

Luzanna smiled. "You got something in mind?"

"I'm thinking."

"Whatever it is, we can't tell Em."

"I know. We'll do something else to make her feel better."

I got my first idea that day when I cleaned the upstairs bathroom. After dinner I drew Miss Baldwin into the office and closed the door. "This is an embarrassing subject," I said. "But I need to remind you not to leave a ring in the bathtub. It's unpleasant for the other guests."

Miss Baldwin's posture was always rigid, but she sat even straighter in the chair, throwing out her chest like an angry bird. "A ring? My bathwater never leaves a ring. And I rinse the tub each time I use it. Always."

"I suppose I must accept your word. But I've checked with the others, and I believe you were the last person to use it, and there *was* a ring."

"And I say you're mistaken. Those watchmen, now. I'm sure they leave a dirty tub."

"We'll forget about it this time," I said. "But in the future, do remember to clean up after yourself."

She bustled from the office, red-faced and sputtering.

Luzanna was responsible for our next portion of revenge, serving pork and sauerkraut three times in the next seven days. Each time Miss Baldwin complained that pork and sauerkraut upset her digestion, Luzanna said, "Sorry, I forgot."

"Everyone else loves it," I said, when Miss Baldwin brought her protests to me.

Miss Baldwin's final embarrassment was accidental, something we saw coming and did nothing to stop. Early Saturday morning she carried a bundle of clothing through the kitchen, headed for the laundry room. Smitty had just returned from the mine and was washing up there.

"Good morning, Miss Baldwin," I said, as she passed. She nodded in the snooty manner she'd maintained since I'd accused her of leaving a bathtub ring. Luzanna and I shared a smile as she opened the door. He hadn't been in there long; I hoped he was at least partly undressed.

"Hey," he shouted. Shrieking, she dropped her bundle and pulled the door closed.

Luzanna raised her brow in surprised innocence. "So sorry, I thought he'd gone."

Miss Baldwin gathered her unmentionables from the floor and hurried back the way she'd come. We smothered our giggles like schoolgirls.

Luzanna sobered quickly. "We'd be fools to drive her out; we need her money."

"She won't leave; no other place in town is as nice, and she loves treating us like servants. Now it's time to help Emmy feel better. We'll have a birthday party."

"Her birthday's not till November."

"I'll say she's getting a party and a gift because it's for school as well as a bonus for taking such good care of Freddy and Hettie. What do you think would make her forget that paddling?"

"I think I know," Luzanna said.

~

My mid-morning walk to the store was a delight, diminished only by the fact that Barlow was not beside me to share the cooling air and the colors on the wooded hillsides. Before we were married, we'd strolled the length and breadth of the valley, prolonging our hours together. Those days had been full of expectation and excitement because so much waited to be discovered. Once we were married, I'd thought our future was settled and secure.

I carried a letter for Barlow. My correspondence glossed over difficulties and embellished the good moments. Though I knew he must be doing the same, I looked forward to his regular assurance that all would be well. Our separation let me know I did not need him to be able bodied; I only needed the support of his presence and his confidence in me. I hoped I would be enough for him.

Luzanna had suggested a pen set for Emmy, stressing that it should not be too costly. At the store, I looked at several, then chose the one that included ink, a variety of nibs, and an instruction book, *The Spenserian Key to Practical Penmanship*. I closed my eyes to the cost and told the clerk to add it to my account.

I collected the boardinghouse mail at the post office window and gave two cents for a stamp for my letter. When I turned around, sorting through the mail to find Barlow's letter, I found Milton Chapman blocking my path. I almost didn't recognize him, because his bushy mutton chops were gone and a new, narrow moustache decorated the space between his long nostrils and thin upper lip.

"Mrs. Townsend. What a fortunate meeting."

"Good day." I stepped to the side and turned toward the front of the store.

He dogged my steps. "Now, now—don't go away mad."

I weaved through a group of Saturday shoppers, aware of his breath close to my neck.

"We haven't talked in such a long time. How is Mr. Townsend?"

Midway through the store, I stopped and tried the door to Will's private office. It was locked.

"You're not being very nice," he said.

"You're bothering me. Should I tell a clerk to call a guard?"

"No need. We have business to discuss. Expect me tomorrow at two o'clock. And tell my wife to be there." He strode away.

I had my mouth open, ready to create a scene that would be described in every house in town, tempted to shout that I'd tell the world before I gave in to his threats. Instead I stopped at the shelves of miners' tools until I stopped breathing like I was in a race. Then I left the store and hurried the short distance to the house at the end of the alley behind the store. Wanda's house.

After I knocked several times, a neighbor called from her porch. "They've went away. Went to see her granny."

"Will they be back tonight?"

"Tomorrow. She said it was a little get-away for the doctor."

I was glad for them, but if I had to endure a visit from Milton Chapman, I needed witnesses. Luzanna would sit with us if I asked, but she did not have the standing of the town doctor. Price Loughrie would be a strong supporter, but I did not expect him to return until Monday.

When I reached home I sent Emmy on the bicycle with a note to Randolph Bell, Barlow's former partner in the Winkler Mine. She returned to report that he wasn't at his house and the guard at the mine said he'd gone to Richmond. Barlow's niece Glory and her friend Virgie White would gladly have witnessed such a meeting, but they currently lived in Richmond, where I imagined they might at this moment be entertaining Randolph Bell.

After lunch I told Rona about her husband's orders, and I asked her advice. "The only one I can think of is my brother," she said. "He will probably attend church tomorrow. I could ask him to come to dinner. Milton will insist that we talk privately, but he won't object to Ebert—he knows I'd tell him anyway. They hate each other, you know."

"Will they come to blows?"

"It's quite possible. Ebert has a temper, and Milton loves to goad him."

"Then I'll ask one of our watchmen to stand by," I said. It was the best I could do.

13

Sunday I woke before light, not prompted by the usual press of duties, but by a positive, purposeful feeling. No matter what lies Milton Chapman spread, Barlow and I would be all right. People had endured much worse.

With the children snug and safe in their beds for another two hours, I dressed and went to the kitchen. An odor of tobacco drifted in from the back porch, where we'd set chairs for the watchmen. The smoker was Smitty, the miner who worked nights and slept through the day. Even on his day off he couldn't change his sleep patterns.

I'd filled the coffee pot and was carrying it to the stove when the front doorbell dinged and rattled. The surprise of the bell at this early hour made me stumble and slop water from the pot. A drunk or a drifter, I thought, but maybe a family emergency—Will sick, Charlie hurt in a fight, Wanda needing me. Or that impossible fear: *Jamie Long.*

Smitty peered into the kitchen. "Want me to check on that?"

I'd lost my waking assurance that all would be well. Silently thanking Barlow for the watchmen. I followed Smitty through the hall and stood aside while he lifted the door's window curtain. Outside, someone held up a lantern, brightening the window. "Mine guard," Smitty said. "Better open up, right?"

My heart thumped. "Let's talk outside."

The worst memories of my life would not stay in their graves, no matter how much I covered them with good times and the comfort of faithful friends. The cool air carried a sharp odor of stove fires smoldering on green wood. I curled my fingers on the back of a porch chair. This felt too much like the morning when loggers had burst into my cabin, looking for Jamie.

The guard removed his hat. "Sorry to bother so early. I'm told Mrs. Chapman lives here."

I nearly fainted with relief, then felt a surge of remorse. The urgent, probably bad news was for my friend. "Mrs. Rona Chapman, yes."

"If it ain't too much trouble, I got a message. Should give it in person, I guess."

I thanked Smitty for his help and asked the guard to wait while I woke her. I tiptoed up the stairs, thankful for the carpet runners, hoping to keep Rona's troubles private. Miss Baldwin had asked to be moved to a room farther from Mrs. Vincent's, emphasizing that she was a light sleeper and was bothered by the other teacher's loud snoring. If her window was open, Miss Baldwin might have heard the porch conversation.

Rona opened her door as soon as I tapped, wakened, perhaps, by the bell, because she was already dressed in housecoat and slippers.

"I'm sorry," I whispered. "You're wanted. A message."

She reached for my hand. "Please stay with me."

Luzanna and Emmy were coming up the walk when Rona and I got to the porch. Luzanna looked briefly toward us before circling toward the back of the house.

The guard lifted the lantern to show his face. "I've come about Milton Chapman. That's your husband?"

Rona nodded.

"Doc Pringle was called to the roadhouse around midnight and he took me along, since he don't trust that place, and rightly so. There'd been a kind of ruckus, and someone commenced to shooting. The place was cleared out when we got there, nobody left but the one that got shot. Said to be Milton Chapman.

I stepped closer to Rona and circled my arm around her thin waist.

"He's alive but not too good. Doc dug out the bullet."

"I see." Her voice came out unnaturally high. "Thank you."

"Well that's not all. Doc said he's gonna need a nurse, and the roadhouse man said no way can he stay there. So. I've brung the message."

I wasn't shocked that someone had shot Milton Chapman, and I wasn't forgiving enough to feel bad for him, but I trembled for her.

"I'll... I'll have to think, won't I," she said. "I'm sorry, my mind doesn't seem to be working. His condition. I should ask about his condition. How bad is he?"

The guard shifted his feet. "Can't say. Doc don't want him moved, and when he goes it'll have to be done

careful, 'cause the bullet went close to his spine. Sorry
to be the bringer of bad news."

I had to ask. "Do you know who shot him?"

"The roadhouse man said he didn't see what
happened, and he said he don't know who was in that
card game. Which nobody's gonna believe. Maybe Mr.
Chapman can tell us later if he gets to talking. Doc's
gonna notify the sheriff."

Irene Herff, I thought. *She'd know*. I thanked the
guard for his trouble.

"Doc said to fetch him if he gets to raving. He can
ease his pain, that's about all."

The guard said good night. Rona gripped the
porch railing. "I thought I was free."

"Let's sit for a minute." I guided her to a chair and
sat too, my heart thumping in sympathy. "None of us
here will think less of you if you leave him."

"*For better or worse*." She uttered a short,
trembling laugh. "I thought I'd already seen the worst."

The sky lightened. Somewhere a mourning dove
cooed its sorrow.

"You don't have to take care of him. You can hire
someone."

"I have no money. I don't even know how much he
has, except he's spent a lot on that house."

We sat for a while in silence, then I decided she
should know. "Mr. Loughrie thinks Mrs. Herff and
your husband have been cheating at cards."

"Nothing he does would surprise me. I suppose I
must go to him. Can your handyman take me to the
roadhouse?"

"As soon as you're ready. I'll ask him to stay a while, so you won't be alone. Let's hope for the best."

"What a ridiculous marriage. I wish I could believe that being shot will make him a better man. But there's one good thing—you won't have to meet with him today. You may be free of him forever."

To my shame, I'd already thought of that. "When it's church time, I'll meet your brother and tell him what's happened."

She squeezed my hand. "Tell him where I've gone. Maybe he'll come to see me."

"I'm sure he will. It's hard to be alone in these things. You'll feel stronger with Ebert to help."

"Unless he tells me what a mess I've made of my life." She gazed at her felt slippers. "I'll need to dress."

"You should eat something."

"I'll try."

I needed to look in on the children, explain to Luzanna, send Smitty for John Johnson, help with breakfast, and pack a basket of food for Rona to take to the roadhouse. She went up the stairs and I peeked in on Emmy and the children. The house smelled of burnt coffee.

When I opened the door into the kitchen, Luzanna paused her rolling pin in the middle of the biscuit dough and waited, wary-eyed. I shook my head and continued to the back porch. Smitty looked curious too, but when I asked him to fetch the handyman and his wagon, he left without a why or wherefore.

Back in the kitchen, I stooped and pulled a basket from a low shelf. "The coffee boiled over," Luzanna said.

"Sorry. I forgot it when the bell rang."

"I made new." Luzanna pressed the top of an empty jar into the biscuit dough to cut rounds. "Your voice sounds funny."

I pressed my hand to my chest and took a deep breath. "Rona's husband was shot."

"Lord a'mighty. Where was he shot? Did you see it?"

I shook my head and laid a checkered napkin in the basket.

"Shot dead?"

"Wounded, badly, I think. I'm packing food for Rona to take to the roadhouse. She's going to take care of him until he can be moved."

"Poor thing. Her, I mean. Who done it?"

"The guard said the place was empty when he and the doctor got there."

"He's mouthed off one time too many," Luzanna said.

"It could have been a fight about cards. Price Loughrie believes both Irene and Mr. Chapman have been cheating."

"If that's true and he was shot for it, you can bet Irene's skedaddled. Whatever you do, don't let either o'them get back in here. If we don't have enough customers to get along, I'll work for nothing."

"You can't do that. You have your children to raise." And I had mine. "We'll think of something."

~

Typically, I felt better about Rona's problem after sending her brother to the roadhouse. She and Ebert might not see eye to eye, but the ties of family were strong—I couldn't believe he'd let her down.

Sunday afternoon, Emmy and Luzanna went home after setting bread, butter, and a bowl of apples in the kitchen and dining room for a light supper. With the house quiet, I decided to satisfy my curiosity and follow my secret hope by visiting the wagon of Magda, the medicine woman. Just a welcome visit, I told myself.

I'd put Hettie in the stroller and was directing Freddy toward the door when the front bell rang. Ebert stood alone on the porch, holding his hat. The teachers were watching from the parlor, and I hadn't explained Rona's absence or told them about the shooting, though maybe they'd heard our morning conversation with the mine guard. I greeted Ebert and asked if he'd help me lift the stroller down the stairs to the path.

"My sister said you had some young ones," he said.

"Frederick and Hester. We call her Hettie." Freddy began running circles in the grass, arms spread wide.

"You've done well," Ebert said.

"Thank you. How is Rona? And her husband?"

"She's going to stay the night. They put a cot for her in Milton's room."

"Is he very bad?"

"He has no feeling in his legs, and he's raving mad, cursing all of us up and down. The owner wants him gone, says he's going to close the roadhouse for a few weeks, maybe for good. Rona doesn't want to move him until she talks with Will."

No feeling in his legs, I thought. How similar to Barlow, and how different. "She's being very loyal," I said, watching to make sure Freddy did not run too far. "She's being a fool. I don't know how she'll put up with him—I couldn't stand him for ten minutes. Can they put her in jail if she just walks away and leaves him there?"

"She won't do that."

Ebert's face was sad. "I'll end up taking them home with me. But I won't promise not to kill him."

"Shh." I glanced toward Freddy. "Little pitchers."

He lowered his voice. "I can hold a gun on him—that might make him shut up. Maybe we'll get lucky and something else will get him. She wants him to go to an invalid hospital but he says it's her duty to take care of him. He doesn't care about her; he wants a free nurse who can't quit. I'll see them again tomorrow. Maybe by then she'll come to her senses."

"And I'll send food in the morning," I said.

"Do you know a lawyer?"

I told him about Barlow's cousin, Clarence Townsend.

"She'll need help to get Milton's money," Ebert said. "If he has anything left."

I caught Freddy's hand as he raced by, and let him help push the stroller to the post where Ebert had tied his horse. "It's too bad Milton wasn't hit somewhere else," Ebert said. "Like right here." He put a hand over his heart.

I shook my head but I understood his feeling. Freddy wanted to pet Ebert's horse, so I held him where he could stroke its neck. We watched Ebert ride away, then set off toward town. Ebert's description had left me in no mood for pleasantries, but I'd sent a note to the Gypsy woman with Emmy, and she'd be expecting me. I'd tucked a quart of tomatoes and a pint of sausage gravy in the stroller as a welcome gift.

The day was sunny but not hot, with the dry odor of dusty weeds in the air. Except for the two hard showers that had marked the departures of Irene Herff and Rona and Milton Chapman, the entire month had been without rain. A dry spell was not unusual for fall, but it was always worrisome. Wells dried up, the river developed a smell, and fires spread easily from careless burning of trash and leaves.

There were many people to greet along the way, for Sunday afternoon was visiting time in Winkler, and women and children were out and about. Freddy's legs soon tired, and I set him in the stroller and carried Hettie. With so much that needed my attention in the house, I seldom spent any length of time out of doors. The pleasant greetings and change of view made me more hopeful about everything.

I stopped to read a sign on an electric pole that said "Rally for the Women's Vote." The sign had been defaced with charcoal slashes. I went on, overcome by a wave of intolerance for the intolerant.

Most of Winkler's houses were owned by the mine, but a few old ones, remnants of the logging town, belonged to Will, as well as strips of empty land not claimed by the railroad and not large enough for a house. Magda's wagon sat on one of these at the bottom of a fenced-in hillside field where Will and Wanda kept their horses.

At the corner of Main Street and the alley leading to the field, I greeted a woman who sat on her step, rocking an infant on her knees. After a few minutes of admiring each other's children, exchanging details of their ages and dispositions, I said I should go, as I was expected for a visit.

"You must of got the wrong street," she said. "There's no one up that-a-way."

"I'm visiting Magda."

"The Gypsy woman? Why-ever would a nice white Christian be going there? Has someone give you the evil eye?"

"I beg your pardon? Why would you say that?"

"Oh, I don't know nothing about it, it's just nonsense told by some. I'm sure you got no evil eye or anything like it. But I'm keeping myself and mine away."

"If it's nonsense, as you say, maybe you shouldn't repeat it," I said.

She shrugged. "I got my ideas. You're welcome to yours."

"Doc Will admires her." I expected his endorsement to make a difference.

"Well a few do, that's the truth. They kinda sneak by, or pretend they're going somewheres else, but I know up from down. What's more, coloreds go there, walking right by my house like they belong here. I might just complain."

"Apparently, the medicine woman supports herself, which you must admit is a hard thing to do. But as you say, we're entitled to our own views." I waved goodbye, gritting my teeth to hide my bitterness.

Maybe tomorrow or next week I'd think of a better come-back, though she sounded like one who'd never believe she wasn't right. Like me, her only guidance was probably common knowledge, and Will said common knowledge was always at least half wrong. He'd suggested Magda had exceptional gifts, and I was badly in need of guidance from someone exceptional, a cure for Barlow, power to manage hostile guests, encouraging words for all occasions, and relief from nightmares about Jamie. Even so, the woman's warning might have caused me to turn toward home had I not needed to show I wasn't afraid. Evil eye? Surely there was no such thing.

I set Hettie in front of Freddy and pushed the stroller with determination up the hard-baked alley. My view of Magda's wagon-house was blocked by Will's hay shed, and I saw the steps first, then the curved wooden top, then Magda herself, sitting in sunshine beside the wagon. She had snow-white hair, wore a yellowed blouse, red velvet vest, and a brightly patterned skirt with a long sash, and she looked old enough to be my grandmother. "Mrs. Townsend, welcome to my home," she said, rising and spreading her arms. She was tiny, and her voice was high-pitched and squeaky.

"Thank you. My name is May Rose." I didn't know if she'd identified me by intuition or assumption, since I'd sent the note.

"I am Magda. Magdalena Müller. Or Miller, if you like." She winked an eye. Already she seemed a woman of contradictions, her appearance strange, but her voice and stature too slight to be frightening. Her speech had a slightly southern accent, and her wink suggested a secret between us.

Freddy climbed out of the stroller and started for the steps, which looked like they were made to be folded against the wagon. Magda waved a bony hand heavy with rings. "The boy is eager to see my little house, as are you. Please, follow him inside."

The interior was dark and warm, with a thick patterned rug on the floor, brightly-woven wall hangings, fringed drapes on the side windows, and shelves of small dark bottles and paper-wrapped packets. The air smelled like a piney wood.

Moving slowly, Magda sat on a wooden armchair and motioned us to a padded bench. Her entire face wrinkled pleasantly when she spoke. "You're wondering about me."

When I sat with Hettie, Freddie leaned against my legs and stared at the old woman. "I've been wanting to meet you," I said.

"It's all right if you wonder. Everybody does. It's good for business. I'm not a dwarf. I used to be tall. Like this." Laughing, she pushed her bony fingers against the arms of her chair and straightened briefly before she slumped again.

"I've heard good things about you from Dr. Herff."

"Many of my remedies were known to these people's grandmothers, but modern doctors have made folks distrustful of grannies. Still, skeptical people come to me hoping there's a bit of magic in my cures."

I hoped she was more than deception. "You want people to think you're a..." I was going to say "witch," but stopped because Freddy had recently begun repeating interesting words.

Magda nodded. "Something like that."

"Couldn't such belief be dangerous?"

"I acquired this wagon from Gypsies for that purpose." She lifted a corner of her vest. "And a few items of clothing."

"Then you haven't always been on the road."

"Indeed, no. I was raised in New Orleans but after I was married we lived in the North. I learned remedies and midwifery from my mother, and helped my husband in his medical practice. I'm afraid he was a lavish spender, and when he died his debts took everything. When I tried to practice without him, I couldn't earn enough to support myself. Meanwhile, so-called Spiritualists were making fortunes. I can't speak loudly enough to speak to a big audience like Spiritualists do, and I think I'd laugh at myself if I tried to fool people that way. My solution was to become mysterious."

"Where there's a mystery, there will always be people trying to solve it," I said.

"Which is why we must keep them on deceptive pathways. But you are close to Dr. Herff, and I do not want to deceive you. He spoke to me about your husband. I think, if his paralysis has progressed no farther, there's a good chance he will recover."

For a few moments I couldn't say anything, and I didn't want to cry in front of the children. "Will wouldn't say anything about my husband's chances."

"I suspect Dr. Herff is not in good health. Currently he seems unsure of himself."

I'd suspected the same thing, but the words were frightening to hear. "He suffers from overwork," I said.

"If that's all it is, rest should help." She stretched her hand and held mine in a strong grip, though her fingers seemed no more than wrinkles and bone. "But other things are bothering you."

"Too many."

"You can speak of them here."

I shifted my eyes to Freddy. "Just dreams," I said, my voice light.

"Something unresolved?"

"I supposed that's it."

"When our bodies rest at night, our minds are free to bring forth problems we can't solve—situations we don't want to think about or have no time for in the middle of days that drain our energy and weaken our spirits. Sometimes dreams suggest solutions. At other times, they connect things we knew but never considered together."

"Do you believe they predict the future?"

"Only if you do something to make them come true. Dreams are most often inexplicable, yet they can give us a new understanding of people we love, including ourselves and the needs of our bodies. What we fear. Something we must do."

"Some days I believe everything will be fine. Then others…"

"Such thoughts are quite natural. To everyone," she said. "They're worse when we feel helpless. So we must keep doing what we can."

Hettie began to fuss. "I brought a welcome gift," I said. Magda followed us outside, and I gave her the jars of tomatoes and sausage gravy I'd left in the stroller.

She thanked me and put a small fragrant packet in my hand. "Put this under your pillow. It may make your dreams sweeter."

"I hope we can talk another time." Alone, I meant.

14

The next day began like a reprieve from bad weather. Near noon, I answered the bell and found John Johnson with an elderly gentleman. Always on the lookout for work, John regularly met trains with passengers and freight that might need delivery to the store or mines in the area. "This feller asked for you," he said. The man hooked his cane over his arm and removed his tweed cap, revealing thin gray-brown hair. His bushy eyebrows, plump cheeks and ruddy skin gave him a look of being extraordinarily pleased with everything.

"Good day, ma'am. Uh, Percy Jones, seeking accommodation." Mr. Jones wore a gentleman's suit with a farmer's stout lace-up boots. The fineness of the cloth and leather said if he was a farmer he probably hired others to do most of his work.

John Johnson set down the man's luggage. "Got anything for me today?"

"Come back in an hour," I said. "I'll have another basket for you to take to Mrs. Chapman." Mr. Jones handed him a coin and John Johnson left.

It was best not to be too curious about our guests, but it was only prudent to know something about them. Mr. Jones said his was not a business trip, but he offered no other explanation. He read the house rules and politely paid for a week in advance, appearing in every way to be the kind of transient guest I'd hoped for, and a most welcome change from Milton Chapman.

As I led him through the hall to the stairs, the bell rattled and dinged again. This time it was Price Loughrie. My pleasure doubled. "Welcome home," I said.

Price stepped into the entry. "It does feel like home. Thank you."

I introduced him to Mr. Jones, who waited at the foot of the stairs. "I need to wash up, and I hope I'm not too late for lunch," Price said. "Do I have my former room?"

"You're not too late, and we've kept your room as you left it." The men followed me up the stairs.

"I believe I saw you on the train this morning," Mr. Jones said.

"You might see me on many trains. In a week, I travel nearly half the state. Are you a regular traveler?"

"Not by train, no. Horses suit me better."

"My horse also travels on the train," Price said. "I'm sorry to subject him to so much time in a boxcar. He should have a home with a pasture, but having him with me suits my work."

"I hope all these new means of transportation do not mean the end of horses," Mr. Jones said. "A horse suits me better than a car."

"A car wouldn't suit me at all," Price said, "and it wouldn't suit most roads where I need to go. But I'm not sure how long Caution and I want to keep traveling."

"Caution?"

"That's my horse. He's a three-year old, not yet cautious. His name is meant as a reminder to myself as well."

"One to take to heart," Mr. Jones said.

Encouraged by this guest's amiable start, I showed Mr. Jones his room and hurried down the back stairs to tell Luzanna we had two for lunch.

"Two nice gentlemen in the house," Luzanna said. "Won't our teachers enjoy that?"

"It's a blessing. Listening to Milton Chapman and Irene at the table was like being battered by a windstorm. But poor Rona. I have no idea what things are like at the roadhouse. If I'm not here when John Johnson comes for her basket, ask if he can find out."

When Price left after lunch, I followed him outside to tell as much as I knew about the shooting at the roadhouse.

"High stakes make men unpredictable," he said. "Milton Chapman must have known that. Did the sheriff come?"

"I haven't heard."

He touched the brim of his hat and mounted his horse. "I'll find out."

From that point the day's events turned discouraging. John Johnson returned from the roadhouse with an empty basket and a note from Rona Chapman. The note was brief. "Oh, no," I said.

Luzanna came to my side. "No what?"

"Rona wants to bring him back here. What can I say? They're paid up through this week."

"Bring him back for a week?"

"Until their house is finished."

"And that's supposed to be what, next spring? She should go home with her brother."

"I think she doesn't want to make things worse between them."

"But it's okay to make things worse for strangers."

"We're not strangers." But I knew what she meant. "I guess paying our way makes us feel better about the trouble we might cause."

"Trouble, for sure," she said. "This ain't a house for invalids. Or looneys, neither."

"She says he can't walk. She says that once we get him upstairs, he won't be coming down."

The doubt on Luzanna's face did not change.

"I can't turn her away," I said.

"So when?"

"Today, if I can send John Johnson and one other man to help move him."

"Ye gods, that soon? He better behave himself."

"If he doesn't, we'll ask Smitty to smack him around."

"May Rose! Just what I was thinking."

"Of course we wouldn't."

"Sure not. But I like that picture."

"Our secret," I said. "And it's time to tell the teachers what's happened."

"I kinda think they know."

That afternoon Luzanna and I added a rubber sheet to the bedding in Milton Chapman's room. She brought water and extra towels for the washstand and I set a chamber pot and a pan under the bed. I wondered if Rona would be a good nurse. It was too much to hope he'd be a good patient.

"I'm sorry for this," Rona said, when we greeted her in the hall. "The sheriff came, and the roadhouse was going to close its doors to us. I wasn't sorry to leave—it's a terrible place."

John Johnson and Smitty came through the door with her husband on a stretcher. They followed Luzanna up the stairs.

"You know you're welcome, but we can't let your husband disturb the other guests."

She showed me a vial of dark liquid. "Dr. Herff said he'd keep me supplied with this. It's to make Milton more comfortable, but there's a limit to how much he can safely take." Though no one was near, she dropped her voice to a whisper. "It could stop his breath. Kill him. I'll be careful about the dose. Naturally."

"Naturally." For a moment, vile thoughts stopped my own breath. "Does he speak? Do you know who shot him?"

"He told the sheriff he didn't know, but to me he said 'Irene.'"

"On purpose?" Maybe he'd stolen her purse and she'd found out.

"He hasn't said anything else. Mostly he yells and groans. It had to be an argument about money. Irene must have left with all of it, because his pockets are empty. But don't worry, I'll be able to pay our way here.

I'm selling Milton's precious car, and my brother is going to buy the farmland that was part of my inheritance. He's going to get a judge to declare Milton incompetent. The same judge Milton expected to defeat in the election. Isn't that rich?"

"Are you accustomed to nursing care? Will he be easy to manage?"

She smiled and showed the vial again. "There's always this. I've hired your handyman to come in the morning and evening to help me change him and the bedding. I can manage his slops. Watching me do that is his greatest pleasure. Oh, one other thing. He wants to smoke, and I think it calms him. Can you provide a bedside ashtray?"

We agreed that he would never be left alone with a lit cigar.

Dinner that evening was a spirited event, with the teachers impressed by two distinguished-looking men at the table, Price being his handsome, inscrutable self, and Mr. Jones encouraging them by showing interest in everything they said. Upstairs, all was not so pleasant. Luzanna had carried dinner trays to Milton Chapman's room. Later she showed me the one on which the invalid had turned his plate of chicken and dumplings upside-down.

I was dressing Hettie for bed after dinner when there was a knock on the apartment door. I carried her into our parlor and set her on the floor beside Freddy, who was turning pages of *Peter Rabbit* and babbling the story.

My visitor was Wanda. "Will's come to see Mr. Chapman," she said.

"I'm glad you've come." I motioned her inside. "I've something to tell you." We moved to the chairs to the other side of the room and spoke quietly. "He told Rona it was Irene who shot him."

"Ha," Wanda said. "She was always my best guess."

"Irene may get away, because he told the sheriff he didn't know who shot him."

"Would anybody believe that?"

"Maybe it was an accident. Price said he and Irene have been cheating at cards. I'm thinking there's a lot more to that story."

"I'd love to know it," she said. "I always feel good when bad folks get what's coming. I can't help it; it's the devil in me. Something else good—if Irene's run off she won't learn about Luzanna and her kids. There's a real blessing."

"Yes, but look how all this has left Rona."

Wanda shrugged. "Maybe he won't last long."

He'd put himself beyond our compassion, but I knew it was wrong to hope he'd die. "I hope she'll leave him. Not leave him here, of course."

"She won't do that to you. Will she?"

"No, of course she won't. Not unless he drives her crazy and she walks off into the night."

"We never know what a feller will do," Wanda said.

How well I knew.

I put the children to bed, then Wanda and I settled down to talk about family. I was eager to hear about her visit to Lucie Bosell's farm, especially for news of Will's brother. "Do Charlie and Blanche seem to be doing all right?"

"Seem to be."

"And Russell?"

"Him and Granny Lucie keep a safe distance from each other. Uncle Russell thinks he needs to watch over Charlie all the time and she thinks she needs to keep Blanche close. I'd say Charlie and Blanche do all the work."

"Is Charlie any better?"

"About the same. He still don't care for company, but he talked a bit to Will, I think about the old days, so maybe he's remembering or he's got more willing to talk. Otis trailed around after him most o'the time, 'cause Charlie was usually outside doing something or other. I think Will was a little jealous. He's never spent much time with that boy."

"Soon Otis will be old enough to spend time on the farm," I said. "Luzanna hopes Tim can work there next summer. She says in town he has too much time to get in trouble."

I leaned back in my chair and put my feet on the hassock. "This has been quite a day. I'll have a lot for my next letter to Barlow. We have a houseful!"

Wanda's eyes shifted. "Well, it's my turn to worry. I thought if I got Will away for a couple of days to where he didn't have to do a thing, he'd come 'round to his old self. But he didn't. And he hasn't. He agrees he needs a long rest, but he don't know how to get it. He drags himself outa bed in the morning and slouches from one patient to the next. He looks like death warmed over, don't you think?"

I winced at the word "death." Living was hard, and death often came too soon. "Did he consult Dr. Pringle?"

"He saw Pringle, but he don't think much of him so he took himself to Magda. She gave him a tonic and said his heart ain't right. Pringle said the same thing. They both said he needs bedrest, right now. Magda said he should go away for a rest cure."

"How long ago was this?"

"Before we went to Granny's. But here he is, working like before."

I didn't know how Wanda had endured our talk about everybody else. "This is urgent. He'll have to get away."

"Talk to him, Ma. He thinks he's got to keep on here, no matter what. Tell him we'll survive without him for a few months. We don't want to lose him forever."

I agreed, though in matters of health, I was used to letting Will tell me what to do, and I doubted I could say anything to influence him. When we heard footsteps on the stairs, Wanda went out and brought him into the apartment. I directed him to my chair and told him to put his feet up.

"I'll see if there's coffee in the pot," Wanda said.

As though lifting heavy weights, Will raised his feet one at a time to the hassock. "Magda said coffee is bad for me, but I need it to keep going."

"You should listen to her."

Even in lamplight, his face had a gray hue. "She says I'm sick. I can't be sick."

"You're over-tired. Go away and rest, please. I'd be grateful if you'd stay a while in that place where Barlow is."

"People need me. My practice will fall apart."

"Perhaps they don't need you as much as you believe. It's such a surprise when the world goes on without us and somebody else steps into our place. You see how it is when people die." I shouldn't have mentioned death, because we were only talking about the suspension of his medical practice, but my judgment veered when I was upset. "You understand what I mean. But nobody can fully take the place of a parent. Hopefully we won't die while our children are young. I worry about that for my family, you see."

He nodded, just barely.

"Your family will need you for a long time. Please stop work and get well. For them."

Will didn't immediately respond, and I wondered if he'd been listening or was thinking about something else. I watched the shallow rise and fall of his chest.

He began with a tired sigh. "Rest may not make a difference. I've been wondering what to do about my patients. If the company should advertise for a new doctor."

"I want you to worry about your wife and children."

"Wanda will be all right. She takes care of everything."

"You have no idea. She almost went crazy when Evie's father died. Please, put your family first."

"They never seem to need me as much as my patients do. Maybe if I can get people to trust Magda, she can fill in until a new doctor comes."

I leaned forward. "You're still doing it."

"What?"

I shook my head.

Wanda entered with a tray of coffee. I took my cup.
"Will said he's not supposed to drink coffee."

"First I've heard of it," she said.

"He's going to join Barlow at White Sulphur Springs and stay there until he's recovered."

"I haven't said I would."

Wanda set her hands on her hips.

"I see you're ganging up on me," he said. "All right, this week we'll introduce Magda to the patients. I'll insist she wear white and a nurse's cap. Maybe folks won't recognize her as the Gypsy."

"Wanda can deal with Magda and your patients. Go tomorrow on the train."

He sighed. "Maybe I should."

"Get someone to ride with you. One of the clerks, or John Johnson."

He stood with a bit of a wobble. "You see, when I give in, I lose all strength."

He and Wanda left arm in arm, and as I watched them go, it looked like he was leaning on her. I returned to my desk and cried until I felt better, then I lifted my pen to write to Barlow. With all the day's comings and goings, I hadn't realized that the day had rushed by with no letter from him.

15

Our house had high ceilings, thick walls and floors, heavy drapes and soft carpet runners in most rooms, all designed to offer privacy by dampening conversation, footsteps and other activities. But the next morning I woke to roars and curses.

Upstairs, I found the teachers and Mr. Jones standing in their open doors. Our night man, Mr. Cunningham, came from his room, pulling suspenders over his shoulders and motioning to the end of the hall. "Him down there," he said, going ahead. Miss Baldwin had the front room directly across the hall from Milton Chapman. She gave me a severe look and pressed her hands to her ears.

I started to knock, but the watchman reached for the doorknob. "Nobody'll hear a knock over that." When he opened the door, bursts of angry sound surged into the hall.

This room was, as Milton Chapman had demanded, the best in the house, with a view of the river through a wide front window, a four-poster bed, fine wallpaper, a chandelier with three bulbs and a thick flowered rug. Today it smelled of urine and carbolic soap.

Rona was bent over her husband, who lay face-down on the rug with his arms thrust to the sides. When we entered the room, he shoved her away. She kept her balance, stood with a discouraged look and said something, but her words were lost in his new roar of outrage. His hair was wildly tousled, and his nightshirt, which barely covered his rear, was twisted around thin, hairy legs.

Mr. Cunningham stooped and spoke close to his face. "Shut yer trap or I'll be shutting it for you."

The roaring stopped.

"I'm sorry. He tried to get out of bed," Rona said. Her hair was loose, and she appeared to have slept in her dress, for it was damp and wrinkled.

"I'm sorry too. We can't have this." I motioned to the hall. "He's disturbed the other guests."

Rona brought a dark medicine bottle from the dresser and poured a spoonful. When she brought it near his mouth, he swatted it away, spattering the liquid on her neck. "It's for the pain," she said.

He yelled again. "It'll kill me. I know you'd like that."

We'd left the door open, and now Mr. Jones entered the room, fully dressed. From the hall, the teachers peered into the room.

Rona poured half a spoonful of thick brown liquid. "It's only laudanum—opium for the pain, thinned with water and alcohol. I added sugar so it doesn't taste bitter. Look, I'll take some." She put the spoon in her mouth.

"Get out of my sight," her husband said.

"I gotta get to work," Mr. Cunningham said. "So here we go." He rolled Milton Chapman to his back, generating a genuine howl of pain. Straddling him, Mr. Cunningham motioned to Mr. Jones and me. "Each o'you hold down an arm." We crouched as directed. He pried open Milton Chapman's jaws and ordered Rona to pour in the medicine. When she held the spoon under the bottle, he said, "Just get over here and tip that bottle into his mouth."

She hesitated. "I won't know how much…"

"Please," I said.

She tipped the bottle. Milton Chapman gagged but swallowed.

"I gotta get to work," Cunningham said. Mr. Jones and I stood.

Rona whispered, "I hope I didn't give him too much."

"Maybe it won't hurt this once," I said. "When John Johnson and Smitty come, I'll ask them to lift him into bed. Then you and I must talk." I'd assured the other guests that having an injured man in the house would not affect them in any way.

~

"You're very industrious," Mr. Jones said, when I hurried fresh coffee into the dining room. John Johnson had come and gone, and Luzanna and I had fixed breakfast and filled lunch pails. We'd all had something to eat, Mr. Cunningham, the teachers and Luzanna's children had gone their separate ways, and Smitty had gone to bed for the day. Through all of that we heard nothing more from Milton Chapman. I hoped we hadn't encouraged a fatal dose.

"I'm glad to be able to work."

"You must have learned that from your family. Good habits."

"Very old habits," I said. "I grew up with an abundance of instruction. And correction." Before her decline, Aunt Sweet had been fanatic about having a place for everything and everything in its place.

"Ah, yes, correction. I remember that." Mr. Jones's face wrinkled with his smile.

Thus far he'd done nothing but attend meals and sit quietly on the porch. I felt ashamed for questioning his reasons for being here. I wished all our guests were like him.

"Thank you for your help with Mr. Chapman," I said.

"I like to work but I've lost the energy. Is it fair to say you're happy in your work?"

I set the breakfast platters on a tray and wiped off the sideboard. "It's not always as..." I struggled for polite words. "As disruptive as this morning. Will you be wanting more coffee?" It was cleaning day, and I needed to sweep the apartment.

"I was in the farming business. It was a good life."

If I'd had a minute of leisure, I might have sat and reminisced about the farm where I'd grown up with my aunt and uncle. Instead, I picked up the tray and backed against the kitchen door to open it.

"I'm glad you're doing well," he said.

He had no idea.

"I can sit with Mr. Chapman from time to time," he said.

"That's a kind offer. I'll mention it when Mrs. Chapman comes down. Enjoy your day." I whirled the tray into the kitchen.

Luzanna took it from my hands and set the dishes in the sink. "How we gonna clean them watchmen's room with one of them always in it?"

"It's vacant for a while after breakfast," I said. I was not going to hear any complaints about Smitty and Mr. Cunningham.

Rona had not come down for breakfast, so I carried a tray of coffee, biscuits and jelly to the sickroom. "He's not wakened up," she said. "I don't know what I'm doing. I'm sorry. I haven't slept."

I could believe it. She also looked as though she hadn't bathed or even washed her face in several days. "Perhaps you should go to your brother's house after all."

"It didn't work when Milton was well. In two days, Ebert would hate both of us."

"You can't stay in this room all the time. Do something for yourself for the next hour or two. If he yells now, there are fewer here to disturb."

"I'm nearly out of this." She held up the brown vial. "Can someone ask the doctor to send more?"

"Dr. Herff will be going away for a rest, but he vouches for the medicine woman and her remedies. Let's ask her for something to keep him safe and comfortable." *And quiet.* "If she has nothing that works..."

"I understand. If nothing will keep him quiet, we'll find somewhere else to go. But I'm so grateful to be here."

I was supposed to say we were glad to have her.

~

The afternoon mail included Barlow's letter, chatty and cheerful with continued stories of the facility and its patients. He was making friends. He felt wonderful. He missed the children. He missed me. He wrote nothing about his paralysis, and nothing to explain what might have happened the day he didn't write. There was no time to tell him Will was on his way.

We heard nothing more from Milton Chapman that day, and I hoped he wasn't saving himself for a nighttime tantrum. With Rona's permission, I sent word for Magda to visit as soon as possible. I had no interest in Milton Chapman's recovery except as it affected his wife and my house.

"He won't take anything from a woman doctor," she said.

"Tell him she's not only a nurse, she's a Spiritualist."

"Is she really?"

"She says she's not. But many people believe in faith healings, and many of those healers are women."

Magda arrived that evening, now carrying a doctor's bag and looking as official as a tiny old woman could be, wearing a plain blue dress and white apron. I showed her to the sickroom and introduced her to Rona, then went downstairs where I found Wanda pacing in the apartment parlor.

"He's gone. I had to talk, and I knew your kids would be in bed." She proceeded not to talk but to cry.

I took her hand and led her to a chair. "He'll be in a place where he has to take care of himself. He'll get better." I sat across from her in silence. Wanda was the least sentimental woman I knew, and it was difficult to watch her break down.

She blubbered into her apron until she was cried out, then used it to wipe her wet face. "It's a sanitarium, isn't it? So he'll want to be taking care of everyone. Tell Barlow to keep him from doing that."

"Barlow won't need me to tell him."

"I know. I'm crazy. When he left, I got the awful feeling that I was never gonna see him again. I can't bear the thought o'that." She bent her head between her legs. "I've made myself sick."

"Wanda, could you be in the family way?"

She straightened. "Ha. That'd be a wonder. I don't know when... Sorry, Ma."

I brought her a glass of water and a damp cloth for her face. She took the cloth but waved away the water.

"I've been a lousy wife. It's like I can't help myself; I'm just contrary. It's probably a good thing he's getting away from me. I could of done this to him, all that grief I give him, going on about every little thing." She cried again.

"You've always been quick to speak your mind," I said, refraining from the word that came most quickly to mind: *sharp-tongued.*

"I want to do different. For Will. Otis and Evie too—I hate myself when I yell and holler at them. But how else are they gonna know what's wrong if I don't tell them?"

We'd had this conversation before without any ensuing evidence of change.

"Okay, enough o'this." She wiped her face with the cloth. "I'm gonna go home and be nice to my kids. Someone should slap me down when I get mouthy."

"Not that," I said. "When you're upset with them, imagine how they feel. Think what they need from you."

She left, claiming she felt better, saying she knew Will was going to be fine. As was usually the case after she unloaded her fears on me, I felt worse.

I was turning off the lights in the parlor when Rona and Magda came down the stairs. We walked together to the porch. Fall was upon us, with warm days and cooler nights, but the nights weren't cold enough to keep mischief-makers inside.

"You shouldn't go alone," I said. "Let me ask Mr. Cunningham to walk with you."

"I'm never afraid. And I brought this." She lifted a cane from the porch umbrella stand.

Mr. Jones stepped from the shadows of the porch, tapping his own cane. "Might I escort the lady? I've a mind to stroll toward town."

"You're welcome to walk along," Magda said.

He put his cane and her doctor bag over one arm and offered the other to her. Rona and I said goodnight to Magda, then gave each other wishes for a good sleep.

The riot in my mind kept my body from rest. After turning over too many times in bed, I put my winter coat over my nightgown and returned to the porch, hoping the sky's quiet progression of stars would calm and lull me to sleep. Like a night creature, I felt drawn to these hours when the senses could not be overcome by the roar and brilliance of day.

In the silence, I heard the tiniest sounds—crickets singing, muted snoring, the tick of the hallway clock. The screen door squeaked and someone in shadow came onto the porch. It was Mr. Jones. "May I sit with you a while? I no longer sleep well," he said. "I think it's because I am no longer tired from work. Yet I do tire, merely from the passing of time."

"I'm about to go inside."

"To be with your children, of course. I saw them outside today. You have fine-looking children."

I thanked him.

"You're a good mother."

I liked Mr. Jones, but conversation this late at night would wake me up, not lull me to sleep. The hall clock struck the four descending chimes of the quarter hour. It was a quarter past twelve.

"I have sons," he said.

I did not inquire about them. He took a chair beside me and watched the sky. "Most of life consists of making it to our rest at the end of each day without disappointing ourselves and our maker," he said. "That has always been my aim."

Moonlight shone on the river. I stared at the sparkling water. Love, I thought. Love of a good person, love of family and friends should be the aim and strength of our days. Even though love opened us for disappointment.

"Will your husband get well?"

The question took me by surprise. Neither he nor the teachers had met Barlow, but since Luzanna and I discussed our guests, I supposed they might also speculate about us. Still, Mr. Jones's inquiry seemed deeply personal. Even my friends didn't question—they only assured me Barlow would recover.

I stood, the peace of night shattered. "I have every expectation."

"Good," he said. "This afternoon I sat with Mr. Chapman."

"I'm sure his wife was grateful."

"I look forward to meeting your husband. Mr. Loughrie says he's a good man."

Price was not one to offer information. Mr. Jones must have asked about us.

"Mr. Loughrie is also a good man. But I must say goodnight." I took a step toward the door.

"I think you've had a struggle," he said.

"Pardon me?"

"Mr. Chapman had a number of unsavory things to say today, mostly about you. I thought you should know, possibly to protect yourself against slander. I must believe the things he said are untrue. He said you met your husband in an establishment that serviced men. A house of prostitution."

With that, I lost the battle to stay calm. "Mr. Jones, I've made my way among some of God's poorest specimens, but I've always been fortunate enough to remain respectable."

"I feel sure you have. Mr. Chapman seems jealous. Obsessed with you as well as with his ideas about himself. His condition, possibly."

"We've tried to treat him fairly, which is more than he deserves. I evicted him once, and let him back in the house only because of his wife." I opened the door, now fully agitated. "I must get my rest."

"I'm not being critical," he said. "I haven't always been proud of my life. Someday I hope you'll tell me about Jamie Long."

With that, my admiration for Mr. Jones perished. He was an excessively familiar old busybody. "Goodnight," I said.

Inside, I lay on my bed and counted sheep.

16

For me, three was a magic number—the third in a sequence of upsetting events, no matter how small, ruined my outlook. Three was also the necessary number of days to regain my balance after bad news or an accusation of wrongdoing. If nothing worse happened, in three days I'd feel positive again.

Mr. Jones was not at fault for hearing Milton Chapman's slander, but he'd been impolite to confront me with it. With that, he'd lost his status as my favorite resident, and I begrudged him even a polite smile. But in the next three days the household settled into a pattern—the regular business of cooking and washing up, the kitchen a congested path between the back stairs and laundry room, the little table regularly crowded with Luzanna's children, my two, or the watchmen, John Johnson coming twice a day to help Rona, trays going up and down for Milton Chapman and us noticing whether he'd eaten or made a mess of his food. I took refuge in the quiet evenings when the linoleum floor and work tables were scrubbed clean, pots and dishes on their hooks and shelves, lights dimmed, teachers retired to their rooms and Mr. Cunningham smoking quietly outside in the cool night air.

The remedy Magda gave Milton Chapman subdued his pain and ended his outbursts. Mr. Jones asked no more personal questions, but continued to sit with him morning and afternoon, earning Rona's admiration.

On a nice fall afternoon she came to the summer house where I sat tearing old clothes for cleaning rags while Hettie bounced in a baby harness suspended from the rafters and Freddy pushed a metal truck across the floor. My children were never content with any activity for very long. Soon they would lose interest and we'd need to move on.

She sat on the edge of a chair facing the river. "Mr. Jones is a considerate man," she said.

Wary, I trimmed a strip of buttons from an old shirt and said nothing.

Freddy placed his truck in her lap. "Very nice," she said. "Show me how it goes." He set it on the floor and gave it a shove that tipped it over. Delighted, he proceeded to make it tip again. I put the strip of buttons in my workbasket and made small cuts in the shirt to help start the rips.

"Milton wants a wheeled chair so he can get out of bed part of the day," Rona said. "He'd said I should ask to borrow your husband's."

"No," I said. For anyone else, I might have added an explanation. For anyone else, I might have been more charitable and said yes.

"I understand."

I doubted she did, unless Mr. Jones had told her about our conversation.

"I'll order one from the store. He'd like me to hire a man to help him get about and campaign, can you believe that? I haven't told him I sold the car. I'm not worried about it—most of the time he can't stay awake. He also wants to be brought downstairs for dinner."

"I won't have him downstairs," I said. "He's already slandered me to Mr. Jones. If he gets the opportunity, he'll do the same for the benefit of Miss Baldwin and Mrs. Vincent."

"I'm sorry. I don't know why he blames you for everything. But Mr. Jones is a kind and sensible man. He agrees that I should not bring Milton downstairs."

This small mark in the old man's favor did not change my displeasure.

"You may depend on me; I have no intention of taking him out of that room until we leave for good. Ebert says now that Milton is not constantly changing the plans, our house may be finished by Thanksgiving."

Two more months.

~

With her husband subdued, Rona now sometimes joined us for dinner, looking more confident and fresh. She urged Luzanna and the teachers to attend Saturday's political rally in the Winkler church, the only structure large enough to hold a gathering expected to be in the hundreds. "A representative of the State Republican Women will be there to enroll us in the party," she said. "Even if you intend to align yourself with the Democrats or Socialists, please come and give a show of support for the women's vote."

Miss Baldwin set aside her napkin, though her plate was half full. "I'll be aligning myself with no political party, and I'm disappointed in the preacher and the elders. The church should be reserved for worship and religious instruction, not tainted by worldly activities." She glanced around the table for approval, but got none from Rona, Mrs. Vincent or me. Mr. Jones did not look up from his plate of boiled beef and noodles.

"Winkler has no other place for a large indoor meeting," I said, "so the church has been used for other things. During the flu epidemic, it was a ward for the sick."

Normally Mrs. Vincent gave no more than a smile to Miss Baldwin's pronouncements, but now she said, "Quite right. The church must be involved in issues that affect the life and well-being of all God's children. For me, that includes equal rights for women."

Miss Baldwin tried to interrupt, but Mrs. Vincent shook her fork. "Some women say we don't need the vote, our husbands can decide for us, but if our husbands are dead, like mine, who's to decide for us? I'm surprised, Miss Baldwin, that having no husband, you do not want a voice for yourself."

"I have brothers," Miss Baldwin said. "And a father to speak for me."

Rona smirked. "Well good for you; I hope they treat you right. In my opinion, we've had our heads in the sand for too long. I have no property of my own. My husband controls my inheritance by law of marriage and will not divorce me. Even if he did, I could end up with nothing, because the laws favor men. And with what kind of work could I possibly support myself?"

"Women everywhere are miserably paid," Mrs. Vincent said. "Men neither recognize that fact nor see the necessity of changing it. Sometimes I think they're afraid we'll take their jobs."

Miss Baldwin delivered her sternest look. "As teachers and mothers, we mold the minds and behavior of young men. That's how we get our say."

"Nonsense," Rona said. "Maybe you mold the minds and behavior of girls, and I do mean 'maybe.' But while a good mother may raise a good son, he will never esteem her in quite the same way as he does his father, not until she's allowed to advance herself with the opportunities and privileges of a man."

Mrs. Vincent nodded vigorously. Still concentrating on his plate, Mr. Jones murmured, "Well said."

Silently I acknowledged another mark in his favor, though I would never feel the same about him again. "The political rally promises to be interesting," I said. "I believe I'll go."

Luzanna brought in the dessert, a warm, delicious-smelling cobbler that sweetened our faces.

~

The political rally turned exciting before it began. I'd put the children in bed and left Emmy to sit with them, because Luzanna said she'd stay and use the evening to run up a new skirt on our sewing machine. Mr. Jones agreed to sit with Rona's husband, so she and I left the house together and followed Mrs. Vincent and Miss Baldwin through town.

Our path passed in and out of the beams of Winkler's four new street lights. A block from the church, we had to slow our steps, hindered by the crowd walking on the brick path and in the street among cars and horses. Public events were rare in

Winkler, and my excitement quickened at the sight of bobbing political signs, strange cars, people too well-dressed to belong to any of our mining towns, and in front of the church, tables draped with American flags.

A group of older schoolgirls, all with bobbed hair and straight bangs, hurried forward and surrounded Mrs. Vincent, chattering with excitement. We stopped a few paces behind them.

"It's good to see young women interested in the cause," Rona said.

"The redhead is my stepdaughter's girl, Evie." She'd always seemed a sweet, quiet child, but now I realized that almost overnight, her childhood had slipped away. I felt a sense of loss, but was proud to see her here. Aunt Sweet had instructed her daughters and me not to be too forward. In her day, young ladies were not supposed to speak out or seek advantage in observable ways. Her caution had taken me years to overcome.

"She's lovely," Rona said. "So Evie's grandfather was...?"

Jamie Long, she meant, Wanda's father. "Yes. We don't speak of him."

"Sorry."

"Evie has the fair complexion of her father, Homer Wyatt. He passed away some years ago."

"Sorry again."

The girls ushered Mrs. Vincent into the church, leaving Miss Baldwin behind. She waited for us to reach her.

"I don't suppose they'll save a seat for me," she said. "Really, there should be a law. She's been preaching women's suffrage to our pupils."

"You're welcome to sit with us," Rona said.

Inside, we saw that though we'd come early, we could not be choosey about our seats. We squeezed into an empty space in a pew halfway to the front. Men and women in the aisles held printed signs advocating their candidates, their party, or their position on the 19th Amendment. One questioned in bold black lettering: "What Will Men Wear When Women Wear the Pants?" The papers had been full of advertisements promising the decline of home and family if women got the vote. Cartoons regularly portrayed suffragettes as old crones, so I thought the women holding "Votes for Women" signs were quite brave. Whatever the outcome, the evening promised to be a historic event for Winkler. The visible dissent made me afraid a fight might break out, but I felt proud to be here.

The church was one of the oldest buildings in town, a survivor of the flood and fire that had ruined most everything else. The well-scuffed flooring slanted toward a raised platform. The pews were new, and a metal-sheeted coal burner had replaced the old potbellied stove in the center of the room, but I could still see the room as it had been for the revival meeting when Hester's cook had stood at the altar to be married. It was the night I'd sat between Barlow and Hester, months before he confessed he loved me, years before we were married. We'd missed so much. I wanted him beside me now.

In the pew ahead, a man got up and offered his seat to a woman. "Ha, look there," Miss Baldwin said. "If you get your equality, there'll be no more of that."

Rona leaned across me to speak to Miss Baldwin. "Hopefully everyone will be considerate of those whose condition is more frail, be they man or woman. There's an old man leaning against the wall. Shall I give him my seat?"

"Let a man do it," I said. "I fear he'd be embarrassed to accept a seat from one of the weaker sex."

She laughed, for her an unusual sound. "Too bad."

To those of us who were accustomed to the same people and scenes every day, this gathering provided great novelty, and among the crowd there was much gawking, pointing, and talking from pew to pew. Rona nudged my arm and pointed to Evie, who'd risen with the other girls to give their seats to older women in the aisles. She asked, "How could a man not want his daughters to have the same opportunities as his sons?"

Not all the same opportunities, I thought. Men did such dangerous work, like going down in the mines. Yet childbirth, the task assigned to women, might be most risky of all, for many women died of it. In their childbearing years, most women were pregnant every-other year, and in the months when I was expecting Hettie, three in our small town had not survived the ordeal. I didn't see how the right to vote would lessen the risk of our most dangerous obligation.

Awareness of a man who'd come to the podium spread throughout the room and gradually stopped the talk. He waited until the room was silent, then introduced himself as moderator and named the evening's speakers.

For this setting, the first need of a speaker was a loud, resonate voice, but the first woman who came to the podium could barely be seen above it, and judging from the shouts to speak up, could not be heard beyond the first pew.

After a few minutes the woman sat down and a buzz of talk filled the room. Miss Baldwin smirked. "There's a poor soul out of her depth."

I had to object. "We only know she hasn't a strong voice."

"I don't know what she said but I like her hat," Rona said. In contrast to the wide brims and flowers of other hats in the room, the short woman wore a close-fitting, nearly brimless hat that covered her ears.

"If women win the vote, we may be required to remove our hats in church as men do," Miss Baldwin said. "Think of that."

"In church," Rona snapped, "men remove their hats in respect, but we are supposed to cover our heads. It's a required sign of submission."

"But hats are useful to cover messy hair," I said, grateful for mine. "If we had to take them off, we'd need time and a private place to restore our coiffeurs." Neither Rona nor Miss Baldwin replied to my practical statement, both watching people in the side aisles who were now chanting and thrusting their signs in the air.

At the podium, the moderator pounded a gavel for order. When the noise subsided, he said, "I'm proud to introduce a candidate for the House of Delegates, Mr. J. B. Thurston."

Mr. Thurston caught the attention of the audience with his ringing, authoritative voice. He spoke of his devotion to the law of the land, and especially to his mother, aunts, sisters, and daughters. "Our forefathers wisely made government the responsibility of men, preserving women, the mothers of our race, from the dirty dealings of politics. I do not claim women are equal—I know they are above us men, queens of their homes, adored and protected, revered and obeyed by their children."

There was a scattering of women's laughter. I wished Luzanna could hear the part about being a queen.

"We hold the virtues of women in high admiration, nay, we adore them, but what will happen to those virtues if women become embroiled in politics? What then of our angels of mercy, our dear wives and devoted mothers?"

This sentiment received substantial applause, it being impossible not to appreciate a devoted mother. Rona shifted uncomfortably in her seat, and I noted that like some of us, Evie and her friends were not clapping. Thurston continued. "All over this land, the great majority of men and women are against ratification. If you send me to the legislature, I'll never vote for anything that threatens the saintly station of our women."

He exited the stage, accompanied by applause and a few hearty cheers.

The woman who came next to the podium wore no hat. Her gray hair was drawn back from her face in the top-knot style of poor women, and her rumpled-looking brown jacket and skirt might have been pulled from the missionary bag. Despite her undistinguished appearance, her rumbling voice lent gravity to her questions and subdued the audience. "How many men in this audience have lost a wife in childbirth? How many sitting here are from families of more than eight children? Was your mother old and exhausted in what should have been the prime of her life?"

This topic was unexpected. I was especially struck that I'd had a similar thought only a few minutes earlier, and I wondered how her remarks would connect to the issue of the evening. Still, everyone had either experienced or heard about the difficulties of big families and maternal deaths, and throughout the audience there were nodding heads and muted sounds of assent.

She shouted another question as murmurs rose. "What does this have to do with the women's vote? Only this: equal rights. Will the law stop a man who beats his wife? Only if he happens to kill her!"

I still couldn't imagine the point of her questions, but her words stunned the audience to an embarrassed silence. We always knew about wife-beatings, but our ideas about the sanctity and privacy of the home meant nobody interfered.

She pounded her fist on the podium. "Remember, I'm not talking merely of the right to vote, I'm speaking of equality under the law. Women must be recognized as equal and worthy to have a voice in every facet of their lives, including what goes on in the bedroom."

Miss Baldwin gasped audibly, as did others in the audience. The speaker stretched her arm and pointed to different sections of the room.

"How many of you are *forced to submit* to intimate acts by a husband who claims they're his right?"

Someone shouted, "Watch your tongue, lady. We're decent people here."

"Pardon me for saying what everyone knows. You who must submit, do you realize that you should be allowed to say no? *No* to the sexual act, *no* to more children than you can care for?"

I glanced at Evie, afraid she and her friends were too young to hear about intimate relations, but they were not whispering and giggling or hanging their heads. I wondered what kind of things they knew and talked about. At their age, I'd been far too innocent.

The moderator had risen and stepped to the stage and he now put his hand on the speaker's arm and tried to pull her away from the podium. She stumbled, but continued to shout. "I know you can't answer, in fact, I doubt you are here; your husbands did not let you attend!"

The speaker did not give up without a struggle, and after the moderator pushed her into her seat and returned to the stage, she popped back up, accenting her speech with raised fist. "Until the government acknowledges us as *equal citizens*, millions of American women will live in *virtual slavery*. Join the cause! In the three months since its proposal, sixteen states have ratified the amendment. Sign the petition for ratification!"

Rona and a few others stood and applauded. Before this meeting, I'd had little awareness of politics, but I stood with them, too keenly aware of women's miseries and unable to approve the ridiculous notion that disenfranchisement kept us safe from worldly harm.

The evening had just begun but I was tired, I'd heard all I needed, and from the lineup of speakers on the front pew, I judged the meeting would continue late into the night. When I excused myself, Rona and Miss Baldwin decided to go too.

Outside the church, tables were set up to register support or disapproval of ratification. Rona and I signed a women's petition in favor, while Miss Baldwin stood in line at the table for dissenters.

"You notice there are separate petitions for men," Rona said, "because in the end, they're the only ones whose signatures will count."

The effort of people who'd come from a distance to influence the men and women of Winkler sent me home with expanded awareness of political activity. But without a doubt, the best feature of the evening was the fact that Milton Chapman, candidate for County Judge, was not in attendance.

17

Barlow was halfway through his intended stay, but his letters told nothing about a change in his condition. "I don't know if he's the same or better," I said to Luzanna. She did not offer an opinion, and I didn't offer my fear that if he was worse, he wouldn't say. He reported that Will looked healthier, was taking the baths, spending leisurely hours in the open air and no longer smoking cigarettes. I always told Wanda what he said about her husband, for neither of them were much for writing. With me she shared her concern that his medical practice was reduced to women willing to take advice and treatments from her and Magda. In every letter, I asked Barlow to tell Will that Wanda and the children were well.

I wrote of a pleasant visit from our friend Piney, not of the loneliness of most evenings; mentioned bills paid, not bills due; the children's recovery from their cold; the upstairs toilet unstopped. I said Mr. Jones was a pleasant guest, ever-present but never in the way. After breakfast, he'd sit on the back porch with Smitty, and when he wasn't sitting at Milton Chapman's bedside he sat alone in the parlor, on the porch, and if the weather was nice, in the summerhouse. At the dinner hour he kindly steered the conversation away from educational and political debate by encouraging the teachers to talk about themselves.

I told Barlow everybody liked Mr. Jones—Luzanna because he complimented every meal, and Rona because when he sat with her husband she had time to herself. I didn't mention my opinion. Since that evening on the porch, Mr. Jones had asked me no further personal questions, and because I observed no change in the attitudes of our guests and staff, I decided he had not spread Milton Chapman's tales. Though he'd said he had sons, he spoke of no wife at home, and I assumed he lived alone. At times I worried he'd come to live out the remainder of his life. I didn't include that idea in my letters, either.

Barlow did write of one concern: he and Will agreed that Wanda and I should stay home during Trading Days. For several years Will had wanted to abolish the market he'd begun when he was the town's only resident, but short of barring people from entering town, there seemed no way to stop it. Before the railroad was rebuilt and the mines opened, those who'd come to the market had spread their camps and their wares throughout the valley. With the expanding population, the event became more crowded, more successful, and less under anyone's control. The hill people continued to come at the full moon to sell what they'd made or grown, and so did many from the mining towns. But with increasing numbers of young men looking for excitement, there were also fights and other rowdy disturbances. Our husbands did not want us to be in the streets unprotected.

"I can take care of myself," Wanda said.

"Barlow said you'd say that. What about Evie?"

"I'll keep her and Otis with me."

"She'll want to walk about with her friends."

"Then me and Otis will go where they go."

Luzanna also said Trading Days meant too much to her kids to keep them at home.

"I can ask Mr. Cunningham to watch out for you," I said.

"Don't do that. He might not even be planning to go."

I asked him anyway, and I also asked John Johnson and Smitty if while they were enjoying Trading Days they'd keep an eye out for Wanda, Luzanna, and any other women and girls who might be bothered by intoxicated men. West Virginia was one of the prohibition states, but moonshine was easy to come by, and there was something about liquor, crowds, and a full moon that made people think they were supposed to misbehave.

Saturday evening I busied myself in the kitchen while I waited for the watchmen to return and tell me the event had progressed peacefully.

"It did and it didn't," Mr. Cunningham said. "Your friends are all right—me and Smitty saw them home. But there was some fuss around that medicine woman's table, whites and coloreds, a good bit of yelling and shoving. Doc's wife brought the guards and one o'them fired a gun in the air and broke it up."

"Was it Magda's table?"

"Don't know her name. Bitty old woman, Gypsy-like. Looked like some folks was giving her a bad time. The doc's wife stayed and helped pack up her goods. After Smitty and me walked the women home we saw a bunch of white boys chasing some coloreds. The crowd was kinda stirred up."

Stirred up. So was I. An altercation of any kind felt a hundred times more personal when I knew someone in it. That night I woke again and again with the sensation of falling. One dream was clear—I was on a train with Jamie and the trestle beneath our car was dropping into a ravine.

~

Sunday morning Wanda came into the kitchen and without a word, poured a cup of coffee and sat at the table like she'd come on business. Luzanna and I were quietly cutting chickens in pieces to bread and fry.

"It's been a bad night," Wanda said.

For her too? I could barely keep my eyes open.

"Magda come knocking before light to get me to help sew up some colored boys. Must have been a dozen, hit with rocks and beat in the head with clubs. Said it was done by whites, four-five to one they claimed, and not just boys. Men."

Luzanna sliced her cleaver neatly through a breast bone. "Sometimes I hate this town. Everybody wants to fight."

"There's always a few bad apples," Wanda said. "Likely there's some in Colored Town too. This coffee's cold." She drank it in a gulp and carried the cup to the sink. "I can't abide people who think they're better because they're richer or smarter or whiter and think it's their job to keep the rest in their place. Each side of that fight is gonna say they didn't start it, and since most folks here is white, you know who they'll believe. I'm afraid for Magda."

Magda? We waited for her to explain.

"Her neighbors don't want her there. It's why I come. I think she's not safe where she is. Can I move her wagon to the lot back of your house?"

People coming and going at night, Magda's neighbor had said. Colored people. Attacks on colored people. "I should ask Barlow."

"Sure," Wanda said, "but you'll feel bad if something happens before you hear back."

"She'll need an outhouse."

"I'll pay John Johnson to build one. You'll let her draw water from your springhouse?"

"It'll be hard work." The springhouse was fifty yards upslope from the back lot.

"She's not afraid of a hard climb."

"In snow?"

"What will you think of next? When it snows I'll move her to the store."

I'd already given in. I knew how injustice felt and what it was like to be alone and afraid. Wanda and John Johnson helped Magda move her wagon house that afternoon, and soon I saw smoke from the pipe through her round roof.

We didn't know how Magda's patients found her, but over the next few days, frequent comings and goings wore a path to our back lot, mostly colored, mostly women and children, but occasionally men, and sometimes after dark. Twice Wanda drove her somewhere to deliver a baby.

I asked Magda if the nighttime visits were emergencies.

"Dark comes early don't you know," she said, "and folks come when they can. You're welcome to stop in too, any time."

The wagon was clearly visible from the kitchen windows, so we were aware that Mr. Jones and Rona were among her frequent visitors. I didn't want to be seen consulting her, so I went with small gifts of soup or dessert. She always asked if I wanted to sit and talk, and I always said, "Another time." I wanted very much to talk, but in a more private place. My dreams had dredged up thoughts that would not go away.

I invited Magda to the apartment the next Saturday evening, providing a tray of nut bread and tea to make it appear no more than a social visit. Luzanna and Emmy had gone home, and the watchmen were in the kitchen, cutting and hammering new soles on their shoes. Mr. Jones and the teachers appeared to be reading in the parlor.

Magda's patient, wrinkled face invited confidence, and in the low light and safety of my parlor I was soon telling about Jamie's death.

"You can't believe he's dead."

"It happened so long ago. But yes, I think that's it. And now someone is trying to find me." I took a sip of tea. "Which could be nothing."

"You never saw his grave. Could you go there?"

"I don't know how. His brother buried him. I know approximately where, but the region is wild and difficult, maybe impossible to reach."

"Even if you saw the grave, you'd still have to take his brother's word that it's Jamie who's buried there. You wouldn't...dig it up."

"I couldn't bear to see it opened. I shouldn't doubt; his brother is Wanda's uncle, and neither he nor Wanda is skilled in deception."

"So you'd know if he was lying. I think you can rest easy about that. Jamie isn't coming back."

I knew. I knew, and I knew, but it helped to hear her say the words.

"Something else bothers you, and you want to talk about it."

Maybe it was because she seemed so different that it felt safe and natural to say what I hadn't been able to confide to family or friends. "All those years ago, people claimed I'd done a terrible thing. It wasn't true; I know it wasn't true, but now I dream about it and it seems real. Some days I doubt myself."

"I see," she said. "And your other dreams, do they describe true events?"

"My dreams are strange and unreal. The other night I was in the train wreck with Jamie. I know that didn't happen, but I so clearly felt the helplessness and terror, people falling on me, all of us falling, screaming."

"It wasn't a nice dream, but it left you with awareness, and that's not bad, if a person is strong enough to bear it. Sometimes when people describe a bad dream, they don't have it again. As for your other dreams, I know propriety is important to you. People who worry about doing the right thing often dream they've done something unforgivable."

We drank another cup of tea and spoke of Barlow and Will, though I had nothing new to report. She thanked me for a pleasant evening. I was the thankful one.

18

Luzanna was the first to mention that Mr. Jones might be sick. "He's got some of Magda's remedies in his room. And this week he ain't been around as much as he was, don't you think?"

I hadn't thought, but I'd been trying not to see him.

Sunday after dinner she said, "He didn't clean his plate." Sunday evening Miss Baldwin and Mrs. Vincent remarked that they hadn't seen him since dinner.

Monday morning Rona asked if he'd ended his stay. "He didn't come to sit with Milton yesterday. Twice I knocked on his door," she said.

Luzanna and I were frying mush and filling lunch pails, so I did not go upstairs myself, but when John Johnson arrived to help Rona, I asked him to look in on Mr. Jones. Shortly after, he clomped down the back stairs, glanced toward Emmy and Tim and motioned me to the porch.

"He's dead to the world," he said.

"Meaning sound asleep?"

"Meaning *dead.* You want I should call the undertaker?"

Unexpected deaths always took a while to sink in "Are you sure? He was quite alive at Sunday dinner."

"He's stiff as a board," John Johnson said. "I closed his eyes."

"Dead. The poor old thing." Two days ago, he'd paid for another week. The handyman was waiting for my answer. "Yes, tell the undertaker. On second thought, tell him not to come until the children have left for school."

An hour later, I showed the undertaker and his helper to Mr. Jones's room and stood a moment at his bed in respect and remorse. Mr. Jones lay on his back. Except for his jacket, he was fully dressed.

"Pardon me," the undertaker said. "Are you going to put him in the ground right away or do you want him embalmed?"

"I'm only his landlady," I said.

"He's got next of kin?"

"He has sons. I'll try to find them."

"Embalming costs money," he said. "And grave digging, if you want him buried here."

"It won't be up to me. I think you'll have to proceed with the embalming."

"You'll pay if the sons don't show?"

"You'll be paid." Mr. Jones's jacket hung over a chair back. I pulled his wallet from the inside pocket. Please witness while I count this money, in case someone thinks I robbed him. The undertaker and his helper watched, then went with me to the office while I recorded Mr. Jones's property as 72 dollars.

They carried away the body, and the next thing I knew, Luzanna was tacking a black drape above the porch steps. "I just felt like doing it," she said. "He was the nicest guest we've had. Polite and cheery."

I was ashamed of myself. His impertinent questions no longer felt important.

Between lunch and dinner, we went to his room to strip the bedding and pack his clothes. In one of his suitcases, Luzanna found a fat envelope with words printed on the front: "To my family." The envelope was brown, with a string fastener. Hoping there'd be at least one address inside, I took the envelope to the office, and when Emmy came home from school, I sent her to the telegraph office with a message to his next of kin.

News of the black drape must have reached Wanda and her Aunt Piney, for shortly after Emmy left on the bicycle, they rushed into the house. I should have been helping Luzanna clean upstairs, but for the last half hour I'd felt stuck to my office chair.

Wanda burst out, "Who?"

I shook my head. "A guest, Mr. Jones."

"What a fright." Piney fanned her face with her hand. "I'm so glad. I mean I'm sorry, someone's dead and I shouldn't have said I'm glad. You know what I mean."

"I know. Wanda, Luzanna is upstairs. Would you ask her to join us?"

Wanda panicked again. "What's wrong? Is it Will? Barlow? Why do you want Luzanna?"

"Nothing's wrong, just strange. I want to tell you together because I'm not sure I can say it more than once."

"Oh, dear," Piney said. We sat in silence, listening to Wanda's footsteps up the stairs then double steps as she and Luzanna hurried down. I motioned her to close the door.

"Okay, let's hear it," she said.

I folded my hands on the desk. "Mr. Jones has four sons and a wife. I sent a telegram this afternoon."

Luzanna was surprised. "A wife? He seemed real settled in here. Did he run away from home?"

"His name wasn't Jones, it was Percy." I unfolded the papers from their envelope. "Jonas A. Percy."

"Maybe he was running from the law," Luzanna said. "Though I can't believe he's a crook. If he's running, it had to be from something he didn't do. Don't tell me he was a crook."

"He left a letter and a will. They explain a few things. I have brothers."

Wanda, Luzanna and Piney spoke at once, variations of "*You* have...? Mr. Jones knew your family?"

"He was my father." They stared like they didn't know me, which was my feeling exactly. For the past hour I'd been trying to identify myself. "This doesn't change anything. It doesn't affect me one way or the other."

Wanda was red in the face. "O'course it affects you. If I was you I'd be mad as all get out. In fact, I'm mad myself. How's come he waited so long to find you? And why didn't he explain himself before he went off and died?"

"There's a letter to me. The short of it is he says he was ashamed. When my mother died, he left me with her sister, my Aunt Sweet. My aunt and uncle never heard from him again. They assumed he was dead."

"He was a nice old man," Luzanna said. "Maybe he meant to tell you. I can't think he planned on dying."

I smoothed the papers on the desk. "He may have had some warning, because he brought along his last will and testament. If I read it right, he's left me half his property. The other half is to go to his wife and sons."

Wanda's mouth gaped. "Half to five other people, and half to you? If I know anything a tall, some folks ain't gonna be happy."

"Their father is dead—a woman's husband is dead. They must have feelings for him. I don't have those feelings, and I don't need anything from him. I hope they come soon and take him away."

Piney stood and held my hand. "When they come, you call me and Simpson. Wanda too. We don't want you to be alone."

I swiped the damp skin beneath my eyes. "We need to get on with dinner. Rona knows he's dead—she was there when the undertaker took him. Luzanna, I'd like it if you'd tell the teachers and the watchmen. Just say he died. Don't say a word about his letter or will, not to anybody, please."

"Half of everything," Wanda said. "He kinda looked well-to-do, didn't he?"

19

Would I reveal myself to the Percy family? I didn't know. My heart was not ticking in excitement to meet them. Maybe they already knew about me and why he'd come. If they didn't know that nor the contents of his will, I didn't want to be the one to tell them.

Writing to Barlow was a comfort. This time I told everything I knew about our dead guest, adding that my friends had promised I would not have to meet his family alone.

The teachers thought it was a fine thing that I was honoring Mr. Jones by placing his coffin in the parlor. I didn't tell them his name wasn't Jones, or that I hoped someone who cared about him would soon take him home.

His family—I could not think of them as mine— returned a telegram with the expectation that they would arrive in three days. Luzanna was in a tizzy. Would they stay for dinner, and if it wasn't Sunday, should we put out a clean cloth anyway? Should there be flowers? More chairs in the parlor? If they wanted to stay overnight, where would we put them? Rona offered suggestions. I left the decisions to her and Luzanna.

And then they arrived, four dark-haired Percy men who mumbled their names as they took off their hats and passed through the door: Robert, Matthew, Woodrow, and Carl, each glancing in turn to a woman named only as "my wife."

The couples were followed by another woman who was left to introduce herself. "I'm the boys' stepmother, Elizabeth Percy." I guessed she might be five or ten years older than me.

The men had black beards and moustaches, and they and the women wore black mourning clothes rumpled from travel and smelling faintly of mothballs. It might have been a time to say I was a Percy too, but I introduced myself as Mrs. Townsend. They looked past me, searching for their father like they were in a hurry to get this over. I agreed with that sentiment.

Wanda, Piney, and her husband Simpson rose from their chairs when I brought the family into the parlor. One of the sons opened the coffin lid and his widow cried. The sons stood behind her, legs apart as though seeking balance, each with his hands clasped, each with his wife at his side, all with fixed, dry eyes. They were a family, nothing to me. My father had been dead my whole life.

One of the sons said, "I thought he was going to visit a cousin in Ohio. How'd he get here?"

I shrugged and shook my head. "Let me know when you're ready to leave. We packed his things."

"You did what? You had no right."

"Pardon me, but we needed to discover his next of kin. We didn't know his address or his true name. He registered here as Mr. Jones."

The room buzzed as they talked among themselves. I heard the word "Addled."

The widow shushed them. "No matter what you think, he always knew what he was doing. Mrs. Townsend, thank you for contacting us. And for arranging..." She gestured to the coffin.

"You have our sympathies. He was a good guest," I said. "If you like, we can provide dinner before you leave." I hoped they would decline.

"Thank you," the wife said. "We'll take him home on tomorrow's train. Do you have room for us, or can you direct us to another lodging place?"

Wanda spoke up. "There's two bedrooms in the company store. It's not fancy, but in this town, it's the only other place to stay."

Against my will, I said, "Two rooms are empty here." Price's room could be rented when he wasn't here, and of course there was the room where their husband and father had died, something they didn't need to know.

"Four rooms. There's nine of us," one of the sons said.

Not my fault, I thought.

Piney said, "Someone can come home with us."

Elizabeth Percy turned and smiled at her. "Thank you. Let that be me."

~

We served two tables that evening, the teachers and Rona at the usual hour, and after them, the nine members of the Percy family. Emmy stayed with the children so I could help Luzanna cook and serve. After dinner, they sat in the parlor with the coffin until John

Johnson arrived to convey two couples and the widow to their lodging for the night.

"I know you aren't the kind to push yourself in," Luzanna said, "but they should know about you."

"I hope that doesn't happen until they're far away," I said.

"I'm disappointed in Mr. Jones, letting all these years go by without a word. Not saying a word once he found you. You could of had a family."

"Maybe this is best." I'd seen the coolness of the sons toward their stepmother, and they seemed less grieved by their father's death than unhappy about its inconvenience.

Their train was scheduled to leave late Friday afternoon. I tried to stay out of everyone's way. "Set lunch on the buffet as usual," I said to Luzanna.

"As usual, just a whole lot more," she said. Later she came to the apartment. "The widow wants to know what she owes for the meals and all."

"Tell her we're even, since her husband paid a week's room and board in advance."

"What if they want to see his bill?"

"Then say I'll add up everything and charge them for the difference."

"I don't blame you for being mad," she said.

"I just want them to leave."

"I know. Such a pity."

As the Percy family sat at lunch, I opened the front door to a surprise visitor, Barlow's Cousin Clarence. "I got here as soon as I could," he said. "When I got Barlow's telegram, I decided to drive instead of taking the train. Connections are always undependable, and he asked me to hurry."

To hurry? I didn't like Cousin Clarence very much and I didn't see why I needed him, but I was glad because he'd come at Barlow's request. I helped him off with his coat and laid it with his hat on a parlor chair.

"Mr. Percy's family is in the dining room. Would you like to meet them?"

"Not yet." He took my arm and directed me toward the office. "Let's see that will."

Ah, the will. Was this Barlow's direction, or his cousin's idea? I'd put the brown envelope in one of the two suitcases now waiting by the front door. "It's in there. I haven't told the family about it."

He scooped up the suitcase and carried it to the office desk, retrieved the envelope and returned the suitcase to its place beside the other. Then he sat in my chair and read all the papers. "That's good, the will was drawn by the same attorney who sent the letter. I brought it along." He stood. "I'm ready to see the family."

"Clarence, what did Barlow ask you to do?"

"To stand by you and protect your interests."

"The family doesn't know I have an interest."

"You haven't told them who you are?"

"I don't think Mr. Percy told them about me. I feel very strange, and I'm not sure I like them. They seem angry because he came here and died so far away. I don't want anything from them."

He pressed my hand between his. "Barlow understands. Naturally, the years of neglect hurt. That's why I'm here. Lead the way; I'll tell them."

Everyone at the table looked up when I opened the sliding doors from the parlor. "Pardon me," I said. "I'd like to introduce my husband's cousin, Clarence Townsend."

Noisily, the brothers scooted back their chairs and stood to shake Clarence's hand. "Please, take your seats," Clarence said. He nodded to the women. "Ladies, Gentlemen, my profound sympathies. If this seems a good time for you, I'd like to read some documents left here by Mr. Percy."

Luzanna came through the door from the kitchen, took one look at Clarence and me and backed out. I stood in a corner, trying to distinguish one son from another, but they looked very much alike. They might have resembled their mother, because their father's coloring, I realized too late, had been like mine.

The son at the head of the table spoke first, directing his disapproval first to me, then to Clarence. "Instead of reading our father's documents, you might more properly have given them to us." His brothers and their wives nodded in support. The widow touched her water glass and did not look up. What they thought didn't matter.

Clarence and Barlow looked enough alike to be brothers, but Clarence was younger, with rounded cheeks and small, feminine hands. He stood near one corner of the table and waited until all eyes were turned his way. "As Mrs. Townsend said, my name is Clarence Townsend, and I practice law. Some weeks ago my cousin asked if I could discover who was trying to locate his wife." Clarence unfolded a paper and passed it to the one who'd spoken. "As you see, the letter is from a Philadelphia lawyer, addressed to Mrs.

Townsend. It seeks to discover if she is May Rose Percy."

I stared at the table, aware of the passing of the letter back and forth, conscious of heads turning as one by one the sons and their wives looked to see if I was the one presuming to be that person.

"Mrs. Townsend was indeed born May Rose Percy in Stillwater, Ohio," Clarence said, "and she was indeed raised by Burt and Sweet Jonson, now deceased. I replied to the lawyer on her behalf, but received no further information. I understand that soon after, a Mr. Percy Jones took up residence in this boardinghouse. I also understand that only after he died did Mrs. Townsend learn that his real name was Jonas Percy."

Barlow and I had on occasion shared a smile when Clarence's name came up, because even in ordinary conversation he tended to pontificate. I stared at the wall behind him, wondering if to others he sounded like an authority or an interfering fool.

"Amongst his belongings," Clarence said, "Mr. Percy left a letter to his daughter, Mrs. May Rose Percy Townsend. This is his letter. Pass it around. See if you agree this is his hand."

There was a rustling of interest at the table, wives glancing at their husbands, chairs shifting. One of the brothers took the letter and let his gaze move over the page before he passed it on. "Might be, might not," he said. "I'm 34 years old and I never heard a word about another family." He frowned toward me. "Or half a sister. Maybe she knew from the start. Maybe that's why he died."

"That's outrageous," Clarence said.

Silently I thanked my husband for sending Clarence.

The widow said, "Could I see the letter?" I watched her eyes follow the script. When she looked up, she said. "This is his writing." She looked at me. "I knew he was troubled about something. So you found each other?"

"Not exactly. Until he died, I thought he was Mr. Jones."

"The letter to you appears to have been written only a week ago."

"It was in his suitcase. Had he confessed he was my father..." I shrugged. "I think I'd still be angry."

The son who'd spoken most rose and faced me from the opposite corner of the dining room. "*You'd* be angry?"

"I'm the one who was left."

"So you say. If you're thinking about getting anything from us, you better be able to prove it."

For most of his stay, I'd liked Mr. Jones, a kindly man whose only fault appeared to be that he was too inquisitive. I liked him less as Jonas Percy, a man ashamed to admit he was my father. So far, nothing made me like his sons.

"I have no need to prove myself, but you may have your lawyer investigate my cousins. It was their home in Ohio where your father left me."

Clarence cleared his throat. "You might as well hear this now."

The widow interrupted. "Mrs. Townsend, you look like you need to sit down." She touched the empty chair beside her. "Please."

She was right. Besides providing a steady base, the chair put my back to the angry-eyed son in the corner. My corner, my room. My house. These people would soon be gone. There'd be no need to see them again.

Nothing but crumbs remained on the plates in front of Mr. Percy's family. We'd shown them hospitality, and my friends had too. I could feel good about that.

Clarence held up another document. "Mr. Percy's effects included a copy of his last will and testament."

Everyone at the table talked at once, a roar of discontent that diminished when the son in the corner said, "I'll take that."

"This document is a copy, witnessed and dated before Mr. Percy arrived here. The original may be in the possession of your father's lawyer. Do you want to hear it or not?" Clarence's voice was buoyant. He was the only person in the room enjoying himself.

Under the leveling of so many hostile stares, I left my seat with the family, where I did not belong, and stood beside Clarence, where I did. "Until a few days ago, Clarence and I did not know about your father's will. We are not responsible for your father's actions. Cousin Clarence, would you like a chair from the parlor?"

"I'm fine as I am," he said.

In the parlor, I turned a chair toward the opening between the rooms and sat with my ankles crossed and my hands in my lap. My new seat let me see and hear from a more satisfying distance. Grim faced, the family moved their stares back and forth from me to Clarence as he read the will. The widow was to keep the house where she lived; the sons had the farms he'd bought for them. His own farm, its buildings, animals, equipment and half his stocks, bonds, and bank account were to go to me. I knew this already, but they did not, and their reaction was much as Wanda had predicted.

"If she's to get his cattle, she can come and feed 'em this winter," one said.

Their spokesman slammed a big fist on the table, rattling the glasses. I uncrossed my ankles and sat straighter. *My table, my room, my house.* "I've asked for nothing," I said. "But now I'd like you to take your father and leave."

"We've worked his land since we were kids," the fist-banger said. "I might tolerate all this if she got the same as us."

Another brother pointed to me. "You bet your life, we'll be taking this to court."

"Well I'm an attorney," Clarence said, "so I know your attorney will appreciate that." Smiling, he returned Jonas Percy's will to its envelope. "A case like this could mean a decade of delay and legal costs."

In the parlor, they filed before the coffin, muttering and sniffing. "She can bury him," one said.

"No," the widow said. "We're taking him home." She offered her hand. "I'm sorry we had to meet like this, and I'm sorry he kept this secret. It's not your fault."

"Thank you," I said. "It's not your fault, either." I meant the hostility of her stepsons.

John Johnson's wagon was waiting in the lane. The sons shouldered the coffin and maneuvered it outside, where a warm, dry wind was whipping the brittle tree branches and whirling funnels of dust. Clarence and I watched from the sheltered doorway.

As the sons went down the steps their hats blew off and tumbled through our parched grass. Dutifully the wives chased and retrieved them, holding onto their own hats and trying to keep their skirts from blowing up.

A bucket clattered across the lane, spooking the horses, which leaped forward just as two of the sons tried to set their end of the coffin in the wagon. I gasped, fearing it was going to smash in the dirt and drop the body out. Swearing, the sons caught the coffin a few inches from the ground.

Then they left, the widow beside John Johnson, the others following well behind the dust of the wagon, a procession in black, two by two, heads bent into the wind, everyone holding onto their hats.

Clarence said he couldn't stay, so we said goodbye as soon as the wagon turned onto the main road. "If you write to Barlow, please don't tell how they insulted me," I said.

"I can honestly report they're no different than most people, fighting over who gets what. At least your father left a will."

Not a father, a guest of the boardinghouse, a stranger, Mr. Jones. "He deceived them too. I suppose they have a right to be angry."

"As do you," he said. "I can represent you in Philadelphia."

"I'll talk with Barlow. Maybe you won't have to go—I don't want their property."

"Now, don't say that," Clarence said. "Your brothers will settle down."

His sons, not my brothers.

When Clarence left, I hurried to the apartment to hug my children. Luzanna met me in the hall. "I'm sorry," she said. "Some family just makes life worse." I knew she'd heard everything.

"It's going to take a long time to get used to this."

"Well I hope to goodness somebody points out how they had a rich father all those years when you was scraping by."

20

Barlow's advice was to let Clarence and the Percy lawyer deal with the will. "We'll talk about it when I'm home," he wrote, responding to my insistence that I wanted nothing. I kept thinking of the Percy son's threats and Clarence's assertion that legal action could take years. The men might be ready for years of fighting, but I wanted it over and forgotten.

Barlow and Will planned to travel home together in two weeks. I started counting the hours, eager and apprehensive. When he left, Barlow had promised he'd walk through the doorway. Surely if he were no better, he'd have prepared me for disappointment.

I stopped trying to imagine how different everything might have been if Mr. Jones had revealed himself in the beginning, but wondered if I should have suspected a purpose in his visit. He'd complimented my work, admired my children, and asked about Jamie. He said he hadn't always been proud of his actions. He'd tried to be helpful. I had to admit he'd seemed like a man trying to do the right thing.

Luzanna took down the black drape and put it away.

We were in a dry and dusty fall, near drought, with crisp leaves thick on the ground and the river no more than pools scattered among the rocks. Because more than one Winkler resident had recently started a grass fire when burning trash, mine guards went door to door asking people to cover their burn barrels and pits with screening and to stay with them until the fires were out. Smoke from cook stoves was normal anytime, but now a smelly haze drifted into the valley.

One evening Mr. Cunningham motioned me to the back porch and pointed to a distant outline of red along the mountain ridge, a wildfire. "Boss says nobody's up there to put it out. If it gets close, half us men will work the mine and the other half will go out to fight it. Me and Smitty should still be here to sleep and eat and such, but I don't know—they might camp us out somewhere."

The gash of red looked tiny against the black sky, yet it persisted, and as I stared, its light seemed to grow. Up close it would be a monster, devouring trees by the minute, driving birds and animals from their homes. And if people were there, them too.

"I was on a fire line when I was hardly more than a kid," he said. "All you can do is shovel dirt on it or set backfires so it'll burn itself out."

"Is it far away?" To fight the fire, the men would have to climb steep slopes and crawl through impossible tangles of undergrowth.

"As the crow flies? Six-eight miles, maybe less. I don't know what it'd be on foot."

The red ridge lay in what I imagined as the direction to Lucie Bosell's farm.

In the morning, a new smoky wind blew into the valley, rattling our gutters and lifting leaves from the ground. Men went to work and children left for school, but by noon, Rona called our attention to wagons and walkers slowly passing on the road north.

"Hill people must be getting out," Luzanna said.

After lunch, the mooing of cattle drew us again to the front porch. Our house sat well back from the road, away from the worst noise and dust of trains but up slope enough that we had a view of the road and the river beyond. At present, a fog of smoke hid the river, and the cattle bunched along the road were barely visible.

"Coming to the stockyard," I said to Luzanna.

She pointed. "Oh, bless me, no. They're coming here!"

Sure enough, men on horseback had opened the gate and were turning a herd of maybe forty animals into the fenced field between our house and the road. The grass there was short, for Simpson Wainwright had cut it for winter hay, but the cattle immediately put their noses down to graze. I was so busy noticing how they raised the dust and filled the space of our field that I didn't tumble to the riders.

"It's Charlie and Russell," Luzanna said. "And I think that one's a woman. Gotta be Blanche."

Russell lifted his arm and rode toward us. "I'll put more potatoes in the pot," Luzanna said.

He stopped his horse near the porch. Russell always looked the same—hair and beard wild and gray, shirt and trousers crusty and faded. He was not much older than Barlow, but his weathered skin made him look like an old man. As always, he was short of words. "Fire's close out there."

"And Lucie? Did she stop at Piney's?"

He leaned to the other side of the saddle and spit. "Sorry fer that—dust in my mouth. The old woman wouldn't budge."

"She's still at the farm? Is she in danger?"

He wiped his mouth with a dusty kerchief. "Fought us like a wildcat. No use losing us and the herd 'cause she's crazy. We decided to leave her to come out by her own self."

This was the worst kind of news. "Wanda will be frantic. And Piney."

"Wanda saw us coming through town. Charlie told how he tried to get her granny up on a horse."

"I know you did your best." Surely Lucie would leave before it was too late.

Russell turned down my offer of rooms in the boardinghouse. "I guess Blanche will bunk at her pa's so she can see her kids," he said. "Me and Charlie will camp near the herd. That field don't have a lot of grass, so we'll move on tomorrow."

"I'll bring your supper. If it rains, you can come inside or sleep on the porch."

"Never fear, it ain't gonna rain."

"Will the fire come here?"

"Could." He turned his horse toward the herd.

Mr. Cunningham's shift ended early, and the night work was called off. Tomorrow both shifts were going out to fight the fire. Because of the wind, Smitty said.

Smoke kept us from seeing the mountain fire until the sun set and a red glow spread into the night sky. At dinner, Miss Baldwin was full of nervous speculation. "The fire is spreading fast. They've called off school, and there's talk of evacuating women and children on the train, so I'll be packing up tonight. If I go before I've used up the days I've paid for, I'll expect a refund, Mrs. Townsend."

I managed to smile.

As we washed dishes, Luzanna wanted to talk about what we should do if the men couldn't stop the fire.

"There's a lot of land between here and there," I said. "Surely they'll stop it. All the mines are sending their workers." I couldn't bear the thought of losing another house. Or this town. What would we do then?

Luzanna said it wouldn't hurt to have a plan. "If there's no passenger train, we can ask John Johnson to take us out," she said.

Together the population of Winkler and Barbara Town numbered more than 2,000, most of them women and children, and trains that came here to haul coal usually did not pull more than one passenger car. If the railroad company put people first, it would send a long train of passenger cars, but passengers would not be the company's priority, not with scores of loaded coal cars waiting on the sidings.

I suggested we might travel as far as Fairmont and shelter with Cousin Clarence. "If no passenger train comes here, we can ask John to take us as far as Elkins. Surely we can go to Fairmont from there."

"Very likely we won't have to leave," Luzanna said.

"I'm sure we won't." I wondered when we'd know.

When Luzanna left for home, I joined Charlie and Russell on the back porch. Mr. Cunningham and Smitty were there too, watching the sky and speculating about tomorrow. Wanda arrived with Evie and Otis. Since they hadn't had dinner, she and I settled the children at the kitchen table with leftovers and went back to the porch.

"I'm riding to Granny's at first light," Wanda said. "If I got to, I'll tie her on a horse."

I wanted to tie Wanda to her chair. "Your Granny will change her mind and ride out. She didn't come with Charlie and Russell because she doesn't like people telling her what to do."

"She'll listen to me. Uncle, I hope you left her a horse."

"She won't ride nothing but that old plow horse," Russell said. "He's about as wrecked as her, but I figure he's smart enough to find his way out of the smoke. I'll go along tomorrow. If she won't come, I'll throw a rope over her."

"Ma," Charlie said.

Mr. Cunningham mumbled, "Who's his ma?"

Russell nodded toward me. "He means her. She raised him."

Charlie spoke from his perch on the farthest porch rail. "You hitch a wagon and come with Blanche and me tomorrow."

"It'd be smart," Russell said.

Charlie's concern made me teary, because most of the time he acted like he didn't know me. "Tomorrow's too soon," I said. "And we have no wagon."

"John Johnson will take you," Wanda said. "Go with them and take my kids."

"All right," I said. "But we'll wait for you."

I didn't see John Johnson when he came to help Rona with her husband the next morning, but I met him in the kitchen on his way out. Before I could ask if he'd drive us to Elkins the next morning, he said, "I'll be hauling supplies to the fire line, next couple o'days. So I won't be here to do for Mr. Chapman. Or for anything you need."

"We'll be fine," I said, not sure at all.

21

Without a wagon, we fixed our hopes on a train. As we'd predicted, engines had moved coal cars all night long. Throughout the day we sent Tim to the train station to see if there was a schedule for passengers.

Mrs. Vincent read in the parlor, but Miss Baldwin went up and down the stairs and from parlor to porch, commenting about people going north on the road, and asking for news of a passenger train. Believing Wanda and Russell might return as early as mid-afternoon, I also went frequently to the porch, as though watching would bring her sooner.

"Bake sugar cookies," I said to Luzanna. The children needed a sweet diversion, and so did we.

Dinner and dusk came without a sign of Russell and Wanda, and I pretended to Evie that I wasn't a bit worried. "They probably decided to get a good night's sleep," I said.

Dawn the next morning was a blurry smear of red sky and bitter smoke. My insides were quivery, but I did what I could to appear calm. Luzanna and I were stewing apples and cooking oats for breakfast when Simpson appeared at the back door. "Piney and me's got the kids in the wagon. We got room for three more, if any of you wants to go."

With Wanda's children, we numbered eight. Luzanna and I had told each other we needn't be in a hurry, yet we'd decided without discussion to make several batches of biscuits instead of waiting for bread to rise. "You and your kids should go," I said.

"We best stick together. There'll be a train."

We thanked Simpson and went to the porch to watch his wagon leave with Charlie, Blanche, and their herd. The animals raised a cloud of dust that hid them from view. Where, I worried to myself, was Wanda?

"Let's bake the ham," I said. "If we have to leave, we can slice it to take along, and it makes an easy meal when we're busy with other things."

Until Rona opened the door from the dining room, I'd given no thought to how she might evacuate her husband. When I saw her, I lifted the coffee pot and motioned to the table. "I haven't eaten anything; would you like to have breakfast here with me?"

"That would be nice," she said. "The fire is worse, isn't it?"

"The mines have shut down so the men could go to put it out. We didn't speak, yesterday, did we? I've been distracted."

"I think I slept most of yesterday," she said. "And all of last night."

I stirred the last of our cream into the sticky lump of oatmeal in the pot, thinking she looked groggy, wondering if she'd helped herself to some of Magda's laudanum. I realized then that I hadn't seen Magda in recent days.

"Luzanna, did you see Magda yesterday?"

"Don't think I did. She keeps to herself."

"She should hitch up her mules and drive that wagon north. Rona, we've been planning what to do if the men can't stop the fire. John Johnson is carrying supplies to the fire lines, but Smitty and Mr. Cunningham may come back. If we need to leave, we'll help get you out." I was beginning to think we should all start walking.

"This might be a good time to leave him." She laughed. "Of course I won't. Maybe I'll put him on a mattress and slide it down the stairs. If I dose him good, he won't feel a thing." She laughed, but I thought we might have to do it.

"I'd better see if Magda is all right." I left my oatmeal and hurried to the wagon house. No smoke came from the tin stove pipe, and she didn't answer my knock, but when I put my ear to the door I heard a faint cough. "I'm coming in," I said.

I found her under a mound of covers. She raised her head. "I'm all right. My lungs don't like this smoke."

"Are you well enough to drive your wagon?"

"I'm awful tired."

"Come to the house and let us take care of you. If we decide to walk north, maybe Luzanna's boy can hitch up your wagon and drive it for you. We'll stay close together."

She was too weak and too reasonable to resist. As I helped her to the house, I made new plans. There was no certainty that a passenger train would come. Even so, Tim had reported that people were crowding the station. We'd be smarter to walk. I'd push Freddy and Hettie in the stroller, and Otis could ride on seat of Magda's wagon with Tim. If Wanda came before we left, she could take Otis on her horse. My stomach churned. She should have returned by now.

The teachers sat in the parlor with their suitcases. "No news," I said. "But I'm told people are waiting at the station. If a passenger train comes, you might have a better chance to get a seat if you're there."

"I'll do that," Miss Baldwin said. "Please ask your handyman to convey us."

I gave her the bad news about the handyman, trying to be patient and concerned though my mind was busy with everything else. I needed to make a list of necessary things to take, like diapers and water. And what would we do about Milton Chapman, even if we managed to pull him down the stairs on his mattress. Could Rona push his wheeled chair all the way to Elkins? "We may walk north," I told the teachers. "We could walk together, if you like."

Mrs. Vincent lifted her suitcases. "I can't walk far and I can't walk fast. I'll have to take my chances on a train." I followed the teachers to the porch and wished them good luck.

I was standing on the front steps, looking for Wanda and watching a surge of black smoke in the southern sky when Price Loughrie rode up our lane, followed by Ebert with a horse-drawn wagon.

"I've come for Rona," Ebert said.

"Oh, thank goodness." I pointed to the new smoke, which seemed near. He and Price turned to look. "It's the school," Ebert said.

"Our school! So the fire has come." The school sat on a knoll at the farthest edge of town.

"It's not the wildfire." Price tied his horse to a porch post. "Talk is, the school was lit. Folks are up there watching to make sure it don't spread."

I felt close to unraveling.

Price carried a rifle and wore a belt with a holstered handgun. "Randolph asked me to help the guards," he said. "There's been some vandalism, 'cause of strangers passing through and houses sitting empty."

"Riff-raff," Ebert said. "Price, I need a hand."

Ebert and Price carried Milton Chapman down the stairs in his wheeled chair. He was thinner, with sagging skin and an uneven shave, and his head drooped. Under his fine jacket coat he wore a wrinkled nightshirt.

The children had gathered in the hall. Ebert glanced at them and spoke in a low voice. "May Rose, you should go with us. The fire does not seem to be spreading toward my farm."

"Do you have room for eight?"

"Two on the bench beside me. The others might walk."

"The little ones can't walk," Rona said, "and May Rose can't push the stroller up those dirt roads. "I want Magda to come too. The boy can drive her wagon, and the children can ride inside."

Ebert agreed, though his face looked like he didn't know what he'd do with all of us.

In the next half-hour we got Magda's wagon house hitched and the children in place. Price and Ebert laid Milton Chapman in Ebert's wagon, and Ebert climbed to the wagon seat and picked up the reins. I'd started to climb into the wagon house when I saw the teachers trudging up the lane, their skirts whipping in the wind.

"No train till tomorrow," Mrs. Vincent said.

I stepped down and went to Ebert. "Please go. I'll come tomorrow. A couple hours' walk—it'll be easy."

"May Rose! Let the teachers take care of themselves," Luzanna said.

"Thank you for rescuing everybody," I said to Ebert. "I'll be there tomorrow." I watched until the wagon with my children disappeared in the dust.

The teachers waited on the porch. "I want to pay for another night but just two meals," Miss Baldwin said. "Dinner tonight and breakfast in the morning. Will those be at the regular time?"

I almost laughed. "There will be no regular times. You may have your bed, no charge. There'll be ham and biscuits in the kitchen. Might be coffee. You may help yourself and wash any utensils you use."

Mrs. Vincent sat heavily into the nearest porch rocker. "Any port in a storm." She giggled. "A storm would be nice right now, wouldn't it? I mean, thank you very much. We have tickets for tomorrow's train!"

The rest of the afternoon I baked unreasonable batches of biscuits. Each time I took a pan from the oven and slid in another, I went to the front to watch for Wanda. The black trails of smoke had disappeared, but haze hid the sun and darkened the day, and soon the figures on the road were no more than gray blots. Four o'clock passed, then five. No Wanda.

~

Price and the watchmen arrived hours later, crusted with dirt. They did not say, but to me their return meant they were resting here because the fire was closer to town. They washed off the worst in the laundry room, and though all said they weren't hungry, they sat in the kitchen and consumed a pot of coffee, a pint of jelly and two batches of biscuits. Months had passed since morning.

I waited until Smitty and Mr. Cunningham went up to their beds to ask Price about the roads to Lucie Bosell's farm. Until then, I hadn't mentioned Wanda and Russell's trip to bring Lucie to safety. He knew all the roads, having lived on the farm several years with Lucie's daughter Ruth.

"They should have been back hours ago," I said. "Yesterday, really."

Price didn't look alarmed, but his face and voice were always bland, maybe tightly controlled. "There's a real web of roads up there. Some might be safer than others. Lucie and Russell know."

"So they might have gone out another way?"

"Wanda's in good hands."

I tried to believe he'd given a reasonable answer, but I no longer felt capable of reason. I was uneasy without the children and restless without the boardinghouse routine. I made another batch of biscuits, stretched out on my bed for a moment's rest and woke hours later, still in my dress. The hall clock struck four.

22

Half asleep, I pushed open the door to the kitchen. Smitty was pouring coffee. "I said you wouldn't mind if they helped theirselves." Price and Mr. Cunningham were packing lunch pails and filling water bottles. Smitty set a cup on the table. "Set yourself down."

"How close is it now?"

He looked at the others. "I'd say about three miles, wouldn't you?"

Their nods seemed unworried.

"The wind's died and there come a bit of rain last night, so I think we'll be setting backfires today," Smitty said. "We'll stop it. Then I hope the mine will give us a day off before we have to go back to work."

"You'll see Wanda today," Price said.

"I'm sure I will." I was afraid I wouldn't. "Do you suppose there's mail?" I hadn't written to Barlow or thought of collecting our mail for days. If he'd heard of the fire, he'd be worrying.

"It's Sunday," Mr. Cunningham said.

No mail, then. "I'm going to join my family at Ebert Watson's today. There's canned sausage and tomatoes in the basement. Please help yourselves."

Price invited me to the field to meet his horse. "His name is Caution. He's young and prancy, but he responds to gentle neck-reins."

I stroked the horse's neck. He was black, beautiful, and as stylish as his owner.

He asked, "I guess you know how to ride?"

"It's been ages."

"He's like most folks—if you treat him right, he'll be good to you," Price said.

He handed me a brush and made grooming motions. It felt odd but pleasant to be brushing this animal in the fearful dawn.

"Don't walk," he said. "You'll be safer on horseback."

"Safer?"

"Above the crowd. I've seen no panic, but you never know."

Price saddled the horse and tied the reins around the pommel, then we went back to the house. In the kitchen, he laid a hand gun on my worktable. "There's looters about," he said. "Keep your doors locked and this handy."

The gun was heavy, with a long barrel. Once again, I doubted. "Are you sure I need this?"

"Barlow would want you to be prepared. Take it with you when you go."

"What about you?"

"I have my key—I'll open the house for Smitty and Cunningham. We'll take care of everything."

"If you see Wanda..."

"She knows the way to Ebert's. I'll tell her you're there."

I wanted to hug him, but he would have been embarrassed. I slipped the gun into my apron pocket.

The gun was still there, its bulge in the sagging apron unnoticed by the teachers when once again I accompanied them outside to say goodbye. We'd heard the passing of a long train but could not see what kind of cars it pulled or even if it was coming or going.

The smoke seemed thicker. Miss Baldwin tied a scarf over her nose and mouth and told Mrs. Vincent she should do the same. I smiled them away. Maybe Miss Baldwin would be so eager to reach the train that she'd stop complaining. Maybe Mrs. Vincent would finally tell her to shut up.

Not long after they left, I came out again wearing special garments for the trip: my garden hat tied down with a scarf, my long car coat, and a money bag secured under a clean dress. I'd tacked a note to Wanda on the front door and moved Price's gun to my coat pocket. I carried the stub of a carrot, something for the horse if I needed to make friends again. I supposed he was still in the field—I saw very little through the fog of smoke.

When I reached the gate, I heard a barrage of angry words, possibly trouble on the road. I gripped Price's gun. Somewhere close, a horse snorted and squealed. Hooves in a gallop, coming close. Not trouble on the road, trouble in our field. I called, "Caution!" Someone, maybe more than one, was trying to steal him. He came into view a few feet from the gate, and then I saw his pursuer, a stout woman, limping as she ran, using a cane like a third leg.

I dropped the carrot and pulled Price's gun from my other pocket. "Bless me if it isn't Irene Herff! Back away from that horse!"

"You ain't gonna stop me."

"I have a gun." I needed both hands to hold it steady.

She peered. "I believe you might. But it don't scare me. You're too prissy to use it."

"Don't tempt me. You make a big target. I can't miss."

She stumbled, righted herself with the cane, and ducked behind the horse. Then she screamed, a high-pitched wail mixed with murderous curses. Snorting, Caution raced away toward the other end of the field.

Someone will come, I thought. All this noise we're making, someone on the road will come to help. I picked the carrot from the ground and went into the field, still holding the gun and watching my steps, for the cattle had manured everywhere. Irene lay on the ground, breathing and shouting in gasps. "The dammed thing kicked me." She tried to get up and screamed again. "My leg is broke."

Perhaps her leg was broken, but I had no sympathy. Caution raced back, and I stepped around the clumps of manure to his head, extending one hand with a carrot, trying to hold the gun steady in the other while glancing back to make sure Irene still lay on the ground.

"Did you hear me?" She roared. "I said my leg is broke!"

Caution crunched the carrot and let me lead him to the gate. My sweaty fingers squeezed the cold metal of the gun as we passed Irene, who was stretched flat and moaning for attention. I led the horse to the porch, hiked up my skirt and stood on the step to swing myself into the saddle. When I was seated, Caution turned his neck and nosed my leg. I gathered up the reins and spoke his name. He seemed willing to go.

Irene screamed again. "I want a doctor. Get Will! He'll not be happy if you leave me like this."

I considered her from the safety of the other side of the fence. "Let's see, you held a shotgun on his pa, slandered me, tried to steal this horse, and best of all, you shot Milton Chapman. I might mention to someone that you're here. Like the sheriff."

"All right I'm sorry for all that. You can't leave me like this. The fire's coming! Fetch someone!"

I was curious. "Where have you been hiding?"

"None o'your business."

"Sorry. I thought you wanted to be friends."

"I do, I do. You can't just leave me here. Get somebody to help."

Briefly the cloud of smoke parted, giving a clearer glimpse of walkers and wagons on the road. If they heard Irene, they did not change their path.

"You're right; I can't just leave you," I said. "I'll get the town guard. He can lock you up until the sheriff comes. Attempted murder and horse theft. I'm not sure which a judge will think is worse."

With a lot of groaning, she rolled over and groped for her cane. She poked it into the dirt to help her stand but fell back down and let out another burst of curses. "Dammit, I'm laying in shit."

Caution pranced like she was making him nervous. I flicked the reins, and he stepped into the lane more quickly than I expected. I leaned forward and stroked his neck, resisting the urge to pull on the bit, whispering, "Slow, boy." The gait he chose was smooth, but I hadn't ridden in twenty years.

The road to Ebert's would take me through Winkler and Barbara Town, then west, away from the fire. That much I knew, but I'd never gone by myself, and I worried about the many offshoots of the dirt roads, none marked, none showing evidence of greater use than the others. Someone at the store might give directions.

With another light touch of the reins, Caution turned onto the paved road, where he slowed to a walk. Silently I thanked Price Loughrie for this sensitive animal. I let him pick his way against the steady current of refugees heading the other way: walkers, riders, and wagons of families—farmers from the hills—some leading a cow or goat, many with dogs. As in a fog, no face or landmark was clear until it was close. The air stung my eyes and made breathing a chore. Many people wore kerchiefs over their faces. I tied my scarf over my mouth and nose.

The travelers stared ahead, weary and slowed by too many miles, but I examined every face that came out of the haze. Not one belonged to Wanda, Russell, or Lucie Bosell. A train chugged by, getting up speed, pulling passenger cars. Finally, the railroad company had recognized its duty. I was glad for Mrs. Vincent and Miss Baldwin.

Price's horse snorted like he didn't like being closed in by the crowd. I bent forward and petted his neck, shushing him as I would a child. In a few minutes we reached town, where the road was broader and the traffic less dense.

One of the town guards sat on his horse by the store steps. "Over there," I said to the horse. "Get up there with that other horse." Caution must have known the words "get up," because he leaped forward, nearly throwing me out of the saddle.

When we reached the guard, I leaned from the saddle to make myself heard. "There's a wanted criminal at the Townsend boardinghouse. Irene Herff. She's lying in the field with a broken leg. Milton Chapman said she shot him."

The guard continued to watch the crowd. "Ma'am, I can't leave. I'm in charge of the company store and the traffic on this street."

"Please. I'd be grateful if you'd get that thief off my property as soon as you can."

"If her leg is broke she won't be going nowhere. We'll get to her sometime." He touched the brim of his hat. "First things first."

23

First things first. What were my first things? I halted the horse and let the traffic flow around us, wondering why I'd thought I had to stay with the teachers instead of leaving with Luzanna and the children, angry for thinking I could find my way even if the air cleared. What was the best choice now? Protect the house against vandals? Go home and deal with Irene Herff? Listen to her rage while I waited for the guard to act on my plea?

The mothers and fathers walking through the smoke carried infants and clutched the hands of small children. Older children ran alongside, holding on to each other or gripping their mothers' skirts. Staying together. In extremity, that was the first thing: stay together.

The store was closed, but the station master or someone waiting for a train might give me good directions to Ebert's. If everyone hadn't evacuated.

"Walk on," I said to Caution. He flicked his ears and complied. As we approached the far end of town I got a full view of the school and a nose full of its odor, the residue, I supposed, of charred wooden floors that for ages had been treated with oil. Evie wouldn't care about the school. Like Wanda, she was no student. Emmy, however, would be devastated, and until the building was rebuilt, our boardinghouse would have no income from teachers.

Loss of the school, however, was not high on my growing list of regrets and sorrows. I hadn't written to Barlow in how many days? And how many days since I'd thought to collect the mail? Barlow, Will. Wanda and Russell, Luzanna and my children—none of us had any way to know how the other was faring. At White Sulphur Springs, Will and Barlow might have access to a telephone, but we had only the telegraph.

I was an idiot. I should have sent a telegram, and I should have thought of it sooner.

I tied Caution's reins to a post outside the railroad station and went inside, composing the telegram in my head. "All well. Forest fire controlled." Even if it was wrong, it was what he'd need to hear.

There was only one clerk in the station. "No more passenger cars," he said.

"I want to send a telegram."

He motioned me to the Western Union window. In the empty waiting room I went to the farthest corner, faced the wall and hiked up my skirt to reach the money bag.

When I'd paid for the telegram, I asked the clerk if he could give me directions to Ebert Watson's place. He tilted his head. "It's out that a'way." That much I knew.

I should have gotten directions from Price. I wondered if ever in my life I'd made so many wrong decisions before finding what was right.

Outside, a girl in a faded print dress and loose pigtails was untying Caution's reins. "You, girl, stop that," I said. She was the size of a child of ten or eleven, and her dress, wide in the shoulders and long in the waist, dragged the ground.

"I need this horse so I can catch up with my folks." Caution stood still as she lifted her foot to mount, but the stirrup was too high. When she turned the horse to the step, I pulled the reins from her hand.

The dust of her face was streaked with tears. "My fault, my fault," she cried. "I got a stone in my shoe and stopped to take it out, and when I went on I couldn't find them. They're gonna be so mad at me."

"Do you live in Barbara Town?"

"Our place is up the mountain. We come from the fire. I thought they'd be waiting somewhere in town. I looked all over, but I ain't seen them nowhere. I'll see them when I'm riding high up." She made a grab at the reins but I held them above her head.

"This horse doesn't belong to me. Come along, I'll help you find your family."

"For sure?"

"It's best you stay in one place. If you go off looking everywhere, you'll be bound to miss them. What's your name?"

"Silby French."

"We'll paint a sign with your name on it and put it by the road. Your folks will see it when they come looking for you." She could stay on the porch when I left again for Ebert's.

"There's a lot of us kids. They didn't notice I was gone, or they would of waited, wouldn't they? Maybe they don't care. Maybe they'll never come back."

"They'll find you." I couldn't leave her. "I'll lead the horse if you want to ride."

"I can stay with you? What about the fire?"

"The men will stop the fire."

I helped her sit astride the horse, then led them back across the bridge to Winkler. When we reached the store, I stopped to speak again to the guard.

He frowned at the girl in the saddle. "Is this your criminal?"

"This is a lost girl, Silby French. If her family comes looking, please tell them she's at the boardinghouse. And I hope you'll come as soon as possible and get Irene Herff. You might have to carry her."

"'Case you hasn't noticed, I've a lot going on," he said. "I'm supposed to make sure there's no thievery or mischief, all these people passing through."

"If you see Price Loughrie, please tell him there's mischief at the boardinghouse. If it's a help to you, I can go back to the station and telegraph the sheriff."

"Well." He considered. "I'm the one should do that."

"So you'll come soon?"

He sighed. "Directly I can get someone to help."

Silby chattered all the way through town. "I figure our place is burnt down. So maybe they won't never come back. I wasn't much good to anybody. The older ones was always saying 'Get outa my way.' There's seven older'n me and three littler. You bet if they come back I'll be in trouble for not watching out for Bias, he's four. I hope he's not lost too. He's probably hungry. You got anything to eat at your house?"

"I think so. We'll be there soon."

She patted Caution's neck. "I like this horse. Pa should see me now. He borrows a horse to plow. He'd rather have a horse than eleven kids. Only the youngest three is boys. Pa says Ma finally got it right, but I don't think boys would be better than us girls. We set out a hundred cabbage plants but I never can get my row straight and sometimes I step on the plants. It don't hurt 'em though. Ma says I eat as many berries as I put in my pail and she always has to go back over my bean row to get what I missed. I'd like to try shooting but Pa won't let none of us touch his gun. My hands ain't strong enough to set traps. I like school but I don't get to go much and now it's burnt."

"We'll get a new school," I said.

"What do you think you might have to eat at your house?"

"Ham and biscuits. Here we are." My nerves were a-jangle. As we turned into the lane, I slid my hand into my coat pocket and touched the cold steel of the gun.

"I'm real thirsty," Silby said.

The air had cleared enough to see the house and field. Irene Herff was nowhere in sight. I was ready to believe anything—that she'd risen up and run off or broken into my house where she might be waiting in ambush.

I peered in every direction as I led the horse past the porch and around to the back door.

Silby slid to the ground and I tied the reins to a porch post. "You look funny," she said. "Are you sure this is your place?"

"I'm watching for robbers." I opened my coat and took the key ring from its pin at my waist.

"That's good. Ma says we can't never be too careful."

Inside, I settled Silby at the kitchen table with a glass of water, ham and biscuits while I checked to be sure the front door and all the downstairs windows were locked. The house was so quiet I could hear the tick of the hall clock from every corner. Someone might have come and helped Irene away. A good Samaritan. A partner in crime. As soon as the watchmen returned, I'd ask them to help me search the grounds. No, I'd get directions to Ebert's house and let them search the grounds.

Silby was a welcome distraction. I carried a can of house paint, a broad brush and a wide board from the basement to the back porch. We decided to paint "Silby French is here." She painted her first name in large uneven letters then said it'd be best if I did the rest.

When the sign was finished, we carried it between us to the roadside.

I'd told myself Irene was long gone, but I'd put on my coat for the protection of the gun in its pocket, and as we walked toward the road I not only looked left and right, I kept turning my head to see behind us.

"You're a nervous somebody," she said "Is there a lot of robbers here?"

"I'm watching for my friends."

"I hope they're not lost too."

"Everybody will come home," I said. It had to be true. Visibility everywhere was better, raising my hope that the fire was out.

At the road, I watched for Price Loughrie while Silby experimented with different locations for the sign, running a distance each way to see how well it could be seen. "It'd be better high up," she said.

"But look, not many people are passing now, so everyone will have a clear view. When they come back, people will see it. They'll spread the word."

Silby left me and walked a few steps with a group of sad souls. Pointing to the sign she said, "I'm Silby French, if you see my ma and pa, tell them I'm here."

When she came back to me she whispered, "Burned out."

"I should go to the house," I said, worried that Irene might be waiting for me in the bushes, and thinking I should have hidden Price's horse in our shed.

She pointed north. "Them riders is coming back. That's a good sign, ain't it?"

Even several hundred feet away the riders were unmistakable—Wanda, Russell, and someone hidden behind the neck of the third horse, either a child or Lucie Bosell. I put my arm around Silby's shoulders and squeezed. "My people."

"Well good," she said. "Probably mine'll be next."

Excited, I waved to Wanda.

"I gotta wait here," Silby said.

"Silby, I'll be leaving soon to fetch my children. If your folks aren't here by dark, go back to the house."

Wanda rode ahead of the others. "We've had a trip of it," she said. "All the way around Robin Hood's barn. Did my kids give any trouble?"

24

Wanda, Russell and Lucie looked like they'd rolled in dirt. "Went off and left my cane," Lucie said. Wanda helped her off the old plow horse and steadied her up the steps and on to the toilet in the hall washroom.

"Ready to go home," Lucie said, when they returned to the kitchen.

"Not tonight," Russell said. "Like to be hot spots all over, even if the farm ain't burned. We'll wait a few days."

I hadn't realized how late it was, but daylight was nearly gone. Like me, Wanda wanted to go to the children. Luzanna was expecting me, and she and Evie would worry. Freddy would be happy playing with Otis, and Luzanna and Emmy would take good care of Hettie, but she'd experience a second confusing night away from her mama. And I needed them.

"Well then if we ain't going home, fix us something to eat," Lucie said.

"I don't mind traveling at night," Wanda said, "but I haven't ate since yesterday."

I set out the last of the ham and a platter of biscuits. While they ate, I told about the school burning and how I'd found Silby.

"Nothing surprises me anymore," Wanda said. "Leaving Granny's place, we rode close to the fire. She led the way; can't remember her last meal but knows all them roads. Do you suppose Will and Barlow heard about the fire?"

"I sent a telegram. I said the fire was out." It seemed like the only sensible thing I'd done that day.

"I should write now and then," she said.

"You should."

"Will knows I'm not good at penning words."

Lucie patted the air around her, looking for something. "I need a cane. Someone go to the store and get one."

"The store's not open," I said, "but I think Mr. Jones's cane is in his room."

"Mr. Percy," Wanda said.

"The name doesn't matter."

She shrugged. "My pa didn't own me neither, you know. I used to feel bad about it."

"I don't feel bad." I was sure I didn't, but I was surprised by a pang of sadness when I opened the door to his room and saw his cane in its corner. I took it to the kitchen, telling myself I'd feel the same about any other kindly-disposed guest who'd unexpectedly left this world.

I told Lucie and Russell about Silby so they'd not turn her away if she came to the house. Lucie said she'd sit on the porch and watch for her, then she saw the summerhouse and said she'd wait there. "Where'll be my bed?"

I hadn't thought. "None of the guest bedrooms have been cleaned."

"It won't matter to Granny," Wanda said. "We slept last night in a ditch. Nasty and cold as a witch's tit. Are you ready to go?"

The night air still smelled of smoke. "Are you sure you can find the way in the dark? Or should we wait for Price?"

At that moment, Lucie struck the cane against the step of the summerhouse. "There's some big woman here on the floor. I don't know if she's dead but she stinks like it."

Irene Herff.

"I'd be ashamed if I was her," Lucie called.

I ran to the kitchen for a lantern and asked Russell to help. Sure enough, it was Irene. Her eyes were closed and what we could see of her leg was swollen. She was covered in brown slime that smelled like cow manure, but her chest moved up and down. She was alive.

Lucie hobbled toward the house. "Throw a tub o'water on that stink pile."

"Draw the water," Russell said. "I'll clean her off."

Wanda and I carried buckets of warm, soapy water to the summerhouse. Returning from her watch at the road, Silby stopped to see the spectacle of the big woman screaming and squirming as Russell doused her. "If you'll stop running your mouth and trying to hit me, I'll wrap you in this blanket so you won't be cold," he said.

I knew it was too late to go. Wanda said she was having trouble keeping her eyes open, and I was afraid she'd get us lost. Price arrived, said he'd remind the guards about Irene, and offered to ride to Ebert's in our place. I was grateful.

He bent and whispered close to my ear.

"Yes, sorry." His gun was still in the pocket of my coat, which I'd laid over the back of a kitchen chair. I put the gun in his hand. "Thank you. It was helpful."

"I'll come back tonight." He patted his pocket. "I have my key."

Wanda turned to me. "How helpful?"

"It's a long story."

After Price left and Wanda settled her granny in a room and went home, I sat with Silby on the porch, wrapped in my coat, waiting for the guards. I pictured Price arriving at Ebert's and telling everyone we were safe. I imagined Barlow's relief as he read my telegram. Any minute the town guards would take Irene away and I'd rest easier. Everybody would sleep somewhere.

Smitty and Mr. Cunningham returned and announced that they'd indeed gotten the upper hand with the fire. When finally the guards arrived and tried to move Irene, Russell and the watchmen came to the porch to see what the noise was about.

She continued to yell loudly enough to be heard all the way to the road. "You bastards! Crooks and suckers! The woman runs that house is a whore. Is this how you pay her or does she give it for free? I'll tell the judge. I'll tell everybody!" She fought so strongly with her arms and one good leg that the men carrying her let go and dropped her a few inches above the wagon bed. She screamed, then whimpered.

"Sticks and stones," Silby said, squeezing my hand. "That woman's nutty, ain't she?"

"Nutty as squirrel turds," Russell said. To me he mumbled, "This'll blow over."

Everyone went to bed, but I was too agitated to sleep. I sat in the office, listening for the turn of Price's key in the lock and trying to soothe myself by rereading Barlow's letters. The mood of his correspondence had never varied, and I found no hints between the lines of an improvement or a worsening of his condition. He felt tired but good at the end of every day. He appreciated every word I wrote. The most recent letter had been mailed before he knew about my meeting with the Percy family. Soon he'd be missing my daily letters and wondering what was wrong. But he'd have the telegram, and tomorrow the mail train might run again.

I went to the entryway when I heard the turn of Price's key.

"Everybody's fine," he said. "Ebert's going to bring them home in the morning."

"We're in his debt. And yours." In hindsight, everyone could have stayed here and been safe. I could imagine Ebert's discomfort with so many extra people in his house, including six youngsters and Milton Chapman.

I put Barlow's letters under my pillow with Magda's sachet. That night I had no bad dreams.

25

I should have been happy and energized—the fire was out, the mines had reopened, and families were trudging back to the hills to see if their homesteads had survived. My children were by my side and my enemies were far removed, yet I resumed work with an almost disabling sense of uncertainty. For the children's sake, I put on a bright face, but my motions and thinking seemed awkward and slow.

"Whatever you can find," I said, when Luzanna asked what we should have for dinner.

Calling me from the apartment to register two guests, she said, "What room will you give them? Will it need to be changed and cleaned?"

I didn't know the state of the rooms, nor which ones were occupied by Lucie and Russell. Emmy went to investigate. I took Hettie and Freddy to the office and set Hettie on my lap while I spoke with Mr. and Mrs. Thornton.

"Our place burned," Mr. Thornton said. "We got our chickens in crates in the wagon out there, and our cow and calf tied up at your gate. I figure I can sell the chickens to pay for a few days' room and board, and maybe I can pick up a mine job. The cow is fresh; I can sell milk too." His face was eager, but his wife looked lost in a fog.

I didn't know what to say. "Excuse me a minute." I carried Hettie through the kitchen, trailed by Freddy, and found Russell in his chair on the back porch. "There are crates of chickens in a wagon out front. Would you take a look and tell me what they're worth?"

While I waited for Russell's report, I sat with Hettie and watched Luzanna peel potatoes. "I can tell men's been messing in this kitchen," she said. She wrinkled her face at the tracks on the floor and crumbs on the work table then gave me a look to pull my gaze to the floor and table top to be sure I got her meaning. "You all right?"

I sighed. "I can't get going."

"It's no wonder. Things is just catching up with you."

Russell returned. "Them hens is scrawny and most has been pecked half to death. I wouldn't give much more'n a dime apiece."

"They belong to a man and his wife who were burned out. They need room and board until he can find a job."

"A job around here being unlikely," Luzanna said. "Let them have two days for a dozen chickens, killed and dressed. That'll be generous."

"And after two days, what are they supposed to do?"

She shrugged. "We got our own troubles."

I knew my trouble then. It was sadness, deadening my limbs and restricting my breath.

When I didn't move, Luzanna said, "I can check those people in or toss them out, whatever you want."

I shook my head. "I'll do it. I'm trying to work up steam."

"It's hard, I know," Luzanna said. "If it wasn't for my kids, some days I wouldn't get outa bed. But I gotta get them up and do my darndest to keep them on the right path. Who knows, when they're grown and gone, maybe I won't know what to do with myself." She dropped a cleanly-skinned potato into a pan of water, stretched her neck and rolled her shoulders. "But you know, I've always got a pleasure outa making things, sewing and such. I'd like to make pictures, but never can afford what it takes to do that. When the kids is gone maybe I'll have more to come and go on. If I should live that long."

"We're all blessed by what you do for us," I said.

"Well that's something too. Now go settle those people, one way or the other."

~

"I'm handy with fixing and building things," Mr. Thornton said, when I offered two days' room and board in exchange for his chickens. "We could be your live-in workers, just for the winter, say. My wife can clean and do your laundry. I could build a shed for the cow, keep you supplied with milk." He turned to include his wife. "Katty could cook, too. She's a wonderful cook, aren't you dear?"

Mrs. Thornton's confusion filled the small room. He linked his hand in hers and gave it a gentle shake. "You *are*. You're a wonderful cook." When she made no sign, he said quietly, "Dear, we're going to be fine."

Her sadness merged with my own.

From her seat on my lap, Hettie tested her reach for the objects on the desk. I pushed the registration book toward Mr. Thornton and gave Hettie the blotter, which she rocked back and forth on the desktop, then on my arm.

"Mr. Thornton, I wish we needed your work. For now, you may put the cow and calf in the field. Deliver the chickens to Luzanna at the back door. Tomorrow will be soon enough for that. She's particular, so please pluck them clean. If you'll wait here a moment, we'll see if there's a room ready for you."

I seldom took the children upstairs, and Freddy considered the stairs and a little run in the upstairs hall as a treat. Emmy said two rooms were ready. I let her show the Thorntons the way.

~

Wanda brought my mail, eager, I knew, for news of Will. There were three letters from Barlow, the first a reaction to the meeting with the Percy family, the second apologizing for not having written the day before, and the third saying he'd heard of a forest fire in our region and was trying to learn from newspapers if it threatened us. I was glad I'd sent the telegram.

"I suppose he and Will are the same as usual," I said.

"Have you wrote to Barlow about the school? Will's gonna feel real bad about that."

"I'll write today. The school board needs to get busy and build a new one."

"They won't, they'll wait for Will. He always says the board's useless. Nothing gets done 'less he does it."

"Construction should start soon so the school will be under roof before the snow comes. Call a meeting. You can go in Will's place."

"Not me," Wanda said. "I barely went to school. I'm not bad at delivering babies and patching up wounds but I don't know nothing about building."

"Talk with Simpson, call a meeting in Will's name and be ready with a plan. You'll be the only one prepared."

"You think I can make those men do what I want?"

"Like nobody else," I said.

She looked pleased. "Better than Will?"

"Like you said, Will doesn't know how to get others to do the work. He does everything himself."

~

The teachers returned, soiled and rumpled by travel and dismayed to discover the school and their jobs gone. "I find myself extremely embarrassed," Miss Baldwin said. She stopped and pressed gloved fingers to her mouth to hold back the quiver in her breath.

Mrs. Vincent finished for her. "She means we have no money. And now no employment. And nowhere to go."

Miss Baldwin straightened her shoulders. "It's not quite that bad."

"It's exactly that bad," Mrs. Vincent said. "Is it all right if I sit down?

I took them into the office and shut the door. "There's going to be a school—my stepdaughter is working on a plan. I know that doesn't help you at present."

"I'm sure it won't be hard for you if my payment is slightly late," Miss Baldwin said.

At any other time, I might have been kinder, but I wanted her to know. "Actually, it will be difficult. I have staff who need to be paid and many mouths to feed." I couldn't ask Lucie to pay. Russell didn't pay either, but I knew in the end he'd do something that more than compensated for his room and board. Silby was still here, sleeping on a cot in my children's room and eating as much as an adult, and Wanda and her children tended to drop in for dinner with little notice. I had no money to buy from the butter and egg man, only credit at the store. "Stay the night and think about what you might do," I said. "Maybe the school board will advance your salary. Or..." I smiled at Miss Baldwin. "Your brothers or father might help?"

Mrs. Vincent lowered her eyes and shook her head, suggesting that for the present, the brothers and father were not a good topic.

"I suppose we must be grateful," Miss Baldwin said. "Our former rooms, then?"

"We have one room prepared, and I'm not sure which it is. Surely you can share? It will cost less."

Miss Baldwin sighed. Mrs. Vincent thanked me.

"Don't expect much of dinner," I said. "We're recovering here, too."

~

I had so many circumstances to report that the prospect of putting them on a few sheets of writing paper felt like one more heavy duty. I knew I'd be better if Barlow were here to offer his thoughts, even if he had no different solutions. Whatever I wrote, I'd receive no response for a week. I wanted to hear him now. I wanted to close the door at the end of the day and whisper in bed.

Each time I saw Lucie Bosell using Jonas Percy's cane, I wondered how I would have felt if the man had revealed himself in the beginning. What we might have said to each other and how much we might have told about ourselves. If eventually I'd have called him "Father" and introduced him to Freddy and Hettie as "Grandpap." Those thoughts were always followed by the uncomfortable sensation that he must not have been sure he wanted to acknowledge me. I wondered if he'd been a good father to his sons, or if he'd been harsh and unforgiving of their trespasses. Except in material ways, the Percy men did not appear to have profited from his parentage.

"You didn't get to know them," Wanda said. She stopped by a few days later to show me Simpson's and Randolph Bell's drawings for the new school, along with an estimate of its cost.

"I know enough. They're rude."

"Doesn't mean they're all bad. Look at it the other way. A feller might be all sweetness and light on the outside but a mean devil in his heart."

"If his sons had any appreciation of family, they'd have been happy..."

"Happy to find you," Wanda said. "Maybe they would. And maybe they'll change."

"They won't. They weren't nice to their stepmother, either. I wish you'd been there when Clarence told them about the will. But they're nothing to me; I don't want to think about them."

"Take the money," she said. "With the distance and all, you'll never have a chance to be family, but you'll have that."

"One of those boys said if the cattle were going to be mine I could come and feed them this winter. You don't think they'd let them starve? From spite?"

"Course they won't. More likely they'd sell them off and pocket the money."

"I'd rather see the widow have them. Anyway, Barlow asked Clarence to go to Philadelphia to represent my interests."

"Good for Barlow," Wanda said.

"I'm afraid if he were here we'd be arguing about it."

"Ma, you don't know what arguing is."

"I'm certain I do." I'd heard her and Will.

"So what does Barlow say about my husband?"

"Nothing, recently." I wanted to say she and Will should do their own corresponding instead of using Barlow and me as go-betweens.

"Tell him I've called a school board meeting," she said. "Tell him about our plan."

~

"They hate my guts," Wanda said. She'd just come from the school board meeting. "Didn't want me to talk, didn't want to build a school until I told them I'd call in the miners' union and the state board of education."

I put my finger to my lips, for with each word her voice grew louder. The teachers had gone to bed, and Freddy and Hettie were sleeping in the next room. At the same time, I smiled, because Wanda might be weak in reading and writing, but when she cared about something, she spoke with fervor and persistence.

She walked back and forth, at times smacking the roll of drawings against her palm. "In the end they said okay to the school but no flush toilets. When they said that I rattled off every disease I've heard Will mention, told them doctors say they're caused by outhouses and dirty hands. Said my own husband was in a sanitarium because of pollution. Which is kind of true. I mean, he worked himself near to death because of everybody's sickness, didn't he?"

I nodded, hoping Will's condition proved to be no more than overwork.

"I said any of them could be next, 'cause even if they never used an outhouse, they touch things touched by dirty hands. I ain't sure of that neither but it sounds good, don't it?"

"It sounds very wise. So the building will have washrooms and toilets?"

"Just like the plan. They wanted to wait till next month's meeting to approve it, imagine that. I said I'd have a talk with their wives, and right off they were dickering about how much each mine should pay. I used the Winkler mine's contribution to twist their arms. I learned some other stuff, too. The high school teachers get 45 dollars a month, and elementary get 40. Can you believe it? It's why the teachers are all women or bachelors. No man can keep a family on 45 dollars a month."

"I never knew." Our teachers could barely afford room and board. I wondered how they managed in the summer.

"Here's worse," Wanda said. "Teachers in the colored school make half as much."

"Oh, my. Maybe their teachers have men to support them?"

"Not fair," Wanda said. "The board thinks if you're a woman somebody else is supporting you so you should work for less than a man. Doing the same work, mind. When I asked why the colored teachers make next to nothing, one of the men said they should be glad they have any kind of school, and another said education on 'those people' was a waste."

"I've never seen the colored school."

"It's up a hollow on the way to Big Bend Mine. Colored Town's out that way too. Most colored men work for Big Bend or the Barbara Town Mine. We got a few at our mine—you see them now and then in the store."

She sat in the chair beside me and abruptly stood again. "I was fired up the whole time. Those men on the board is idiots. I don't know how Will got through the meetings without being struck by apoplexy."

I didn't like the thought of anything upsetting him. "You should take his place on the school board, permanently."

She winked in wicked amusement. "I should. Them others would have a fit, wouldn't they? But our mine can put whoever we want on the board. I'll bet I care more than any that's on there now, and I'm way better at talking back."

I knew all about her gift for talking back. I wrote Mr. Thornton's name on a piece of paper. "When you return the drawings to Simpson, tell him I hope he can use this man to help build the school. I'll send Mr. Thornton to him tomorrow."

"I mean to do something about the colored school," she said. "And the teachers' pay."

"I know you will. I might not tell that to Barlow just yet."

"I'll fight the battle and leave Will out of it."

"Good."

"But I don't want him to think we can get along without him."

"Wanda, please write to him."

"I don't know," she said. "You do it better."

"He needs to hear from you."

"What do I say?"

"Something nice. Say the store is busy and the children are doing fine in school. Say you're doing well but will be better when he comes back."

She sniffed and wiped her nose. "I can't do without him, Ma. *I can't.*"

I knew exactly how she felt.

26

"I seen a few people I know," Silby said. "So I guess my folks will come for me any day." She touched the round collar of her dress, a hand-me-down, originally a gift to Evie from Will's sister Glory, who loved beautiful clothes. The dress reached not to Silby's ankles, but evenly below her knees, like the dresses of every schoolgirl. Because the wind had turned cold, she also wore long cotton stockings and a plaid coat in blue and brown with a matching tam, first owned by Evie and then Emmy. Because they had no shoes to pass along, I'd added to my store account a brown pair with laces and thick soles suitable for mud or snow, not the shiny leather pumps with buckles she adored.

She was happy with the gift anyway. "Ma says it's good when we can't have all we want, 'cause then we still have something to hope for."

I was sorry about the shoes.

Silby was driven by an abundance of hope. Insisting she must not leave the roadside while there was light in the sky, she ate an early breakfast each morning with my children and did not return until evening. On the fourth day she said, "There's a mangy dog comes and watches alongside me. I think somebody's forgot it, like my folks forgot me."

"They'll come when they can," I said. "Nobody could forget a girl like you."

"I know."

Her talk was brave but her expression most often looked afraid and strained. I worried her family might have given up the search.

Except for regular shifts at the mine, regular meals and bedtimes, everything that happened in the house felt not only different, but temporary. With no school in session, Wanda often left her children with me. The older ones took turns riding the bicycle in the lane, regularly bursting into the kitchen for a glass of water or a slice of sweet bread. Mrs. Vincent sat in the parlor of a morning, reading or knitting. Miss Baldwin commanded the parlor desk every afternoon, filling sheet after sheet of writing paper with perfectly spaced words. Mrs. Thornton kept to her room.

Supposedly the sheriff had taken Irene Herff to the county jail, but we didn't know if she'd been charged or released. Price said the roadhouse had reopened, and he'd talked to the acquaintance who'd sometimes played cards with Milton Chapman. The man claimed not to have been at the roadhouse the night of the shooting, but said he'd keep an ear to the ground. Price predicted that others present that night would be as reluctant to testify as the one who'd been shot.

Lucie Bosell moved herself to her daughter Piney's house when Simpson and Piney came home, and Charlie and Blanche once again left their herd in our field, this time while they traveled to Lucie's farm to see if anything had survived the fire. They came back after a day with news that was only partly good. Blanche talked for Charlie, who was in a black mood. "The stone house is all right," she said. "Everything else got burned. The barn, the hay, the shed Russell built for hisself. The fire stopped at the swampy ground by the pond. It saved the house. We're gonna go back and build a barn and maybe stay out there this winter, but Charlie says we can't take the stock till the grass grows again."

There was also no grass left in our field, and the cattle had been bawling about it. Russell and Charlie left to talk with other farmers about choices, including Ebert Watson. Blanche rode with them, unwilling to be parted very long from Charlie.

Without school in session, groups of boys roamed the streets, bent on trouble, Luzanna said. She asked Simpson if he had any work Tim could do, and he not only hired Tim, but also a crew of boys to remove debris from the burned school building, supervised by Mr. Thornton. Tim was happy to be earning money, and I was happy when after his first six days of work, Mr. Thornton handed over his wages, catching up on his bill and paying a few dollars in advance. His payment felt like Silby's new shoes—not all that was wanted, but enough to leave me hopeful.

~

I needed to talk about Barlow, and not just about his condition. I wanted to tell someone how good he'd been to the children and me, because saying those things made him seem not so far away. I didn't like to say too much to my friends, who knew how lucky I was, and except for asking if Barlow was better, nobody mentioned his name. I felt like a widow, full of reflections vital only to myself. A real widow would understand, and there was one in our back lot. I waited for a time when neither of us were busy with other demands.

The kitchen window gave us a view of the wagon house as well as the patients who took the path to Magda's door. As she worked, Luzanna kept her eye on them. I did too; we couldn't help being curious.

"I think I'll take this bit of custard to Magda," I said one day after the children went down for their naps.

"Better wait a while," Luzanna said. "She's got somebody with her. Colored woman and a boy. He carried a bundle of wood. They been in there a long time. What could she be doing?"

"Maybe just talking. She's good to talk to."

"Smitty says she does some o'that voodoo stuff."

"I'm sure she doesn't—she made that clear to me. Ask Smitty not to say things like that."

"Ask him yourself."

Maybe it was Luzanna's turn to have a bad day. "I will, if he says it to me. But Smitty didn't say it to me; he said it to you. You should talk with her."

"Magda? Why, do you think something's wrong with me?"

"She's just nice to talk with. I like her. Will thinks she's almost as good as a trained doctor."

Luzanna sniffed. "A lot of people are going to have to bring a lot of wood if she's to keep warm in that thing this winter."

"True enough."

"There they go," Luzanna said. "You can take your custard now, if that's what you want to do."

"I won't stay long." I put on a sweater.

"It doesn't matter."

When I reached the door, Luzanna said, "It wasn't no picnic, out there at Ebert's. He made clear he didn't like the kids underfoot and he and Rona argued about every little thing."

"I'm sorry. I shouldn't have stayed for the teachers. I should have gone with you."

"Right. Well, it's over. And maybe it was meant to be. If you'd gone with us you wouldn't of found Silby." Luzanna wiped her eyes with a corner of her apron.

"It's sad about them that was burned out," she said. "No matter how much they work at it, some people's life won't never be nothing but hardship. Which is why I tell my kids we gotta be as good to others as we can."

It was true. Nobody knew the importance of being helpful like those who'd suffered.

"But you now, you got a rich father. Or had one. You could be one of the lucky ones."

I had my hand on the door knob. "I'm lucky in friends."

"Friends ain't everything. Your father gave each of his boys a farm. I'll bet he didn't work no harder than anyone else, he just got lucky. Or maybe he was crooked; we don't know."

"I thought you liked him," I said.

"I'm just saying. There's no chance I'll have a thing to pass on to my kids, so I'm gonna be real mad if you throw this chance away so you can keep your pride."

I had to let her think she was right. Maybe she was.

~

Magda's wagon was cold. "I'm saving wood for later," she said.

A small stack was piled under the wagon. "Have you ever wintered...in this?"

"Last spring was cold, but no."

"We might find room for you in the boardinghouse."

"That's kind, but I have a plan. I'm going to move into a little house in Pleasant Grove."

I'd never heard of the place. "Is it a mining town? Is it far away?"

"It's just a few miles from here. You probably call it Colored Town."

"Magda, why on earth? And will you be allowed?"

"They're generous people. I'm needed there, and this winter the men will keep me supplied with wood."

"We need you here." *I* needed her. "*We* can keep you supplied with wood."

"You'll soon have a new doctor, and he may not want or need my help. But I have stronger reasons, May Rose. I feel an affinity. Maybe you see it. My mother was of mixed blood: white, colored, and Indian."

I didn't know what to say.

"I know what you're thinking. I may have only a drop of color, but in the eyes of many the smallest drop means I'm not white. When my father was alive, we lived among immigrants from Europe, many with dark complexions, like mother. Because no one questioned our race, I didn't think about it."

"I wish you didn't have to choose one side or the other."

"I wish there were no sides. I've always been more privileged than other people. I feel a calling now to discover my heritage."

"Will I be welcome there, if I come to see you?"

"It's a poor place, but the people are kind. I'm glad you came today. I think the men will help me move soon."

I wanted to talk about Barlow, Will, the Percy family and this new resentment in Luzanna, but it didn't seem to be a good time. I wished her the best.

"You'll work everything out," she said.

~

I finally got the courage to ask Barlow the one thing we hadn't written about, the state of his paralysis. He was coming home in a week—I wanted to be prepared. But given the delay of mail, I knew he'd be here before his reply. His letters that week showed the lag in our correspondence. He thanked me for the telegram, commiserated about my experience with Irene, and said he hoped Lucie's farm hadn't been burned out. The letter I received three days before he was supposed to come home had a message for Wanda. I was angry that Will had left the duty of telling her to me.

Deciding it would be best to deliver the news in her own home, after dinner I rode the bicycle to her house. The street was dark and empty, and I bent my head against a cold wind all the way.

Wanda opened the door and stood in the opening, shadowed against the lighted room. "Ma. What's wrong?"

I said it quickly, as she would have done. "Will's going to stay on at the hospital a few more weeks."

"I knew it. He's working there, isn't he?"

"May I come in?"

She stepped back to let me enter. I glanced around to see if her children were near.

"The kids are in bed."

In their early days, Will had built their parlor furniture and hired Luzanna to upholster cushions. These now looked lumpy and stained, but the room was neat, the result, I assumed, of Evie being at home to pick up, wash and polish. Wanda did not care about fine touches.

We stood in the middle of the room under the ceiling light. "He's not working." I handed her the letter. "Here, you may read for yourself."

"Skip all that. Tell me what it says."

"His doctors say he needs to stay." I said this as gently as I could. "It's to help him get well."

"All right. Then me and the kids will go down there where he is. We'll get a room till he's fit to come home."

Plainly, she needed to go, and I couldn't help agreeing. "I'd have gone with Barlow if I could have afforded it. But what will you do about your patients? What about the school board?"

"Barlow's coming home, right? Ask him to take my place on the board for a while."

I sat in one of Will's chairs, fingering the places on the wide wooden arms where Otis had gouged the letters of his name. "I don't know if Barlow will be able to walk," I said.

Wanda sat in the matching chair. "He hasn't said nothing? Well he's coming home, so I'd say that's something. He'll surprise you."

One way or the other. "And if he can't walk?"

"Then it'll be time for you-all to buy a car."

"Wanda, Barlow and I are not well off. The house..."

"You can borrow Randolph's car till you get that inheritance."

There we were again. I closed my mind to the thought of Jonas Percy's money.

"Randolph knows the mine's gonna have to hire a new doctor," Wanda said.

"Did Will contact him?"

"I don't know. It just makes sense. Turns out, not a lot of the people who need real doctoring trust Magda and me. Now she's got this idea of moving to Colored Town."

"Pleasant Grove," I said. "They call it Pleasant Grove."

"Who's they?"

"The colored. Their town is Pleasant Grove." She hadn't mentioned Magda's drop of color. "Do you think it's a good idea? Her moving there, I mean. Mixing in?"

"Be all right with me if everybody was mixed around, and not just where they live. 'Course folks here won't never go for it, but Will says some of the smartest, strongest folks he knows is mixed. He says it's a whole lot healthier than always breeding with your own kind. I never thought much about it but you know me, I don't think till I'm forced to it."

"I have to get back."

"You don't think I'm crazy? Going down there to where Will is?"

"I think you're smart. And loving."

She looked as startled as Silby.

~

The next morning, Evie came to the boardinghouse with a list she'd written for her mother, ideas for the school board. "She wants you to give this to Mr. Barlow. We're going now. Her and Otis are waiting in the car."

I should not have been surprised, for Wanda never wasted time in decision or preparation, and often seemed better tuned to essentials. "You're going by car?" I'd assumed they'd take the train. "Does she know the way? Will the roads be suitable? Will there be places to buy fuel?"

I shouldn't have mentioned these things, because Evie was a worrier. "Mr. Randolph made her a map," she said. "I don't know about the rest." Evie was prepared for the trip in a coat, scarf, knitted hat and gloves, for unless the days suddenly turned hot, the car would be warm as an ice box. She didn't look happy. "If it wasn't for Otis, Ma would let me stay with you. The only reason I gotta go is so I can watch him while she's off somewhere."

"That's not true. Your ma wants to be with you. And maybe you'll like that town. Will said it's nice. Maybe there'll be a place that shows motion pictures. Even if you're there only a few weeks, you and Otis can go to school."

"I won't know anybody."

"You're a popular girl. You'll find new friends." I linked my arm in hers and walked her to the porch. "You know that gauge on the car that shows the fuel? Watch to be sure it doesn't get too low, please, and remind your ma to stop every time you see one of those filling stations."

She turned on the path and waved goodbye, looking sad.

"Write to me at least every week. Your ma won't, and I need to hear about all of you. Write to me as soon as you get there. Tell me about your trip."

Wanda and Otis waved from the car, and I waved back, then the car pulled away.

27

I thought I'd received Barlow's final letter, but another arrived the day before he was due to come home. I read quickly down the front and back of the single page, looking for words meant to prepare me for a worsening condition or to tell of a change in plans, but the only thing new in this letter was his hope that Wanda wasn't too upset by Will's decision. My husband was still coming home tomorrow, and I still didn't know what to expect.

By now, Wanda should have arrived in White Sulphur Springs, and I hoped Will was pleased. I had to believe that no news meant she'd arrived safely, but cars, roads, and roadside conveniences were all so uncertain. They might be stranded in the middle of nowhere. And had she telegraphed Will to expect her?

I sat at my desk and wrote a confident note to Evie, resisting the desire to inquire about trouble, and asking only that she send an address as soon as they were located. I enclosed the note in an envelope addressed to Will at the hospital, and sent Emmy to the store to mail it. Then I cleaned the apartment and adjusted furniture for easy movement of a wheeled chair, should Barlow come home unchanged. Surely he wouldn't surprise me with a condition that was worse. In one letter he'd said the hospital stay was doing him good, but I didn't know if he meant it was healing his body or strengthening his spirit. I should have insisted he be clear. Maybe he thought I was afraid to know. Maybe I was.

He was due to arrive on Friday's passenger, and this time I asked our friend Randolph Bell to drive me to the station in his car. Barlow hadn't said he'd need help getting home, so I swallowed my pessimism and didn't wake Smitty to go with us.

As the train rolled slowly to a stop, Randolph took my arm and we hurried along the platform to the passenger car. The first passengers to leave the train were women and children, helped off the high steps by other women and occasionally by a man. Randolph and I stood back until Barlow appeared in the doorway. He stood tall, a cane in each hand. My sight blurred; my head felt too heavy for my neck, and my chest too thick to breathe. I leaned on Randolph's arm.

"There he is," Randolph said, patting my hand.

Still in the passageway, Barlow spoke to a man behind him, who moved forward and came down the steps, then turned and extended his hand. Barlow gave him one of the canes, then gripped the rail and took the first step. I cried.

I knew Luzanna had been watching for us, because she opened the door and came onto the porch when we drove up to the house. Smitty stood beside her. They clapped their hands when Barlow stepped out of the car.

Under his trousers, he wore braces of leather and steel, buckled above his knees and attached by rods to his shoes. He walked stiffly and used the canes, but he walked, and the smile on his face was a match for mine.

We made a happy entrance to the house, causing Miss Baldwin to turn from her usual place at the parlor's writing desk and frown at the noise. I did not bother with introductions, because Emmy was waiting with Freddy and Hettie in the apartment, where Luzanna had provided tea and sweetbread. Randolph brought Barlow's luggage inside, and everyone left us alone with the children.

The canes and the braces on his shoes fascinated Freddy and frightened Hettie. "I may not have to wear these forever," Barlow said. "The doctors think they'll strengthen my legs."

I couldn't stop smiling. He was home. He was walking, and he looked proud.

Hettie finally toddled to her father and lifted her arms to be pulled into his lap, and Freddy gripped his fists around the canes and prodded them around the parlor. We stayed there for the rest of the day, attending to the children and catching up on details omitted in our correspondence. Just this week, Russell had arranged to winter his stock at Ebert's, and he'd moved from the boardinghouse to Will's old apartment in the store. Barlow said he'd been at the hospital when Wanda and the children arrived, and reported that Will was extraordinarily pleased to see them. If Wanda had experienced any trouble on her trip, he hadn't heard about it.

Luzanna and Emmy carried our dinner to the apartment. "I'll take Silby home with me tonight," she said.

"Oh." I'd forgotten about Silby, who'd been sleeping every night on a cot in the children's room. "Thank you, Luzanna, for thinking of her. And of us."

Barlow and I spoke of nothing serious until after we put the children to bed. Then he wanted to know more about Irene, Milton Chapman, damage by the fire, and finally about Jonas Percy.

I showed Barlow the letter he'd left for me. The letter wasn't dated and hadn't been folded for an envelope. Barlow read the first words and looked up. "The greeting is quite affectionate. *'My Dear Daughter, Sweet May Rose.'* While he was here, did he call you by name?"

"Never anything but 'Mrs. Townsend.'" The greeting's endearment irritated me. "His sons suggested he was dotty. His wife didn't think so."

"And you?"

"He was helpful to Rona. He gave no trouble. Everybody liked him"

"You liked him before you knew who he was."

"I liked him until he asked about Jamie Long."

"I see. You didn't tell me about that." Barlow read silently. "He says he's proud to know you. And he's heard I'm a fine man." Barlow looked up, smiling. "Good judgment, there."

"He couldn't tell me in person."

"Do you think he was going to mail it after he left? Or did he suspect he'd die here?"

"I haven't thought about it. His intentions don't matter."

"He says he's sorry he left you. That he always meant to find you. He says, "I've lived with a great burden of guilt."

"Being a guilty burden doesn't make me feel better."

"May Rose, guilt was his burden, not you."

I knew that. "It makes me feel evil, but I'm glad it bothered him. If I'd had a chance, I'd have told him I didn't miss him for a moment. I had a good family—my aunt and uncle, my cousins."

"You regretted never knowing your mother."

"Yes."

"But sometimes you felt abandoned."

"Not until I knew he hadn't died. And had another family."

Barlow sighed. "In my experience, women are more likely to work at maintaining connections than men. Look at Charlie, out of touch for years, and Will, exemplary in so many ways but poor at communication. Their sister is the only one who tries to make them a family."

"That man came here to satisfy himself. Please don't say he came for my sake."

"May Rose, he left you half his wealth. That's a lot more than he'd might do if he only wanted to rid himself of guilt. If his sons are as unfriendly as you described, he must have known for a long time that including you in his family would not be a kindness."

"You may be right. They made all of us angry."

"I'm not trying to excuse him, but sometimes a man does whatever's at hand, taking the first job that's available and staying in it the rest of his life. Marrying the first woman who's interested because most of the time, he needs a wife like he needs a job. We seldom get far from our roots. When Hester and I were growing up, my mother made ends meet by taking in boarders, so that's what Hester knew how to do. My cousins got me into the lumber business, and since then, I've always been in business. I never had a chance to try other things, to learn if I might be better suited for farming or law or ship-building. After you left Winkler, I was sure I'd never marry, but when Hester and I moved to Grafton, Alice kept bringing herself to my attention, and I married her. What I'm saying is, coming back to Winkler and marrying you were the first clear-sighted, deliberate acts of my life. Everything else just happened."

His sweet testimonial made sense, and it made me happy, but didn't bridge the distance I felt from Jonas Percy.

When I said nothing, Barlow went on. "If he was like most men, he did whatever was at hand, maybe not what he wanted; maybe he never had time to think about what he wanted. Near the end, he did something clear-sighted and deliberate. He traveled to meet his daughter."

"He didn't introduce himself to his daughter. He spied."

"I'd say he didn't know how to ask forgiveness. He thought he deserved your contempt. Maybe he didn't feel strong enough to bear it."

"Luzanna says I should remember him as a kind and helpful guest, but all I can remember is what he didn't do. I confess, the thought of him makes me feel mean, and I'm not proud of that."

"Your father didn't do things right, not in the beginning, and not in the end. I'd say he was a decent man because on paper he tried to do the decent thing. If he'd lived, I think in time you would have forgiven him."

"I don't know. Maybe if you'd been here. I'm terrible without you," I said.

"I'm here now."

"You are." I turned off the light. Barlow followed me to our bedroom and sat on a chair while he slid down his suspenders and unbuttoned his trousers. He stood, using the canes, so the trousers could fall below the braces, and sat down again. I watched while he untied his shoes and unbuckled the braces. The shoes and braces were attached, and his trousers lay around his ankles. "I can't yet handle this part," he said.

I pulled off the shoes and their connected braces, laid everything aside, and had my first view of his thin legs.

"The muscles have shrunk," he said. "We need to continue the therapy."

I knelt at his feet and pressed my cheek against the flimsy calf muscle of each leg.

"Ah," he breathed. "How I've missed you. I'm better already."

28

"The doctors were hopeful from the beginning, but I was always afraid," Barlow said. "Poliomyelitis—*infantile paralysis*. Imagine, I could have passed it to Freddy and Hettie. To you."

I knew people died of it, usually children. It was easier to talk about, sitting side by side under the covers, slowly waking up with a quiet cup of coffee. I'd rested well, though I'd opened my eyes many times through the night, surprised by the novelty of the warm body stretched beside me.

"My infection was not the worst, but my leg muscles will never be what they were. There were setbacks, days when I felt too exhausted to move. I didn't want to talk about those or give you too much hope. Your letters always gave me a lift, and I wanted to do the same for you."

"I hope each of our children marries someone who makes them as happy as you make me."

I'd made him laugh. "You do think ahead!" He paused and listened. "Did I hear a door?"

"It's Smitty, back from his shift. He tries to be quiet. If no one is in the kitchen by the time he cleans up, he makes the coffee. In a minute you'll hear the upstairs toilet flush. That will be Mr. Cunningham.

Sometimes if we're very busy in the kitchen, he packs his own lunch pail."

"You like them, Smitty and Mr. Cunningham." It wasn't a question.

I'd come to think of them as indispensable. "During the wildfire, when the mine closed and the men went out to the fire lines, they felt like family." Since then Mr. Cunningham had cleaned leaves from the roof drains, no bother, he liked to work about the house, just let him know if we had any other jobs he could do of an evening. "They've been firing the furnace, too."

"I'd say they want to stay on," Barlow said.

I told him of Magda's decision to move to Colored Town. Not Colored Town, *Pleasant Grove*.

"I'm afraid the houses there are poorly built," he said. "The town was a joint effort by the Coal Association, and you know how those men think."

"You're not surprised? About Magda's race?"

"Stands to reason that there's a bit of another race hidden in most family trees. People don't know it or won't admit it. Could be in mine—I know nothing about my grandparents. If I had a colored ancestor, would that change your mind about me?"

"Impossible."

It was Saturday, which meant Luzanna and Emmy would be with us only until noon. While Barlow dressed, I woke the children and took them to the kitchen for breakfast. Emmy was chopping vegetables for stew, Smitty was coming from the laundry room, and Silby was scraping oatmeal from her bowl. Her constancy made me sad. I bent and squeezed her shoulders. "You're a good girl. I like having you here."

Smitty stopped short of the table, Luzanna turned from the stove, and Emmy paused her chopping and looked up. "All of you," I said. "I like having all of you here."

Luzanna winked, angling her head so only I could see. "It's a relief to have Barlow back, ain't it?"

~

As my aunt used to say, everything was up in the air. It seemed everyone who was going to return to their homes in the hills had already walked or ridden past Silby's sign, and she'd spoken to no one who knew anything about her family.

"I want to go home," she said Tuesday morning.

Luzanna and I spoke together, "Not by yourself."

"What if they're there, waiting for me? I won't get lost."

"We'll find a way. If I ask, Russell will go with you." He appeared regularly for Luzanna's biscuits or potpie, bringing an offering of trout, squirrel, or a portion of beef he'd slaughtered. Silby had convinced me she knew the way home but I didn't want her to be by herself if she found her house in ruins.

Luzanna and I were alone in the kitchen, talking about her when Mrs. Thornton came down the back stairs with her laundry. Normally she said no more than "Hello" but now she stopped and listened.

"Is that the girl who waits at the road every day?"

"Her name is Silby French. Do you and Mr. Thornton know her family?" I hated that I hadn't thought to ask.

"I don't recognize the name."

"She wants to go home... to see if anything's left."

"I feel bad every time I see her out there," Mrs. Thornton said. "She makes me think of that dog and her pups some fool tossed out on our road. The poor mama kept watching that road, watching and waiting. Tell the girl me and Mr. Thornton will take her to her homeplace the next day he don't work."

"That's very kind."

"It's gotta be done, but likely it'll be hard on the girl."

We agreed it would.

~

Wednesday I had my first letter from Evie, saying the trip was long and cold and she was mad as hornets because her ma had enrolled her and Otis in school. Otis liked it but she hated her classmates and her teacher.

I did not immediately reply to her letter because I was full of Silby's need and strongly tempted to say Evie should be ashamed of herself—she had her family.

"It tears my heart out, seeing Silby so hopeful," Luzanna said, when the girl left the next Saturday with the Thorntons. "Do you suppose her folks really don't care where she is?"

"All kinds of things could be keeping them away."

"If her pa is like either o'my husbands, he might be in jail," Luzanna said.

"Or sick. Maybe they're all sick. Silby was poorly nourished."

"I'll whip up a batch of cookies," Luzanna said. "Don't let them men eat 'em all. The most is for Silby."

Barlow's departure that morning with Randolph was more satisfying. Inspired by Wanda's list for the school board, he and Randolph were going to talk with Simpson about needs for the new school, then inspect the school at Pleasant Grove. On the way, he said they'd work on a strategy to make the other mine operators cooperate. He seemed so excited by these challenges that I hoped Wanda would not be disappointed if he took her place on the school board. There was work to do, we had no idea when she'd be back, and after all, she'd left a list.

The Thorntons returned late in the afternoon, Silby holding onto Mrs. Thornton's hand, the look on their faces all we needed to know. "There's some things I'd like from the store," Mrs. Thornton said. "Silby, come walk with me."

Mr. Thornton watched them go, then said, "Betcha anything my wife's gonna buy something for her—it's the first she's cared about anything since we was burned out. Her and the girl cried most o'the way home. Wouldn't surprise me if she wants to keep her."

Luzanna and I had both talked of keeping Silby. I'd given her name again to the town guards, and splurged for a telegram to the sheriff, asking if he'd inquire among the authorities in other regions.

"We're trying to find her family," I said. I'd tried to make allowances, but I was angry because her parents did not seem to be trying to find her.

"Sure and that'll be the best thing," Mr. Thornton said. "I'll warn my wife not to get too attached."

"When she and Silby get back, please invite them to the kitchen. Luzanna made a surprise."

~

By November, days in the boardinghouse settled into a new routine. A combination of hired workers and volunteers got the school building under roof, and the school board approved classes in the Winkler church. Silby gave up her roadside vigil in favor of school, Mrs. Vincent and Miss Baldwin paid on their accounts, and a teacher who was already a friend came to stay at the boardinghouse, Miss Bertha Graves.

Bertha was engaged to Jonah Watson, Ebert's son, and she'd helped us feed and entertain the children during the miners' strike. I knew she lived with her brother when school was not in session, but I hadn't known her brother was Ebert's hired man. When Bertha arrived, I was eager to hear news of Rona.

"She moved into the house," Bertha said. "But she opened only three rooms. She says she'd need a staff of servants to maintain the whole place, and she has enough to do, taking care of her husband. He's furious, of course. I'm sure you know, he's always furious."

"Does she have help? Managing him, I mean?"

"My brother goes to the house twice a day. Jonah helps when he's home, but he's at the Agricultural College now. Ebert doesn't go. Mr. Chapman throws a tantrum if he so much as hears his name."

That evening I wrote to Rona and tried to entertain her with every bit of news I could think of—Barlow's braces and his fights with the school board; Wanda's decision to remain in White Sulphur Springs until Will's doctors said he could come home; Silby and her attachment to the Thorntons; and the latest news of Irene Herff, who had not been jailed, according to Price Loughrie, but had lost a leg and been sent to the county home for the indigent. Price said she'd put up a fight about that, being positive, for some reason, that she was being condemned to the asylum for the insane.

~

The best part about having guests in the house happened when they stopped feeling like strangers. I'd walk into the kitchen of a morning and find Luzanna and Smitty laughing, and many nights after dinner I'd see her and Mr. Cunningham drinking coffee or bent over the sink, scrubbing sticky pots. I began to look and listen for clues that she favored one over the other.

One night, conversation between her and Mr. Cunningham stopped when I opened the door from the hall. Nodding a greeting, he took his coat and cap from a chair and hurried out to the porch.

When the door closed, I whispered, "What was that?"

"He was telling me about his ma and pa. He was devoted, and he got real sad. I don't think he wanted you to see."

"Ah, what a good man. And Smitty too. It's a shame you're not here on Sundays, when both your admirers are lounging about at the same time."

She carried their coffee cups to the sink. "Don't start."

"It can't be denied; you've got a man for the morning and one for night."

"They appreciate my cooking, which is something I like to do, seeing how for most of my life I never had enough to cook with. They don't want no wife nor no kids, and I don't want no husband, but it's nice having men friends. Smitty calls me 'Ma'."

"I've heard you call him 'Pa'."

"Just friendly. It's fun."

"Whatever you say."

"I'm no schoolgirl."

"Thank goodness—I'd be worried sick. Since you're no schoolgirl, I'll just wink if I get wind of any goings on."

She took her coat from its wall hook. "I'm leaving now."

"I imagine somebody will walk along, be sure you get home all right?"

"I better not see you watching from that window."

"Yes, Ma," I said.

~

With three teachers in the house, a lot of table talk had to do with education. The Winkler church was not large enough to hold all the students at once, so younger students attended in the morning and older ones in the afternoon. No one was surprised when the board refused to give the teachers full-time pay for half a day's work, and no one was surprised when the teachers stayed on, finding it better to accept starvation pay than to locate another job in the middle of the year. Since my income was closely tied to theirs, the new school was important to me, too.

I was surprised when our teachers showed interest in another school, the one in Colored Town.

"Pleasant Grove," I said. I could see the name wasn't going to take hold here.

After his visit to the Pleasant Grove school, Barlow reported that volunteers were digging ditches to divert water from the building's foundation, and wanted wood, block, tar paper and nails to add a second school room. "They'll never know," he confided. He was speaking of the school board and the fact that he and Simpson were going to send the Pleasant Grove school what it needed. "I'll put those materials at the end of a report so long that none of the board will read it."

I didn't tell the teachers what Barlow and Simpson were doing for the colored school, but I shared one thing that evening at dinner. "At present, the Pleasant Grove school has no teacher."

Miss Baldwin straightened like someone had given a smart smack to her head. "And why is that?"

"The teacher and her husband moved away. My husband says nobody will travel such a distance for so little pay. And there were about sixty children in one room, all ages."

"Our conditions aren't much better," Mrs. Vincent said.

"But they are. For one thing, teachers at the colored school make half as much."

"Half? And the children have nobody? The board should be hanged," Miss Baldwin said. "Mr. Townsend excepted, of course. Please tell him I'll take the job if I can continue my afternoon classes in the church."

Bertha Graves spoke up. "I can work half a day too. Instruction will be better if we divide the children by age. Miss Baldwin can teach the upper grades, and I'll take the lower, as we do here."

"I think the board will accept your offer," I said. "But do you know the school is nearly two miles away? How will you come and go in time to teach in both places?"

"I'll take you in our wagon," Mrs. Thornton said.

Her voice startled us into a silent, inquiring turning of heads. We'd been so immersed in school talk that I'd forgotten anyone else was at the table.

"I'm here all day with nothing to do," she said. "Maybe I could help at the school while I'm there?"

"What a kindness," Mrs. Vincent said. "I'm sure you'd be welcome. I'd offer to go too, but this year it's all I can do to work half a day."

I wished Barlow had been at the table to see the bright faces.

~

We were joyful and sad when Silby's father came to claim her. She bawled like a calf, and I teared up. Emmy and Tim stared with their mouths open, and Luzanna sniffed and dabbed at her eyes, seeing Silby hugging a strange bearded man in an oilcloth coat and dusty boots. Mrs. Thornton, who was sitting in the parlor mending socks, bowed her face over her workbasket for a long time until her shoulders stopped shaking.

It was dinner time, and because Silby did not want to be separated from her father, we granted her the privilege of eating in the dining room with the grownups. It was my turn to stay in the apartment for the children's dinner, but I traded with Emmy and helped Luzanna serve the dinner.

Silby sat beside her father, pecking at her food and watching like he might disappear. He cleaned his plate and hers too. When he began to tell his story, Luzanna and I stood by the sideboard and listened.

"It was hard to keep everybody together in the crowd, so the kids' ma told Silby and her sisters to keep track o'each other," he said. "I didn't know she was gone till I stepped on a board that was under some leaves and run a nail right through my foot. After that a man came along and offered us a ride in his wagon. We counted off the kids—no Silby. One of the girls said she was ahead of us and one thought she was behind. My wife said me and the kids should go on in the wagon to where there was a doctor, 'cause my foot puffed up and I couldn't hardly walk on it. She said we could watch for Silby along the way and her and the baby would wait to see if Silby caught up, she didn't think it'd be more than a minute or two. The road was crowded and other folks were asking to get in the wagon and my wife said I better get in and go. We never thought how it might be hard for us to find each other again. I stayed a while in the Elkins hospital and the kids that was with me got took in by a preacher's widow, but my wife didn't come and didn't come. I always hoped her and Silby had found each other, and soon as my foot healed, I struck out to find them. Don't you know, there's a lot o'mining camps between here and there, and in one o'them I found my wife and baby. The baby had turned sick, then her. Thank the Lord for good people. She's housed up there yet, waiting for me to come back with our Silby."

"I saw our house, Pa," Silby said. "It's burned."

"I found you," he said. "The house don't matter."

At the start of dinner, he and Mr. Thornton had compared the locations of each other's property and the kind of work each had done, a little of everything: farming, building, blacksmithing, logging. "And begging," Mr. French added. Nobody had laughed.

When Mr. French ended his story, Mr. Thornton suggested they might help each other rebuild in the spring. His wife looked anxiously from Silby to Mr.

French and then to her husband. "We're awful attached to Silby. She could stay with us until you get your family together."

Silby shook her head. "It's real nice here, but I gotta go see Ma."

"We'll all miss you," I said.

Everyone echoed my words. When Mrs. Thornton blotted her cheeks with her napkin, her husband looked toward Barlow. "Simpson said we could use another carpenter on the school."

"True," Barlow said. "We might find a house for your family."

Later in our apartment, Barlow said he hoped he hadn't jumped the gun by hiring a man with unproven skills.

"He passed my test," I said. "Silby's happy."

~

I was straightening papers on Barlow's desk one morning when I picked up an envelope from Cousin Clarence, addressed to Barlow in White Sulphur Springs. The envelope contained a clipping from a Philadelphia newspaper, the obituary of Jonas A. Percy, a landowner well known in the region. He'd been born in 1855 to Hammond and Violet Parker Percy. I supposed I might write those names in my mother's bible. I read on. Mr. Percy was survived by his wife, Elizabeth, and four sons. Each was named. His grandchildren were named. He was preceded in death by his first wife, Marion Wagstaff Percy. No mention of my mother, my children, or me.

I showed the clipping to Barlow. "You didn't tell me about this."

"It hurt me to read it. I thought it would hurt you, too. I feel sorry for the man. He missed his chances."

"I suppose he did. He liked watching Freddy and Hettie."

"I'm sure he felt the loss."

"He gave me no chance to care for him." I dropped the obituary to the desk. "And this is what his family thinks of me."

"We can go to Philadelphia, or you can give Clarence the power to act on your behalf," Barlow said.

"I'll sign the power of attorney papers."

"It's the practical solution." Barlow dropped his canes and held me close.

It was more practical than I admitted. Barlow might never walk without his braces. If I accepted the inheritance, we could buy the car he needed to get from place to place. Beyond that one purchase, I had no plans for Jonas Percy's bequest, but I remembered Luzanna's words. It might give my children a better start. It might do something for her children, too.

Sometimes we wait and wait for healing, reunion, reward or restoration, a broken thing to be fixed or life to go back to the way it was, but as time slides on, the thing we set our hearts on becomes less and less necessary to our days, and when at last the wound is healed or the quarrel is dead it all has happened so gradually that if we notice it at all it comes with no sense of triumph. It's just over.

I thought often of the dog and her pups thrown out at the roadside, confused by where they were and the abrupt change in their lives, watching and waiting for the ones in charge to make things right again. Until they knew it was useless to wait and they lifted their feet and traveled on.

~

"Oh, my," I said, unwrapping newspaper from the first item in a large box sent by Will. I held up a wooden carving for Barlow to see. It was a hawk with wings elevated, head bent, legs stretched down, talons poised to grip. It was beautiful, and I'd seen it before, or one nearly identical.

"I knew Will was carving," Barlow said. "I didn't know he was so good. Even the feathers look real."

"There's more." There were six in all, hawks and squirrels. "Do you remember his father's carvings? They hung on the walls of his house."

"I knew Morris did that kind of thing, but I never saw anything he made."

I'd admired and hated Morris Herff's carvings. "He made such beautiful things, yet to my mind he was a poor human being. He disregarded his most important responsibilities. He forgot to feed his children. He forgot to go to work." Someone had stolen the carvings and burned them. It might have been the Donnelly boys, for the theft had happened while Morris was married to Irene, but Wanda and I had suspected Charlie.

"A bit of forgetfulness might be good for Will," Barlow said.

"I think it's a good sign that he's given these to us. His father sold his sons' bed, but he wouldn't part with his carvings."

At the bottom of the box, I found an endpaper torn from a book with a message in Wanda's scrawl. "Coming home."

Coming home! We didn't know if that meant Will too. I worried that when he returned to Winkler, he'd feel responsible for everything again. But the time might be right. The town had a new doctor, Randolph was attending the Coal Association meetings, and Barlow had taken Will's seat on the school board and was managing the store and the company rentals. If Will wanted to stay home and carve, his income from the mine would let him do it.

We hung some of Will's carvings in the apartment and some in the entryway for all to admire. I wondered what Charlie would think of them, but he rarely came to the boardinghouse, and at those times only as far as the back porch or the kitchen. Very likely he wouldn't see the carvings, and even if he did, they might mean nothing to him. We had no idea what he remembered.

While we expected to see Wanda and Will any day, Charlie was the first to return to Winkler, and his return was a surprise. Blanche had taken to crying all the time, Russell reported, carrying on about her kids, so he and Charlie were getting rid of junk and dirt left behind in one of the company houses. They intended to live there through the winter so Blanche could see Ruby, Robert and Ralphie whenever she wanted. I felt bad for my friend Piney, who'd raised them all these years while their ma flitted from man to man, and I hoped Blanche had no ambitions to take the children away. They were all in school now, and shy of the woman who called herself their ma. Until Charlie and Russell acquired some furniture, Blanche was staying in the little house on her father's property with Lucie Bosell.

Russell often came by when Price Loughrie was in town, and the next Monday night, Charlie came with him. They drank coffee and talked around the kitchen table with Price and Barlow while I popped corn. Charlie and Russell had helped dig a grave that day, and the men's talk turned to stories of forgotten graves, Indian mounds, graves that had sunk, and graves that had bubbled up in what they called a wet weather spring.

"Russell," I said. "I'd like you to show me Jamie's grave." It was a new idea, but it felt right. Barlow passed me a worried look.

"I told you about it," Russell said.

"Is it down in the ravine?"

"Kinda hard to remember." He sounded evasive.

"Are there roads nearby? Would horses be able to go there?"

"Don't know what it's like these days. I know it was a lot of walking, and I don't think I could do it again. When I found him, I pulled him up to a level place. The ground was too rocky to dig, so I just piled the stones."

"I seen it."

Who'd said that? Russell, Barlow and Price looked at each other and then at Charlie, who wasn't looking at anybody.

"Charlie," I said. "What did you see?" I could imagine him spying, a boy no older than nine, as Russell pulled Jamie's body to its resting place.

We stared. "When? Where?"

"When we went to Fargo. You remember." He still didn't look up.

I remembered my surprise when they'd boarded the train at Jennie Town—Russell, Wanda, young

Homer Wyatt, and Charlie, who'd been lost to his family and me for months. "What did you see?"

"I was just watching for the place where the wreck was."

The popcorn was done, but I left it in the pot. "And?"

"And?" He shrugged, eyes still down. "I don't know. You remember when you and me and Wanda jumped on the work train to go down to see the wreck."

I wondered if Charlie was just now getting his memories back or if he'd remembered all along. I hadn't wanted to see the wreck—Wanda and I had jumped on the train to escape the Donnelly boys.

Charlie looked up with a nod toward Barlow. "He was right mad at us."

I remembered that too. Barlow and I exchanged a look. Back then he'd hidden how he felt about me.

"Then when Russell and us got on the train to Fargo, I watched to see if any of the wrecked cars was still there. I saw a pile of stones on top the hill."

"I see that pile winter and spring," Price said. "Rest o'the time it's hidden by brush. So that's the grave of Jamie Long?"

"I reckon it is," Russell said. "I know for sure it was him I covered, flattened and broke as he was. He was my brother."

"We could take the train to Elkins," Barlow said. "See it that way. Maybe Wanda would want to go."

I set the popcorn on the table. "I doubt she would. And there's no need."

Charlie's memory was good enough for me.

~

"We don't know where Aunt Rona went," Jonah said. He was on his way back to agricultural college, and had stopped to say goodbye to Bertha. Ten days earlier Bertha had told us of Milton Chapman's death. There'd been no public funeral, and Jonah and the hired man had dug the grave in the Watson family plot. Since then I'd hoped to pay Rona a condolence call, but first we'd had an ice storm, and then the weather warmed and the roads turned to mud. I'd sent a letter. Eventually the rural delivery would go through.

"Pa's not sure when she left. One day he noticed there was no smoke from her chimney. The shades were pulled down and the doors were locked. He had a key, so he went in. She'd covered the furniture, taken most of her clothes, and left a note on the table. All it said was, 'Don't worry about me.' Of course we've been worrying. Pa says if she comes here or writes would you let him know? He's afraid she's not in her right mind."

"I'm sure she's fine," I said. "If she were not, she might have walked away without her coat and left the door open." I knew where she might have gone, but I felt almost as abandoned as Ebert and Jonah. I'd thought we were friends.

With Barlow home, I dreamed better dreams. Will and Wanda returned to Winkler at Christmas time. Wanda went back to work in the store, but Will spent his days in his workshop, isolated from the weaknesses and concerns of his town. Wanda seemed happy, so I supposed that meant Will was happy too.

A few months later, March 10, 1920, West Virginia ratified the 19th Amendment to the U.S. Constitution, granting women the right to vote. The vote in our senate was narrow, 15-14. A week later I received a postcard from Charleston, West Virginia, with no return address and no signature. The message said only, "Yippee!"

~

We bought a car, knowing it might be months or years before we received my inheritance. And though Luzanna and I still worked hard and suffered the daily irritations of trying to please strangers, we discovered we perked up if one of us could say, "Today wasn't too bad." "I'm sure she meant well," or "I feel pretty good," even if those things were only half true.

We took that advice from Magda, who came to see us now and then. "Tell yourself you're happy," she said. "Love every little thing you can. You'll be surprised how good things will grow."

~~~

Thank You

I'm grateful for the suggestions, edits, and proofing of these smart and generous people: sister Diane Plotts, author friends Bob Summer and Lindy Moone, and sister-in-law, Carol Martin.
Thanks for having my back.

A Note to the Reader

Thank you for selecting *The Boardinghouse*.

If you enjoyed this book, please tell others about the series, and consider leaving a review on the Amazon page or your favorite review site. For announcements of new books in the series, follow me on Amazon.

I'd love to hear from you.

Email: carolervin2012@gmail.com.

Facebook: https://www.facebook.com/carolervin.author

Website: www.carolervin.com

Other Books by Carol Ervin

The Girl on the Mountain

Cold Comfort

Midwinter Sun

The Women's War

Kith and Kin

Ridgetop

Dell Zero

1

According to the calendar, spring had arrived. Our weather was milder, but the hillsides surrounding Winkler remained an ugly black tangle of trees and brush, our streets and houses were gray and gritty with soot, and in place of the glitter and cleansing curves of winter's covering of white we had gray skies, rain, piles of black snow, and mud. Even so, we saw fresh glimpses of color and new life—pale green shoots of wild onions in the poor soil of our yards, tiny leaves on bramble branches, and pretty girls in their fresh Easter dresses.

I was especially taken by the blooming beauty of the girls closest to my heart, Wanda's daughter Evie, and Luzanna's Alma. Evie had her father's red hair and her mother's stature, and at 16, was taller than 19-year-old Alma, who was petite with black hair and lovely brown eyes. They sat together in church that Easter, for though they'd grown apart, separated by Alma's college and work in Richmond, they'd been each other's first friend in our early Winkler days.

The weather that day felt more like winter, but the service was marked not only by greater than usual attendance but also by lighter dresses and shirts for the children, either new or made-over. My friend and helper Luzanna was not much of a church-goer, but she usually attended on Easter with her own observance for the season: a pair of new gloves and a fresh ribbon in her summer straw hat. Later I wished she hadn't been there that day because of the spectacle caused by her daughter.

Our preacher was good at dramatizing and personalizing the horror of crucifixion, the pain of the spikes, how it would feel to hang by our own flesh there on the cross, the sun scorching our nearly naked bodies. And it was our fault, he said, because our sins were keeping Jesus on the cross, perpetually in agony. We'd heard this frequently, for it was one of his favorite themes. Barlow and I privately agreed our preacher's interpretations were often extreme. Surely if Jesus was seated at the right hand of the father he was not still being tortured on the cross.

The preacher's other favorite theme was Hell, specifically flames, demons, and other evil creatures that kept sinners in eternal agony. He also had an explanation for unanswered prayers: either we were more sinful than we acknowledged, or we hadn't completely devoted our lives to God. In the year he'd been here, attendance numbers had dropped off. Barlow, who'd read his Bible front to back many times, said people might be like himself, tired of being battered by the same sermon each Sunday. Everyone needed to be uplifted occasionally, especially when lives were already hard and troubled. The preacher had a few loyal followers, however, and I often wondered if those most sensitive and least sinful were the very ones most susceptible to fits of guilt.

Seizing the opportunity to convert those whose attendance was limited to Christmas and Easter, that morning the preacher gave a highly emotional plea for repentance. In the quiet of prayer following the sermon, someone began to cry, great deep gut-wrenching sobs. Opening my eyes and lifting my head to sneak a look, I saw that Luzanna and others were also looking around, either curious or disturbed by the outburst.

Alma and Evie sat close to the front, several rows down from where Barlow and I sat with Luzanna and her younger two children. The bowed heads gave us a better view of what was happening down in front. Luzanna and I exchanged a troubled glance. A woman beside Alma had put her arm around her, and one behind had reached forward to pat her on the shoulder. The one sobbing was Alma.

When the congregation rose to sing the next hymn, Alma slid out of the pew and knelt at the altar. This practice was not unusual in our church, and the preacher often let us know he didn't think he'd done his job unless someone came forward to repent. Immediately Luzanna's daughter was joined at the altar by two women, the same ones who ended every service on their knees.

The three remained at the altar when the hymn ended, and everyone else remained standing. Like most people in our small society, I was uncomfortable in the presence of public displays of emotion, whether excessive affection or distress, which could be as unnerving as witnessing a mental breakdown or painful death. All of that was best kept at home, we believed. Now here was Luzanna's lovely young daughter, making herself the object of everyone's attention, as shocking to her mother, I was sure, as if she'd taken off her clothes. At the altar, the preacher bent over her, saying something. Then he took her hand and helped her to her feet.

The service had been excessively long, and now a few families with cranky children edged out of their pews and moved toward the exit. Instead of waiting for her friend, Evie left too, flashing me a frown as she passed toward the doors, as though saying, "What's wrong with that girl?"

I was equally perplexed. Alma was so helpful and so new to life, what terrible sin could she have committed? Barely into her teens when we'd met her family on our journey to Winkler, she'd done her best to help me manage her small dying stepsister. When poverty had separated her from her mother, she'd stayed with me, and had faithfully sat at my bedside through my episode of Typhoid fever. The same winter she'd fallen into a ruined basement, attempting to rescue her brother and sister. I would never forget the chill in my feet and hands as Luzanna and I had stooped amid the wreckage, holding her face out of the icy water while our friends struggled to free her. I loved Alma like my own.

Luzanna, Barlow and I stayed in our pew through the final hymn and benediction, frozen by courtesy and tradition. However, we'd left chicken baking in the oven for Sunday dinner, so we did not wait for Alma or linger outside the church to greet others, but hurried away toward home. There, Luzanna displayed her annoyance by complaining about everything—the mud tracked from the back porch, potatoes that defied all effort to mash without lumps, water that was barely lukewarm—how was she going to clean the greasy pans, and what was wrong with the water boiler? We said nothing about what we'd witnessed in church.

If Alma had been someone else's pretty daughter, we'd have been curious and probably sympathetic, and maybe we'd have spoken about her in confidential tones. But because she was our Alma and we felt shocked, hurt, and a little afraid, it took a while for us to speak of what we'd witnessed. Luzanna brought it up after dinner as we were scrubbing the pots and pans. "She hasn't said a word to me. About nothing."

Why Alma had suddenly left her teaching position and come home from Richmond, she meant, why the girl who'd gone away with confidence had returned so nervous, and what guilt had driven her to the altar. The usual trespasses came to mind, distasteful events and situations we could not bear to connect to Alma. We spoke no more of her that day.

~

Our kitchen was truly the heart of the house, proved by its six doors—one to the outside, others to the laundry, basement, back stairs, hall, and dining room. With guests passing through to the laundry room, our part-time watchmen sitting down for meals, Luzanna's children popping in after school, delivery men setting their produce on the worktable and often three of us preparing meals or cleaning up, the kitchen at times seemed as busy as the store. It was also the place for exchanging news.

Tuesday morning when I brought the children to the kitchen for breakfast, I was surprised to find Alma there, washing dishes as fast as Luzanna set them in the sink. "She doesn't expect to be paid," Luzanna said. "She just wants to keep busy."

Luzanna knew I couldn't afford to pay additional help. I was already paying Emmy, Alma's younger sister, to watch my children when she wasn't in school.

"Alma, you know you're always welcome here," I said. The children put their hands together for our prayer and Freddy mumbled the words with me.

"Amen," Alma said.

Luzanna gave me a weary look. I could see she wanted to talk.

I didn't get time for a private conversation with Luzanna then, but later when I was alone with Alma, she revealed something about my family I didn't know. Thinking she might benefit from company nearer her age, I'd asked if she was seeing any of her former friends, like Evie.

"Oh, no," she said. "Evie's too busy to have time for me. And she's mad. When I told her what people are saying she stuck her nose in the air and told me to keep my notions to myself."

I was standing on tip-toe, reaching a heavy platter to the top shelf of the wall cupboard. I wobbled and nearly dropped it. "About Evie? What are people saying?"

"She's keeping bad company."

"Boy? Girl?"

"Boy, of course."

About anyone else, this bit of news might have been intriguing. I slid the platter into its place. "Who's the boy? And how bad is he?"

At that moment, Luzanna came from the dining room and Alma shook her head. We went on with dinner preparations as if nothing had been said. I couldn't stop wondering about Evie and her bad company.

Gossip about who was fighting, who was sick, and who was in love was a main source of entertainment for women in our town, and maybe for men too, though I didn't let myself wonder what men talked about. I had good reason to dislike gossip, but like everyone else, I never tired of talk about a new romance and its potential for bliss or disappointment. If the stories ended happily at the altar, we were happy too, whether we knew the lovers or not. If a girl was jilted or her entanglement led to disgrace, her story served as good warning, and I frowned and shook my head like all the old grannies. Most love stories centered on the young, and everyone, including our teachers, knew which boys and girls were pairing off and which ones might be up to no good.

I wondered how Alma knew about Evie and if she'd told her mother. I asked Luzanna later, when Alma went to the washroom. "Has Alma said anything about Evie?"

Alma's help had lightened our duties, but Luzanna looked as tired as if she'd spent the day scrubbing miners' work clothes on a washboard. "Like what?"

"A boyfriend? She said Evie's keeping bad company."

"Yeah, that," Luzanna said. "She'll of heard that from her sister."

"You knew?"

"It's not my business. The kids brought that tale home from school. And I heard one of the teachers say something."

"One of our teachers is talking about Evie? I wish people would tell me these things!"

"I thought probably you'd heard. I didn't want to bring it up."

Our talk was cut short because the butter and egg man appeared at the back door and I had to go to the office for money to pay him, then there was a new guest to register.

When finally we had a private moment, I said, "Who's the boy?"

Luzanna answered as though our conversation had not been interrupted. "Maybe talk with Wanda." That meant she didn't want to repeat what she'd heard.

The store closed at six, and I could count on Barlow arriving home half an hour later. I asked Luzanna's younger daughter, Emmy, to have dinner with the children so Barlow could eat with the guests while I paid a quick visit to Wanda's house.

~

Wanda was currently in her fifth month of pregnancy, spotting and cramping and ordered to bed by Will, whose doctors had ordered him to stop practicing medicine for the sake of his heart. It seemed a bad time for Evie to give them grief. She'd always been a sweet, compliant girl, but I knew how girls changed when they got interested in boys.

"Junior Doddy's a nice one," Wanda said. She was propped up in her bed, working knitting needles like her life depended on it, a stack of "funny papers" from the Richmond *Times Dispatch* on the bed beside her. She had always been uninterested in both needlework and reading but did not know how to be idle.

The room was small and dark, though its windows were open and someone had tied back the curtains to bring in additional light. Wanda's Granny Lucie sat in the corner, weaving one of her grapevine baskets and letting chaff fall to the floor. I was glad to see Wanda was following doctor's orders. She'd helped with enough births to know her baby was in danger, maybe herself too.

Junior Doddy was the boy. I sat on the chair beside the bed. "Nice? Says who? Evie?"

"Says his teacher," Wanda said. "Evie told me. Junior Doddy's a nice boy and the smartest in his class. He'd like to be a teacher."

"Doddy?" Lucie leaned forward, cupping her hand to her ear. "What's that about a Doddy?"

"Evie's boyfriend," Wanda shouted. "Junior Doddy."

"You'll have to put a stop to that," Lucie said. "We're not getting mixed up with no Doddys."

"Evie says he's a nice boy," Wanda repeated.

Lucie Bosell reminded me of one of those winter garden weeds, pale and withered but with roots too strong and deep to be pulled from the ground. She opened a large pair of shears over a vine's knobby end. "He won't be nice for long if he's from that Sweeny-Doddy clan," she said, squeezing the shears and letting the knob fall to the floor.

Wanda's ancestors had lived in the hills near Winkler long before it was a town, and though Lucie couldn't remember what she'd said a minute ago, she had a detailed recall of her people's history.

"The Sweeny sisters was around the same age as your aunts and your ma," Lucie said. "They's our distant cousins. They might of been all right at one time but they made bad choices for husbands—ever last one o'them married a Doddy. Maybe because their father was a bad'n, and that was the only kind of man they knew. He died when he fell off his horse into a creek, too drunk to know he was drownding, and after that the girls married off pretty quick. The Doddy men is known to chase women and drink like there's no tomorrow."

I waited to see if Wanda would disagree with her granny, as she did half the time, or ignore her, as she did the other half.

"Good can come out of any bad family," Wanda said.

"Well, maybe," Lucie said. "As far as I know, not one of them Doddys ever lifted his hand to his woman in fury. Folks say they beat their wives for pleasure." She paused, eyeing Wanda and me like she wanted to be sure we were appropriately impressed. "There's two kinds of girls in that family--the kind that's sassy and sneaky, and the kind that says nary a peep. The boys, well, the boys got no choice but to give as much as they get. They's bootleggers to this day, and that business has got dangerous. They's all nice looking, though."

I'd heard enough. If Lucie said the family was bad, it was bad. She'd been a moonshiner herself, though never in profitable times like now, and her family had never been high in respectability.

Wanda laid aside her tight, crooked knitting. "Evie's 16. That's almost grown up."

"A perfect age for bad decisions," I said.

"I married her pa when I was 15."

"We all knew Homer. He was like family."

"I know how Evie feels."

I understood that too. I hoped Evie and Wanda were right about Junior Doddy.

"Don't say anything to Will," she said.

We agreed we should do nothing to disturb her husband's new peaceful life. No one said, but it had to be hard for him to stop serving as the region's doctor, leader of the school board, representative to the coal association, and manager of several properties in town. He now spent every daylight hour undisturbed in his workshop, thinking only of the emerging qualities of the wood under his knife.

"I'll have another talk with Evie," Wanda said. "The boy might do better if he gets away from his family. Now you tell me—what's this about Alma going around telling folks they need to be saved?"

"Who's Alma?" Lucie screeched. "We're talking about *Evie*. We gotta get her away from them Doddys."

2

Supposedly, I was the beneficiary of a wealthy estate, a fact disclosed six months ago following the death of Jonas Percy. Such news should have brought joy and excitement—not confusion, irritation, and the financial burden of hiring an attorney.

The elderly man I'd known for a few weeks last autumn as Mr. Jones had seemed a decent sort, a gentleman farmer traveling for personal reasons never explained. He'd settled nicely into our boardinghouse routine, ever polite and occasionally helpful, and as days went by I stopped doubting he'd come to Winkler for no more than a change of scenery. I never asked how he'd found it, a town with no tourist attractions, on no road to anywhere, and not at all scenic. To outsiders it was a dead-end kind of place, starting life as a valley trading post, then a logging town, now coal. Like other small towns in our region, coal was the only business here. Mr. Jones had not been interested in coal.

Until he began to ask personal questions, he'd been my favorite guest. Unfortunately, after hearing the phony stories about me showing myself naked to the logging crews, he'd overstepped and asked if it was true.

In the months following his passing, I accepted the fact that the painful, probing questions that had turned me against him were part of his belated attempt to be my father. He wasn't Mr. Jones; he was Jonas Percy, a man who'd died with his blunders unrevealed and therefore unforgiven. Near the end of his life, as my husband pointed out, he'd tried to do the right thing— he'd searched for the daughter he'd abandoned as a baby, and he'd left her half his considerable wealth. His bequest came as no solace, and it was the root of my present anger.

Barlow had come home for lunch with the children and me, a routine I treasured, and a benefit of managing the company store instead of traveling as a sales representative of Winkler Coal. Following lunch I'd put Hettie and Freddy down for their naps, and when I returned to the table in our parlor he'd handed me the letter from Elizabeth Percy, my father's widow. For the last several minutes he'd been listening to me in his calm, nonjudgmental way.

"It's not worth the aggravation," I said. "The Percys can have it all—his collections, his cattle, his land. And we can stop paying your cousin to represent us."

In disagreeing, Barlow never raised his voice or suggested my ideas were wrong, but he had a way of presenting a side of things I hadn't considered, and at least half the time his sober comments moderated my judgments. This time he might not succeed, because any event involving the Percy family raised my ire, even one meant to help, like this letter.

"I'm sure it will make the Percys happy, if that's what you want to do," Barlow said. "When your father's estate is settled, you can liquidate your share, send

your brothers a bank draft and end all this
unpleasantness."

I'd stopped objecting when people referred to
Jonas Percy as my father, but I could not make myself
think of his sons as my brothers. In every instance,
they'd proved themselves the opposite of decent, and
their manner to me as well as to Elizabeth Percy, their
stepmother, was hostile.

"*His sons,*" I said. "*Jonas Percy's sons.*"

"Sorry, I keep forgetting."

"If you'd met them, you'd understand."

"I do understand. You don't have to like your
father's family or feel kinship with them. You also don't
have to fight for what he clearly wanted you to have.
I've said this before—Cousin Clarence will do that for
you. But I hope you'll write to his widow. It was good
of her to write, and I feel sorry for her. She seems
caught in the middle. And alone."

When the family had come to Winkler to collect
Jonas Percy's body, I'd gotten the impression that
Elizabeth's home was surrounded by the farms her
husband—my father—had bought for his sons. "We
don't know she's alone."

"Her closest family live in New Jersey."

"She's young enough to remarry." I knew little
about her, but my father's third wife looked not much
older than me, perhaps as young as 40. Grown children
commonly felt bitter about a parent's remarriage, and
after seeing his sons' reaction when they learned about
me, I could imagine them calling their young
stepmother a fortune-hunter. Perhaps she'd married
the father too soon after their mother's death, or
perhaps his sons would never accept anyone he cared

for. There might be good reasons for their dislike, such as laziness or bad character, but I could not associate those traits with Elizabeth, the only member of the Percy family who'd tried to be kind.

"She's trying to do the right thing, letting us know about this," Barlow said. "His sons are stealing from the estate, helping themselves to tools and anything else they can drag away, and now she says they're arguing about his collection of Indian artifacts, arrowheads and such. She says someone should do an inventory. It's disturbing to think that hasn't been done."

We had only a vague description of the land, cattle, and farm equipment that were to be sold and distributed to the heirs. I'd always been relieved, hearing about families who squabbled over their parents' possessions, that I had no connections and therefore no such trouble. *Now this.* But I had to agree with Barlow—Elizabeth's situation might be worse than mine. "I'll write," I said. "Do you want the Indian artifacts?"

"You're not curious? I think I'd like to see them. Who knows, someday we might be sorry we didn't save them for Freddy."

"Or Hettie."

"Or Hettie, of course. I forget that girls might be interested in such things. We may have to go to court to get an inventory. I think we should ask for a new administrator, someone impartial."

I dreaded the tangles of legal action, but fortunately for us, Barlow's Cousin Clarence thrived on it. Because Jonas Percy's will hadn't designated an administrator, the court had appointed his oldest son,

Robert. I didn't want to fight, but as my husband pointed out, we had young children to consider.

"Shall I discuss everything with Clarence?"

"I should do it. I don't like to push my responsibilities onto someone else."

"I'm not someone else," Barlow said. "I'm part of you."

"You always say the right thing." I kissed his bald spot. "I'll try to make it up to you."

He swiveled his desk chair and pulled me onto his lap. "And that, Mrs. Townsend, will make everything worthwhile."

~

In Barlow's capacity as manager of the store, he'd asked Alma if she'd like to clerk in the store as she used to do, and she'd agreed, so the next day she did not come to work with her mother. Several days went by before he complained to me about her work. We'd put the children down for their naps, and were enjoying a few minutes of peace and private talk in the middle of an ordinary busy day. "I don't know what else to do," he said. "Customers are complaining about Alma."

"About Alma?" *Surely not.*

"About Alma. I told her she should refrain from witnessing her faith to people who don't want to hear it. It wasn't easy for me to say; she's so eager to please, and I didn't want to disparage her beliefs or hurt her feelings. I don't remember, was she always intensely religious like this?"

"Not like this." I wondered if religious enthusiasm had anything to do with her unexplained return home.

"What did she say when you asked her to stop witnessing in the store?"

"She agreed to speak of her faith only if someone inquired. But she hasn't stopped, and I'm afraid she may interpret a polite 'How are you?' as a desire to hear the passions of her heart. It's not just her witnessing, though that's the root of it. She's neglecting work, watching for opportunities to spread the Gospel. If she can't change, I may have to let her go."

"Shall I talk with Luzanna?"

"I'd hate for this to come between you. I mean, if I have to fire her daughter."

Only a few weeks ago, Alma had sent enthusiastic letters describing her teaching job in Richmond and hinting of a special interest. Then she'd unexpectedly arrived by train and said she wasn't going back. She was such a good, hard-working student; we couldn't imagine she'd been anything but a fine teacher, but we agreed she was in a fragile state. If Barlow had to fire her, she might fall apart.

"Maybe you could suggest a different job. Could she be our telephone operator?" Randolph Bell was constructing a phone system to connect the Winkler and Barbara Town mine offices, company stores, doctors' offices, railroad station and a few other locations to each other as well as to the outside world. We were excited about the possibilities for our town, and Barlow had promised we'd have a telephone in the boardinghouse, available to our guests for a small charge. We'd imagined him being able to telephone from work, and to telephone Cousin Clarence instead of communicating by letter or telegram. We could ring the railroad station to check on departures and arrivals, and instead of taking an hour or more from my work each day to see Wanda, I could call to see how she was faring.

A line had already been strung beside the telegraph wires from the railroad station to Elkins. Randolph planned to install the switchboard in the home of a suitable operator, probably a woman able to work as early and late as the system required. She'd have to be pleasant and trustworthy, Barlow believed, and not encumbered with children or other distracting duties.

"I think Randolph has someone in mind," Barlow said. "Until the system has income to pay for more than one operator, the job will be confining, probably not suitable for a young woman who'd like to be out and about."

I no longer knew what Alma might like. I'd known of people so totally caught by religious fervor that they stretched the bounds of ordinary behavior, but never anyone as close to me as Alma. She might have been gifted with a holy spirit, but to me she seemed lost.

"Fire Alma if you must. I'll do what I can to help her."

Barlow stood and leaned over to give me a goodbye kiss, balanced on his canes. "You take too much on yourself. Sometimes you need to stand back and let events play out."

He was right, but what else could I do? The radical change in Alma's ideas of herself and how she should approach others was already causing trouble.

As it turned out, I did not have to say anything. That evening, Luzanna confided that the store work was making Alma upset and she was going to quit. "Tell Barlow I'm sorry she didn't work out."

"I'm sure he'll understand," I said, trying not to show my relief. "Maybe she needs a spell of rest."

Luzanna sighed. "If she can make herself do it. She can't sit still. Or stop talking. She goes on all the time about how me and the kids need to get saved. It's got so when she starts, the kids get up and walk off. I don't know much about it but I think she may be going about this religion thing the wrong way."

"Do you suppose she might talk with the preacher?"

"She says he's weak in the Lord, whatever that means. I can see her trying to set him straight. If it's all right with you, she wants to come to work with me tomorrow. I said she's not to bother any of the guests or workers in this house. Maybe you can say something that will help her."

Barlow had advised me not to get involved, but I was sure he knew I would.

End of this sample.

The print edition of *Kith and Kin* is available at
Amazon.com, CreateSpace.com,
Barnes & Noble, and other retailers.
The ebook is available at Amazon.com.

Made in the USA
Monee, IL
02 April 2023